YOU WILL NEVER BE FOUND

ALSO BY TOVE ALSTERDAL

We Know You Remember

YOU WILL NEVER BE FOUND

A NOVEL

TOVE ALSTERDAL

ENGLISH TRANSLATION BY ALICE MENZIES

HARPER

An Imprint of HarperCollins*Publishers*

YOU WILL NEVER BE FOUND. Copyright © 2022 by Tove Alsterdal. English translation copyright © 2023 by Alice Menzies. All rights reserved. Printed in Canada. No part of this book may be used or reproduced in any manner whatsoever without written permission except in the case of brief quotations embodied in critical articles and reviews. For information, address HarperCollins Publishers, 195 Broadway, New York, NY 10007.

HarperCollins books may be purchased for educational, business, or sales promotional use. For information, please email the Special Markets Department at SPsales@harpercollins.com.

Originally published as *Slukhål* in Sweden in 2021 by Lind & Co.

Lines from the poem "Childhood Scenes" by Verner von Heidenstam, translated by Charles Wharton Stork in *Sweden's Laureate: Selected Poems of Verner von Heidenstam*. New Haven: Yale University Press, 1919. Originally published as "Ensamhetens tankar," in *Vallfart och vandringsår* (Albert Bonniers Förlag, 1888).

FIRST EDITION

Library of Congress Cataloging-in-Publication Data has been applied for.

ISBN 978-0-06-311511-8

23 24 25 26 27   FB   10 9 8 7 6 5 4 3 2 1

YOU WILL NEVER BE FOUND

MALMBERGET, NORRBOTTEN

The ground shook that night, with a quake more powerful than the usual rumbles, making beds jump and crockery and glasses fall out of cupboards.

When morning broke, an elderly woman would call the mining company and ask to be moved higher up the relocation list. A twenty-seven-year-old father would do the same, having gone out into the garden and discovered his daughter's trike was missing. Stolen, he would assume, cursing the thieves and the scum and the rising crime levels in society—at least until he spotted the crack that had opened up beside his house and realized that her bike had plummeted towards the bowels of the earth.

It was the kind of thing that made people leave Malmberget and never look back, though they would forever long for the place they had once called home.

The tremor didn't wake Tommy Oja. It was his phone, which started ringing an hour later. A cup of black coffee, a quick sandwich. The sun wouldn't be up for hours, and the car's headlights swept through the darkness. Many of the streetlights had stopped working over the past year, others had been dismantled. He turned off towards the Hermelin neighborhood and parked by the fence marking the area at risk of collapse. Several of the old wooden houses there were still waiting to be moved to their new locations, the kind of buildings that captured the spirit of Malmberget's hundred-year history, chosen as particularly valuable. Tommy himself had grown up in one of the apartment buildings that were torn down years earlier. It was what it was. The fence crept closer and closer and his childhood disappeared, swallowed up by the enormous hole known as the Pit at the heart of the mine.

Tommy Oja didn't bother waiting for his colleague from Gälli-vare. He just grabbed the keys and camera and made his way inside.

Insurance, that was what had dragged him out of bed. If a din-ner service had smashed or a flat-screen TV had broken during the night's quake, it was the mining company's responsibility to replace it, not the contractor's.

In a month or two the movers would empty these apartments of all possessions. That was when the real work would begin, digging around the foundations, wedging pallets and steel beams beneath the structure, and securing the chimneys so that the houses could be transported to their new addresses. Once there, their owners would put all their furniture back and everything would look the same as ever, aside from the fact that their breathtaking views over Malm-berget, the church tower, and the mountains had been replaced by a patch of forest outside Koskullskulle.

The people who lived here were the lucky ones, Tommy Oja thought as he moved between the rooms, documenting everything. They got to take their homes with them—or at least some part of what made a home, whatever that was.

A set of books had fallen from a shelf. The glass had cracked on a black-and-white wedding photograph, slightly yellowed with age. He took a picture of the damage and thought he could hear the cou-ple's moaning, staring down at their faces, the solemnity of a special occasion some hundred or so years in the past. The crack cut right across the man's throat, split the bride's face in two.

"Pull yourself together, Tommy Oja," he told himself.

As a native of Malmberget, it was important to keep any senti-mentality at bay. Everything around them was temporary, and they didn't try to kid themselves otherwise. There was no crying over long-lost cinemas or the newspaper kiosks where they bought their first hockey cards. The ore had to be mined, and if it wasn't for the mining company there would be nothing, no society or jobs, none of the riches that had built Sweden; there would be nothing but reindeer pastures and an expanse of untouched mountains. Certain people in Stockholm would probably think that was wonderful, of course, the ones who hung out in fancy bars and didn't give a single thought to how their good fortune had been made, blasted from the rock beneath him.

There it was again. For God's sake.

He couldn't make out any words, just a quiet moaning, as though their voices were lingering in the walls.

"Shut up," he barked.

"Who you talking to?"

The kid was standing in the doorway, a young temp who had been brought in after one of the other guys slipped a disk. Bad timing. Moving these buildings was a prestigious job; they couldn't afford for it to go wrong. The slightest imbalance and the walls could crack. The local press would be following the procedure, people lining the roads along the way.

Finally watching their community disappear.

"Dragged yourself out of bed, did you?" said Tommy Oja, heading back out into the stairwell, making his way upstairs.

The young man stood still.

"What was that?" he asked.

"What?"

"Sounded like an animal or something."

Tommy Oja stepped back down.

"You heard it too?" he said.

"Fuck, did someone forget the cat or something?"

A jolt rattled through the pipes, a faint knocking. They stood perfectly still, neither uttering a word. The sounds traveled around them, muffled and evasive, then with renewed force.

"The basement," said the young man. "It must be coming from down there."

Tommy rummaged through the keys, trying one and then another.

The door opened, a curved staircase leading down into the darkness. That was where it came to an end, by a metal door with a sturdy handle. They could no longer hear anything; the noise must have been transmitted some other way, possibly through the chimney. None of the keys fit the lock.

"Shit," Tommy muttered, turning around. He climbed the stairs first, the young man right behind him as they slowly made their way around the outside of the building. There it was again. He dropped to his knees by the basement window and turned on his torch. The pane of glass bounced the light straight back into his eyes, dazzling him.

"Smash it," said the kid.

"We can't start causing damage, damn it."

"It's just one window. What difference does it make?"

Young people, Tommy Oja thought as he trudged back to his car to fetch his tools and then aimed his pipe wrench at the small window. They're bloody right sometimes.

The last few shards of glass hit the stone floor inside, and then there was nothing but silence. For a split second, Tommy Oja wondered if it had all been a mistake. His apology to the boss flashed through his mind as the kid grabbed the torch and shone it inside. There was a drop of over two meters to the floor, Tommy Oja knew that, he had been involved in every single calculation and plan for shoring up and moving the building. The window was also too small to squeeze through—assuming anyone was willing to risk their life for a fucking cat.

The young man yelled and dropped the torch. He scuttled backwards, scrambling in the gravel like he planned to make his way to Gällivare on his arse, a wild look in his eyes. Right then, the morning sun broke over the mountains, making his hair glow like a halo.

"You see a ghost or something?"

Tommy reached in through the broken window and moved the beam of light across the walls. It was eerily quiet. He could hear his own heartbeat, the young man cursing. There were boxes inside, folded chairs. An old Ping-Pong table, posters on the walls. Then he saw something move. Hands being raised, shielding a face. The person was half sprawled, hunched up like an animal, pressed against the wall. Surrounded by cardboard and junk.

Tommy stared in, unable to make sense of what he was seeing.

The temp was still mumbling behind him.

"Shut up," Tommy barked.

He could hear it clearly now, the sound from the corner, rising among the bricks and concrete, cutting like an arrow through the air. It was the cry of a caged animal, something not quite human, from before we became human and discovered language, like the panicked cry of a baby upon being born. Tommy Oja had three children, he knew what that sounded like. This was much worse. He searched his pockets for his phone, hand trembling as he hit 112 and incoherently stuttered for both the police and an ambulance to come to Långa Raden. He had to repeat the address three times, the call handler was in Umeå, five hundred kilometers to the south, what did they know about the geography of Malmberget?

He crawled back over to the window and shone his torch on his own face to avoid blinding the man inside.

"They'll be here soon," he shouted into the darkness. There was no answer.

ÅDALEN—OCTOBER

Eira Sjödin was busy wrapping coffee cups in towels when her mother started unpacking the first box.

"What are you doing, Mum?"

"Oh, there's no need for any of this."

"But you said you wanted to take your books with you?"

Kerstin pushed a few of the books onto the shelf, in the gaps left behind by the ones they had picked out.

"It'll probably never happen," she said. "It's all just so unnecessary, the whole lot. I can live so cheaply here. Two thousand kronor a month."

Eira slumped onto a chair. She was exhausted. They had been at it for over a week now, the painful procedure of whittling down a lifetime's worth of objects and trying to make them fit into eighteen square meters.

She had managed to convince her mother that she really did need to move into the care home, thirty times, if not more, only for Kerstin to have forgotten by morning—sometimes only a few minutes later. Eira made a mental note of everything her mother had unpacked so that she could repack it that evening, once Kerstin was asleep.

"Which of the pictures do you like best?"

The frames had hung on the walls for so long that they left pale marks behind. The black-and-white etching of the river, from the days when the logs used to pile up in a jam; a framed drawing

Eira's brother had done before she was even born. Mother, father, and child, the sun shining down on them with its thick golden rays.

And the curtains. From a home spread over two floors to a room with a single window. Her clothes, too. The municipal care budget probably didn't stretch to ironing pretty blouses, Eira thought when she saw what Kerstin was unpacking from her suitcases, the neatly folded fruits of yesterday's efforts, they were now going back onto their hangers. Kerstin was still young when the dementia took hold, just over seventy. Eira had seen how old the other residents were, and she wondered how long it would be before her lovely mother adjusted to a life in sweatpants, the occasional skirt with an elasticized waistband when she had visitors.

They only had one week for her to move in, otherwise the place would go to someone else, but Eira picked up when her phone rang anyway. She still couldn't say no.

"How're things?" August Engelhardt asked when she got into the patrol car fifteen minutes later.

"All good," said Eira.

He glanced over to her as he slowed for the turnoff, giving her a smile that was more than just collegial.

"Did I mention that it's good to be back?" he said.

August Engelhardt was five years younger than Eira, a fresh-faced police assistant who was back in Kramfors after a lengthy posting down in Trollhättan. Trying out different areas of the country to see what they had to offer, no doubt.

"What have we been called out to?" she asked.

"Missing person. A middle-aged man from Nyland, no criminal record as far as they could see."

"Who reported it?"

"His ex-wife. Their daughter's a student in Luleå, but she called her mum to say she was worried. It's been three weeks."

Eira closed her eyes. She could see the road even with them shut, her mind on the old chest of drawers that had been passed down through the generations, was that one piece of furniture too many?

They might have to navigate the room with a wheelchair before long, it could all happen so damn fast.

The missing man lived in an apartment just behind the supermarket in Nyland. They pulled up by a cluster of two-story buildings that looked like countless others across the country, well tended but anonymous. The property manager who was supposed to be letting them in was running late, but the man's ex-wife was already waiting outside. Wearing a blazer and a pair of trendy white glasses, not a single strand of her short hair out of place.

"No one's heard from him in three weeks," said Cecilia Runne. "Hasse can be a real shit sometimes, but he's always gone to work."

"What does he do?"

"He's an actor, technically, but he does a bit of everything to stay afloat—you have to, living up here. Simple building jobs, maybe even the odd shift for home help, I don't really know. Our daughter said he was meant to be filming a part in Umeå last week. Hasse's useless with money, but he'd never let a job pass him by. Not after last year, when he didn't have anything for seven months."

The virus that had struck the globe, the cultural world, and the elderly with such force. It had also pushed back Kerstin's move into care, until the situation at home became unsustainable.

August jotted down everything the ex-wife said.

When was Hans Runne last heard from, who did he hang around with, did he have any history of mental illness, a drinking problem?

"Is there a new partner in the picture?"

"No, I don't think so," Cecilia Runne replied, possibly a little too quickly. "Not that I know of, anyway." Her eyes darted around the yard, to the leaf-covered lawn, a walking frame outside a doorway.

It wasn't a priority case—an adult male who hadn't turned up to work and wasn't answering his phone—barely even a matter for the police, but they would take the report, help her into his apartment. Worst-case scenario, they would find him dead up there.

That was the most likely explanation. A heart attack, a stroke, something like that. Suicide. Or maybe he had succumbed to a mid-life crisis and gone wandering in the mountains—which also wasn't a crime.

"I just hope he's not lying dead in there," said the woman, the fear in her voice now palpable. "There's been so much of that lately, people who've been left like that for weeks. It happened to an acquaintance and several others I've read about. I don't know if Paloma could live with that."

"Paloma?"

"Our daughter. She's been calling and calling, she was going to come down from Luleå, even though she's got exams right now. I told her I'd take care of it. I promised her an explanation."

The property manager arrived to let them inside. Hans Runne lived on the first floor. They stepped over bills and junk mail, the air ripe with old rubbish or possibly something else. The hallway led straight into the kitchen. A few cups and glasses in the sink, wine bottles on the counter. The smell was coming from the rubbish bag beneath the countertop.

"He might drink a bit much," the ex-wife said behind them. "It could've gotten worse since we split up, I don't know."

There was no sign of Hans Runne in the living room. A few more glasses and bottles, an enormous TV. The bedroom door was closed.

"It might be best if you wait in the hallway," said Eira.

The woman raised a hand to her mouth and backed away from them with a terrified look in her eyes. August pushed the door open.

He and Eira both breathed a sigh of relief.

The bed was unmade, a tangle of bedding and pillows, but there was no one inside. They ducked down and checked beneath the bed. No sign of anything out of the ordinary, just a man who didn't make his bed. Who read before going to sleep, a thick volume of Ulf Lundell's diaries. And who, judging by the tooth guard in an open plastic case, ground his teeth in his sleep. The air smelled like it could have been standing still for three weeks, give or take. Stuffy but not exactly unpleasant.

Cecilia Runne had slumped down into a chair when they got back to the kitchen.

"He can't do this, disappearing on his daughter. Leaving me to take care of everything. It's so fucking typical of Hasse. He's all talk, but when it comes to actually taking responsibility for other people . . ."

"How long have the two of you been divorced?" asked Eira, opening the fridge. She heard the woman say something about three years, that she was the one who had left.

Milk that had gone out of date a week ago, a ham sandwich that had hardened at the edges. If Hans Runne's disappearance was voluntary, it definitely didn't seem like it had been planned.

Cecilia Runne began to cry, calm and composed.

"I've been so angry with him," she said. "And now it's too late."

Eira saw August studying the free newspapers in the hallway, the dates.

"We don't know that," she said. "It's too early to say anything."

Fanom and Skadom and Undrom. There were villages with strange, incomprehensible names like that dotted throughout the forests around Sollefteå. Tone Elvin slowed down to thirty as she drove into Arlum och Stöndar. The village really did have two names on the map, as though two smaller communities had come together to form one. She had no idea why, it was the first time she had ever come out this way; she knew nothing about the people in Arlum och Stöndar. She just drove slowly through. A few houses on either side of a narrow road, that was all. One or two seemed to be empty, but none were dilapidated enough to catch her eye. She continued towards the old ironworks, her heart skipping a beat as she passed Offer.

It sounded so ominous, naming a hamlet after the Swedish word for victim, yet somehow it was also beautiful.

Tone was looking for the places people had forgotten. Roads that had been used some fifty or a hundred years ago, then abandoned to their fate.

Spotting an overgrown forest track, she pulled over and hung her camera, an old Leica, around her neck.

The forest seemed to close in around her. The September air smelled earthy, ripe, the scent of death that follows life, bringing resurrection. A raven flapped up and soared high above her, soon joined by a second. She had read that they tracked bears, and her heart started racing again. What were you supposed to do if you came across a bear, meet its eye or not?

Bright autumn colors replaced the uniform darkness of the spruce trees. There was a glade up ahead, a neglected garden full of deciduous trees and bushes, a real abandoned house. Tone took a deep breath. It was incredible, exactly what she had been looking for. The paint had flaked away, and the facade was an expanse of gray. She raised her camera and waded through the tall grass. Caught the past through her viewfinder, the sorrow of what once was. The sunlight danced between the leaves, making the spiderwebs shimmer.

The ravens landed in front of her.

It was almost too much. The black birds were like omens of death among the beautiful greenery, against the backdrop of the weather-beaten house. One of them hopped along the cracked foundation, another had landed on a branch. Tone backed away with her camera raised. She shouted to make them lift off again, to capture their black wingbeats.

She loaded a new roll of film, fumbling and stressed. She needed to capture everything before the daylight faded. *Oblivion*, that was what she would call the exhibition. Either that or *Loss*. Her psychologist friend had told her to face up to her grief, to the fact that she was all alone in the world, but she would do more than that. She would document it in black and white, in all its grayness, her very own project that would take her back to what she loved most: photography.

No more home-help shifts to pay the rent.

The porch outside the front door was rotten, weeds poking up through the boards. She used tight, tight framing to capture the grain and the detail, the pale remnants of paint and the different layers of the aged wood. All the years, all the lives that had passed through.

Tone tried the door handle, forged from iron. It wasn't locked, and the door swung open.

Silence. The sunlight filtering in through the dusty windowpanes filled the room with slanting rays of gold, light that would have made Rembrandt jealous. There were a couple of broken chairs in one corner, and Tone dragged one of them into the middle of the floor. Oddly enough, it stayed upright, despite missing a leg. She photographed it from various angles, adding a broken stool. Suddenly she had drama, a fight from years ago, someone who left, someone who stayed. She turned the chair and the atmosphere changed. The light dipped slightly with each frame. Evening was approaching. Tone peered through to the next room.

An old iron bedframe. A ripped, disgusting horsehair mattress. She shot a few frames that made her feel uneasy. The room was north facing, which meant there were no shadows, just gloom. She stepped on a floorboard that creaked loudly beneath her, and her mind turned to the dead, she saw images of something violent. Outside, one of the ravens screeched. The house was on its guard, groaning and sighing and driving her away.

It's all in your mind, she told herself once she was back outside. The sun had dipped behind the trees, and the cool air felt rawer. That's just the sound old buildings make, she thought. Maybe there were swallows living in the roof, there were almost certainly mice in the walls.

Her art required her to delve into her own fears, touching upon the things she found painful. That was what she had to convey in her images.

Just not right now, she thought, making her way through the aspen and birch trees in what she thought was the direction of the trail. She could no longer see it.

Just like that, everything was in place. The chest of drawers and the bookcase and all the rest of it, shabby and old against the pale walls and the metal bedframe, an adjustable hospital model. Eira would have to get going to work soon, but she still took the time to hang the curtains. She couldn't leave her mother with this mess; everything had to be nice and cozy, it had to feel like home.

Or an illusion of it, anyway.

"I'll come back and help you with the books tomorrow," she said, unpacking the last few glasses. Four of each, in hope of visitors. The only cupboard was getting full.

"No, no, I can manage that myself," said Kerstin. "You don't know how to organize them anyway."

The librarian in her was the last part to disappear.

Time was different in the care home. Slower. It felt wrong to hurry her, possibly inhumane, but Eira had no choice.

"You'll be happy here."

She hugged her mother as she left. Something they rarely did.

"Mmm, I don't know," said Kerstin.

The autumn air, crisp and clear. Eira paused for a moment to catch her breath. There was a path down to the river, outdoor furniture that hadn't yet been brought in. The forecast kept talking about a warm spell. Everything would be OK, wouldn't it?

She drove to the station in the rented van, would just have to pay for another day.

A young woman was standing by the main doors. She seemed lost.

"Are you looking for someone?" Eira asked as she held her card to the reader and entered her code.

"Yes, but . . ."

Eira paused midstep on her way into the building.

"Do you want to report something?"

"Maybe I shouldn't have come." The young woman's voice was as delicate as a dragonfly wing, her hair bleached. A ring in her lower lip.

"I'm a police assistant, you can talk to me. Has something happened?"

"It's not about me." The young woman ran a hand through her hair, neither smoothing it nor messing it up. "It's my dad. We've already reported him missing and Mum says there's nothing else we can do, but surely there has to be something?"

"Would you like to come in?"

It was only after Eira had showed her over to one of the vinyl sofas in what had once been the reception area, back when the station actually had opening hours, that she asked her name.

Paloma Runne.

That wasn't the kind of name you forgot. It brought back melodies, a cheesy song from the past. *Una paloma blanca . . .*

"I was there when we went into your father's apartment last week," said Eira.

"Oh, that's lucky. I wanted to talk to one of you, because over the phone they just said they couldn't tell me anything, blah, blah, blah."

"Would you like a coffee? Water?"

Paloma nodded, giving Eira a chance to get away, up the stairs, waiting as the machine ground the beans. She needed time to think.

Hans Runne.

Had they made any progress? She had used her time off in lieu to help her mother move and hadn't given the missing man a single thought in days.

Healthy, some would say. Being able to forget about work and focus on what really mattered in life: our nearest and dearest. But Eira thought there was something suffocating about that approach, as though it implied that our nearest and dearest would be neglected otherwise.

She spotted August as she was heading back down with the two coffees.

"What's the latest on the missing man in Nyland?" she asked.

"Don't know, I guess he's still missing?"

"His daughter is downstairs."

August got a vague look in his eye and half turned to his computer. The call records from the man's network provider had come in a few days earlier, as had his bank statements. Since there hadn't been any indication of a crime, requesting them hadn't been the natural next step, but they had done it anyway. Eira remembered how she had felt on leaving the apartment: the fading adrenaline, the slight suspicion of suicide or an accident. Hans Runne could have run off to Mauritius with his lover, of course, but most grown adults would take the rubbish out first. If he had waded out into the river or gone off into the forest with a gun, it might be a long time before they found his body—if they ever did.

And yet there had been something that bothered her, something that didn't quite add up.

His home was messy, but it wasn't chaotic. It looked like somewhere that had been left in a hurry, but not with the intention of it being for good.

They had put out an internal alert. That likely wouldn't help them find the man, but it would make things easier if his body turned up.

"I forgot to ask if you took milk," said Eira, setting down both coffees on the table. One black and one beige and milky. Paloma Runne chose the latter.

"Thanks."

"I'm sorry, but there isn't much I can tell you."

Eira laid out the documents she had collected from the printer on her way back down.

Hans Runne's last phone calls, made in the middle of September. That was four weeks ago now. Paloma pointed to her own number in the list, two days before his phone went quiet.

"He sounded happy, a bit overexcited like he gets sometimes. He didn't have time to talk, but we were supposed to be seeing each other soon anyway, this weekend, while he was filming in Umeå. I was going to take the bus over there, he said he'd book a table at Le Garage. That's hardly the kind of thing you'd arrange if you were planning to kill yourself, is it?"

Or maybe it is, thought Eira, because those last few days fork off into parallel worlds, one in which everything will be OK and another that plunges into darkness. Unless Runne had already made up his mind when he placed his last call to his daughter, and that was what he wanted to give her: the prospect of a nice meal at one of Umeå's trendiest restaurants.

"Maybe he didn't want to worry you," she said.

"I still don't believe it," said Paloma. "Dad wasn't like that."

She quickly corrected herself.

"He isn't like that."

"Like what?"

"Depressed. The kind of person who gives up. He's always so happy, even though things have been tough with work and everything. And the divorce too, obviously, he didn't take that so well . . ."

"Do you recognize any of the other numbers here?"

"My godfather's," she said after a moment, pointing to one of them. Four days before his disappearance. "He's an old friend of Dad's."

"Have you spoken to him?"

"He said Hasse was on great form, that he was working, dating, seemed to have come out the other side—like life was one big party, basically."

Eira told Paloma what August had managed to find out from the other numbers, that his last call was to a broadband company, the second last to a painter decorator.

"Can't you trace his phone?"

"It doesn't seem to have been switched on in weeks, unfortunately."

"But that must mean something has happened. Surely you can see that?"

"He could have turned it off, or lost it . . ."

"No one turns off their phone."

What was she supposed to say? That yes, people do actually want to disappear sometimes, to be unreachable, to vanish into the silence.

The last time the phone connected to a mast, it was in Härnösand. From his home in Nyland, that was a distance of sixty kilometers, between them the powerful Ångerman River with its raging currents and dizzying depths, heading straight out into the endless Bothnian Sea.

Where were they supposed to look?

Eira gathered up the documents. His bank account was overdrawn, Hans Runne had been out drinking in Härnösand, gambling online, but no huge sums. Over the past four weeks, he had neither used his card nor made any active payments.

That was as far as they had looked, which wasn't a neglection of duty; they could easily have done far less. The whole case was a gray zone, though that was hard to explain to a young woman who looked like she might burst into tears at any moment. Paloma held up her phone, scrolling through pictures.

"This is him as Hamlet . . . he really wasn't a bad actor, he just didn't have much luck, probably because he moved back up here, but he did get a few small parts on TV, you might have seen him. Do you remember that show about the doctor in the archipelago? He was in that once."

"I do understand, but . . ."

"I just want you to see him as a person." Yet more acting parts flashed by, a Midsummer party, Christmas celebrations, laughing in a Santa hat. "A person can't just vanish off the face of the earth without anything happening. Like he never even existed, like no one cares."

"Is there anyone you can talk to?" asked Eira.

"I'm not the problem here, am I?"

Eira's phone buzzed in her pocket, and she heard quick footsteps on the floor above. A call she had to attend.

"I'll see what I can do."

She finally had time to set up the darkroom. Without anyone banging on the bathroom door, wanting to take a shower, shouting to be let in to the toilet. The students she sublet her master bedroom to had both gone home to see their parents over the weekend.

For two wonderful days, Tone had the apartment to herself.

Yet here she was, doing laundry. She threw the students' books back into their room and went to the supermarket to buy enough ready-made soup to last all weekend, feeling increasingly anxious about the moment when the images emerged in the developer solution. The light could be wrong, the exposure off, or she might simply have failed to capture what she felt in the abandoned house. The sense of melancholy and the passing of time, everything you couldn't see.

She had cursed herself for taking the risk of shooting film, but it was an artistic choice, and she had to stand by it.

Honesty. Quality. Her father's old Leica, his favorite camera. Whenever she used it she could feel his hands on hers, back when she was a child, his voice teaching her five-year-old self about the relationship between aperture and shutter speeds. Tone had no memory of her father ever turning the camera on her. She was never the subject. What he wanted was to show her how to see. In all honesty, he wasn't the greatest photographer, he had never made anything of his dreams. During his last few years, he had sold insurance.

What artist isn't chasing their father, she thought, lifting the enlarger onto the washing machine and locking the bathroom door to block out even the slightest chink of light.

Working in the dark, she loaded the film into the developing tank and poured the chemicals inside. When the timer blared, she added the fixer, then rinsed the negatives and finally dared turn on the light. Chamois leather, her father had taught her, to carefully dry the negatives. Tone plugged in her hairdryer to speed up the process.

She still felt the same sense of magic she had as a girl, when she first discovered this inverted world. It was a world that revealed itself only to her, but which may well be the true world, one in which the ravens were white, flapping against a dark facade. What was light and what was dark, good and evil, truth and lies; everything around her carried its own opposite.

Tone studied the negatives with her loupe, took out some photographic paper, and got the trays ready. Time ran away from her. It could be evening, could be night. She felt no hunger or anxiety, no sense of longing that stretched any further than the next image.

One of the ravens, caught midlanding. Perfect diagonals against the shabby facade, right where a crack ran through the foundation, black wings by a small basement window. But there was a bright spot, right in the middle of the frame. Damn it. She just hoped it wasn't a mark on the lens, or the entire series would be ruined. Tone fixed and dried the image, turned on the lamp and grabbed her loupe.

Just the thought of having to retouch the photograph made her lose all enthusiasm. She became aware of the sharp chemical smell and the headache that always followed. What she wanted was to get closer to the truth, not distort it.

The bright spot took shape beneath her magnifying glass. It wasn't a scratch, wasn't reflected light. There really was something there.

A hand.

Tone remembered the sound she thought she had heard, the sense of something awful. She rubbed her eyes, swallowed hard, and bent down over the loupe again.

The Leica's sharpness was second to none, her father had been right about that. It caught every contour. Left her with no doubt.

The hand was reaching out through the window, towards the grass, where the raven was heading.

She rummaged through the negatives, hands shaking. Picked out another frame, from a moment later. Four seconds, aperture set to f/8. The darkness pulsed through her. The seconds it ate up, the minutes before the image emerged in the solution.

The light was hitting the window. The black bird was still hopping around on the ground.

But the hand was gone.

The last few customers of the day pushed their overloaded carts across the car park outside Ica Kvantum in Sollefteå. Things were still quiet, but within an hour or two the music would be pounding from oversized stereos, beer cans scattered across the tarmac.

"So this is the place to be, is it?" said August, looking out across the near-empty car park.

"Just wait."

Eira finished the last mouthful of her noodles and crumpled the carton. During the pandemic, when the pubs closed and festivals were canceled, more and more young people had started hanging out in various car parks, and it had continued ever since. Invitations were shared on social media, and up to three hundred cars might show up, either here or outside the supermarket in Kramfors—not to mention the area by the station in Örnsköldsvik. There had been weekends when Eira had done little other than drive from one car park to another, helping to keep the peace.

She called the duty officer to ask whether he had seen any indication that the meeting had been moved. He hadn't.

"But something else has come in, not far from you."

"What?"

"It's pretty inaccessible, as I understand it, in the middle of the forest outside Undrom." He was thinking aloud rather than giving orders. "So maybe it'd be better to wait until morning, once it's light. Assuming it's actually anything, that is."

"We're currently watching the supermarket staff bring the carts in."

"OK."

Eira got into the car as the duty officer summarized the call. Her phone pinged when the directions came through.

"Where are we going?" asked August.

"An abandoned house twenty minutes from here."

"Exciting," he said with a laugh. "What's going on there?" He had that teasing look in his eyes, in his smile. It was really quite irresistible.

"Probably nothing," said Eira.

When August was last in town, they had spent the night together a few times. More than a few, in fact. No strings attached. Eira didn't know where they stood now, whether the spark was still there or whether it had faded. There were no clear signals. Just a certain tension, which she felt as she pulled out onto the road following the river east, all too aware of his body. Those hands and their softness, how agile they could be, no calluses or rough skin, a body built in the gym, on the jogging track. She remembered an awkward good-bye, a kiss and a bye, see you later. No hard feelings, no longing messages.

"We need to take a left at Undrom," she said, handing him her phone with the directions, "and continue towards Nolaskogs."

"Where?" August searched the map, zooming in. "I can't find that name anywhere."

Eira laughed.

"I always forget you're from Stockholm. Nolaskogs isn't on the map; it's just what people call the area to the north of Skuleskogen National Park."

"Nice to get out in nature, anyway," said August. He sounded like he meant it.

The last set of oncoming headlights disappeared when they turned off the main road. There were a few streetlamps as they passed through a small village, then more darkness, one of those black October nights before the first snow arrives. Remote-controlled lights in some of the summerhouses, in the hopes of keeping the thieves at bay.

"Offer," August read from a sign lit up by their headlights. "Seriously, that's what they called the place? D'you reckon you have to be a victim to live there?"

"There's a lake called Offersjön a little farther up . . . ," said Eira, racking her memory for any further clues. She knew there had been a sacred well near Sånga, a place people had gone to make offerings since the pre-Christian era. Place names rarely meant what people thought they did, particularly not in areas where the first settlers had arrived so long ago that the language had had time to evolve. Skadom, she had heard, came from an old word for shadow, a farm in shadow. Bringen came from the ancient bringur, which meant height. If anything, the place names said more about age, about how long people had been moving around these regions, coming up with words for the land when they first arrived.

Their headlights painted the spruce trees around them white.

"There should be an overgrown track somewhere," said August. "But no signposts, apparently . . ."

He yelled, and Eira slammed on the brakes. In the glow of their taillights, she could make out the grass growing over the ditch, saplings on what had once been a road.

"There are bears around here," she said.

"How do you know?"

"I just do."

She got out and shone her torch between the trees. Doubted they would be able to get much farther in the car. These old trails had a tendency to get narrower the deeper into the forest you came, sometimes disappearing completely. Once a forest was left to its own devices, it quickly regained control, growing over all trace of humans.

August took the lead, holding back branches for her. They had been walking for five minutes, no more than ten, when the beam of light hit a building, gray and dilapidated.

"I think this is it."

It couldn't have been abandoned for too long, Eira thought as they came closer. Ten years, perhaps. Twenty, max. The roof still looked intact. She had crept around enough abandoned houses to be able to read their decay, a bit like the rings of a tree. It often began before the last residents left, in the weariness of the elderly, legs that could no longer manage stairs, the hopelessness of having no one who was willing to take over. The family tree simply continued elsewhere.

August climbed up onto a rock and peered in through a broken window.

"Man, what a place. There's still furniture inside, and a tiled stove—don't people know what those are worth? How can they just leave everything behind?"

He sounded like a young boy on an adventure, as though he had forgotten why they were there. Eira pulled on a pair of latex gloves before trying the door handle.

"It's probably nothing, just someone crashing here overnight," she said. "Assuming the person who called it in was serious."

"Surely there's no harm if the place is empty?" said August. "Why don't they send all the homeless people up here?"

"Sometimes they do," said Eira, thinking about the revelations that had come to light in recent years, wealthy Stockholm councils handing their benefit claimants one-way tickets north.

They were quiet as they stepped inside. There were net curtains in the windows, wooden chairs and a four-seater table, a sense that life had stopped midbreath. Their footsteps were the only sound.

"Shit," August muttered as one of the floorboards gave way.

"The caller saw someone in the basement." Eira used her torch to work out where each of the doors went, peered into the pantry. Empty jam jars, bottles, a crumpled flour packet. There was another narrow door in the kitchen, and it was locked. She looked around for a key on a hook, pulled out a couple of drawers.

"Should we try to see in from outside before forcing entry?" she said.

There was one spot around the base of the house where the otherwise tall grass had been cleared. By a small basement window, the ground was bare, the earth disturbed. The insulation had been pulled out. Eira got onto her knees. Reached inside and let the beam of her torch slowly sweep the room. Plenty of junk, an oil drum, a broken chair, a torn bale of insulation, a crib. A heap in the corner, an old blanket. Her torchlight wandered farther, a few seat pads that had been chewed to pieces by mice or similar, scattered piles of foam padding. The sight of the crib seemed to be lingering in her, the sorrow of the dreams it must once have contained, and her mind turned to the child who had grown up and left, the idea that every house like this was someone's childhood home, before it hit her.

Something she had seen but not quite seen, a discrepancy.

The awkward angle was making the muscles in her arm ache, and she had to carefully pull back, turn her body into a half-sprawled position, switch hands.

The far corner. The heap of blankets, or whatever it was.

"August. Come here." Eira got up and handed him the torch, told him where to look. "Is there someone there?"

She jumped when August shouted into the cellar, announcing that they were from the police.

"If it is someone, they're not moving," he said.

"Let's go in."

It took them fifteen minutes to break down the door. Solid wood, quality work, iron hardware. She had been expecting the usual smells of a basement, moisture and earth, but the stench that hit them as they picked their way down the steep staircase was something else entirely. Urine and excrement. August stopped dead when he reached the bottom, meaning Eira couldn't see anything but his neck and back, his arm holding the torch.

"Jesus Christ."

He moved to one side so that Eira could step down. The bundle was in the corner right by the stairs. It caught the light. A sliver of a face, half hidden beneath the blanket, beneath a tangle of hair, an eye staring past her and beyond them and through the solid walls, a gaze that had faded.

She took another two steps.

There was also a foot sticking out. The person's face was so sunken, possibly emaciated, that it was hard to tell whether they were male or female.

"Poor bastard," August said behind her. He was clinging on to the handrail and looked like he wanted to be sick, his own face deathly pale, though that was possibly down to the torchlight. "Do you think they came down here to sleep and then just never woke up?"

Eira checked the door as they made their way back upstairs.

"There's no key on the inside," she said.

"It could be in their pocket," said August.

"Yeah, that's possible."

She stepped out into the fresh air ahead of him. August leaned against what was left of the old bakehouse. It was a calm, clear night, the moon hanging low behind the forest, its light spilling between the trees. The smells at a crime scene rarely affected Eira. She became efficient and methodical, doing her job, and it wasn't until later that it started to creep up on her, the knowledge that there was evil out there, in people and places, an awareness of grief and loss that she found it harder to keep her distance from.

She managed to find some phone reception in the middle of the overgrown yard. Two bars, enough to call it in.

"It'll be a while before they get here," Eira said as she lowered her phone. "We might as well start cordoning off the area."

The night cracked and whispered all around them. Eira had allowed herself to nod off for a while, sitting on the floor in the old bedroom. In the darkness, there was nothing she could do but let her thoughts drift to the man in the basement.

They had gone down there again, carefully lifting the blanket to reveal the lower section of his face. That was all they needed to see that he was male. Facial hair, possibly several weeks' growth, an entire month? He was curled up in the fetal position.

As though he had lain down to sleep, crawled back into what came before life, the blanket a cocoon around him, ripped to shreds by some animal, of course, barely providing any warmth.

Two fingers to his skin.

His body was the same temperature as the air around him, which meant he had been dead for at least a day. In a basement, on an October night when the temperature hadn't yet dropped below zero, they guessed it must be somewhere between 39 and 43 degrees. Eira had spoken to the duty pathologist in Umeå over the phone. The man's body temperature could no longer tell them anything useful about the time of death, and as a result there was no reason for the medical examiner to drive 250 kilometers in the middle of the night. They had other ways of establishing a rough timeframe, but that would be done once the body arrived at the lab in Umeå.

The lead investigator on duty had said something similar from Härnösand. If it turned out to be a crime, any physical evidence was no longer fresh. Eira and August should stay put and guard the scene, wait for daybreak.

The other responding officers on duty had to drive eighty kilometers from Härnösand to deal with the car park meet in Sollefteå, which spiraled out of control sometime around midnight.

She and August had spent the first few hours putting up the cordon around the house, before grabbing some blankets from the car and taking it in turns to keep watch.

The night had grown quiet around them, time passing without a trace. A slight shift in the darkness; the sun would soon come up. August was sitting on the steps when she came out. It could only be another hour, at most, until they were relieved.

He broke off a piece of protein bar and handed it to her.

"I saw a fox," he said. "It was just standing there, over by the shed, staring straight at me. I thought it was a bear at first, when I heard it rustling about. I shone the torch at it, but it didn't move. Wasn't scared of me at all."

"It would've been dumb to shine the torch at it if it was a bear," she said.

"What are you supposed to do?"

"Talk to it."

"Seriously?"

"Never turn your back on a bear. Slowly move away, throw yourself on the ground as a last resort."

In the breaking dawn she could see that he looked jumpy. Tired. He had a half-empty bottle of cola by his side, which they shared. Eira felt like taking his hand, lowering his head to her lap, his tense neck on her knee, but she didn't. She was in uniform, as was he, and they hadn't touched since he got back from the west coast.

"This is hardly the kind of place you'd find by chance," he said.

"No."

"So whoever dumped him here must've known about it."

"Mmm."

A buzzard rose into the air beyond the trees and dived back down towards the ground. Eira thought about all the abandoned houses she knew of, had snuck into. They were the kind of places people told others about, their abandonment bringing a certain temptation, the draw of the past and the hope of finding something of value. Hundreds of people might know about this house, anyone who had grown up in the area or simply happened to be passing by.

A woodpecker began pecking a tree nearby, distant voices growing closer. Eira brushed the dust and dirt from her uniform and got up to greet their colleagues.

There were strict rules about working hours and daily rest. That meant she and August had to leave the scene once they had accounted for their movements in the house, explaining how they had forced open the door to the basement and so on, enabling the technicians to rule out any trace of them. It bothered her. Eira wanted to stay and see what happened, to try to understand and grapple with the questions now that it was light. She hadn't even been able to get any real sense of the basement, just scattered snapshots in the glow of a torch. That was what happened when you were the responding officer: first to the scene, then on to the next one.

"Looks like he's been down there awhile." Georg Georgsson—or GG as he was known—had been brought in from Violent Crimes to investigate, and had just reemerged from the basement. "Judging by the amount of excrement, at least."

The dead man had used one corner of the room as a toilet, screening it off and covering it up with loose planks of wood and other junk.

GG filled his lungs with the cool morning air and lit a cigarette. His fitted suit jacket looked out of place, his shoes dusty from the house.

"Dignity," he added. "Right down to the last, people want to maintain some sense of dignity."

Eira looked around for August, who had been tasked with moving the cordon to make way for the forestry equipment that was en route. It wasn't time to head home to bed just yet.

"Have they found anything to tell us who he is?" she asked.

"No personal items on him," said GG. "And it'll be hard for anyone to make a positive ID. A man going without food for . . . well, God knows how long." He studied his own hand, the ash falling down from his cigarette. "They've sent his prints off for analysis."

Eira thought she could detect an undertone, something he was holding back. She waited. They had worked together two years ago, on the murder of an old man in Kungsgården. That case had grown increasingly complex, entangling her to the point where she eventually had to walk away. Looking back now, she realized just how much she had missed working with her colleagues from Violent Crimes. And standing beside GG, she realized just how much she had missed him, too. Their conversations, the feeling that he trusted her. Six months earlier, Eira had been asked to apply for a temporary vacancy in Sundsvall, where the unit was based. She spent three evenings struggling with her application, but never actually sent it off. She had her mother to think about, for one thing, and liked having a more predictable work schedule, but that wasn't all. As a responding officer, she was sent out to do whatever was needed, then she changed out of her uniform and went home. Tomorrow was another day. Her work didn't take over, and rarely haunted her dreams.

"The ones he's got left, anyway," said GG.

"What?"

They had been standing quietly for a moment or two, which wasn't to say that the area around them was quiet. The air hummed with engines, tree trunks breaking. The forestry machine had arrived, and was in the process of clearing the trail so that the vehicles could reach the house—above all the van that would transport the body to Umeå.

"He's missing two fingers on his left hand."

"Accident at work, maybe?" Eira had seen countless mutilated hands. Her neighbor had lost three fingers in a forest harvester, an uncle had had his thumb sawn off. The old men happily held up their damaged hands as proof of a lifetime of hard work, another era.

"Sadly not," said GG. His gaze wandered beyond the dilapidated shed that had likely been used to store wood at some point in time, maybe even housed a few hens. "The wounds are fresh and his shirtsleeve is covered in blood."

Eira swallowed.

"That sounds like . . ."

GG nodded.

"God knows what we're dealing with here."

She couldn't smell smoke. There hadn't been a disaster. Nothing but a few confused flies that didn't seem to realize summer was over.

Eira poured herself a glass of orange juice. No one had touched the open bottle, there was still exactly the same amount in it as yesterday. The leftovers of her dinner from the Thai restaurant in Kramfors were still in the fridge from the day before last. She reheated them, eating straight from the carton.

No one said: come on, use a plate.

Just over a week had passed since she took her mother to the care home, and Eira still wasn't used to the silence. The freedom, you might call it. All the time she suddenly had to spare, responsibilities that had vanished overnight. Kerstin Sjödin was now sitting in a dining room with pine tables and watercolor landscapes by local artists on the walls. She wasn't alone; they were taking care of her. It was time for Eira to put her feet up, watch terrible TV shows, start dating, and call old friends. Time to run a bath.

She checked her phone again. No missed calls, no emails. There was no reason for the detectives to keep the responding officers up to date, of course. She would run into GG or one of the others at the station in Kramfors sooner or later. Or maybe not, they would probably set up camp in Sollefteå, which was closer to the crime scene. They might not even do that. They might do most of the work from Sundsvall. Either way, her part in the case was over.

She should take a nap to catch up on sleep after her night in the abandoned house, but knew she wouldn't be able to doze off.

Instead she went over to see her neighbor. He was busy raking leaves on the lawn, and the black dog came bounding towards her. Eira crouched down and let him bury his nose in her armpits and neck.

"He's missed you, poor lad," said Allan Westin. He was in his eighties and had spent the past few years living alone. His wife had moved to Stockholm to be closer to their grandchildren, and the plan was for him to follow her down, he just had a few things to sort out first. But almost four years later, he still hadn't managed to leave the house.

That was why he had been happy to help look after Rabble, so the dog wasn't alone when Eira was at work. His rightful owner should have been to pick him up by now, but time passed and Olof Hagström never called. He had been the prime suspect in the murder of his own father. That was the investigation that had ensnared Eira in a way she struggled to escape. She was still feeling the effects of it now, partly in the form of this crazy mongrel the dead man had left behind. Rabble had breathed life into both her home and her mother, the eager yapping of a dog who needed to pee, the presence of something fluffy and alive.

But then Allan Westin had started chatting over the currant bushes, telling Eira how much he missed the dogs in his life. She barely claimed her share of custody anymore. Rabble had taken up what seemed like permanent residence in the house next door, where he had his very own basket and everything—though he preferred to jump up on the bed, "the great big lump, I barely get a wink of sleep," her neighbor said with such warmth that Eira understood. She cut back her involvement to long walks. Throwing sticks down by the river helped to clear her mind.

Her phone started ringing just as Rabble came trotting towards her with wet feet. Eira hurled the stick for him and turned her back to the wind.

"Are you at home?" asked GG.

"Yeah. Well, out with the dog," said Eira. She could hear that he was in the car, shouting into his phone over the loudspeaker, the low hum of the engine.

"Do you still live in Lunde?" he yelled.

"Yup, still there."

"Perfect," said GG. "I'll swing by in five."

•   •   •

She waited for him outside Wästerlunds Konditori. The old café had already closed for the season, but the sun was warm on its wide steps.

"And here I was hoping for a bit of mille-feuille," GG said as he got out of the car and glanced up at the neon sign that, at one point in time, had been the largest in the whole of Norrland.

"Too late," said Eira. "You should've come in August. Or some-time during the sixties."

He sat down beside her, a quick gesture to make sure she didn't mind him smoking. She could see mud on his shoes, dirt on the hems of his trousers. A bit of leaf, or possibly wood shavings, in his nicely graying hair.

"We know who he is," said GG.

"Already?"

Eira could taste his smoke when she breathed in.

"He'd carved his name into the wall. Forensics didn't notice it until we moved the body."

There was a soft creaking sound as the flags by the door to the café flapped in the breeze.

"We found him in the missing persons' database. Seems like the officer who wrote the report was pretty thorough. I'm wondering if she had a sneaking suspicion there was something else going on. That's the sense I got, reading between the lines."

Eira saw his smile fade and realized he was talking about her. A disappearance, a man, something she had been called out to.

"The one from Nyland? Hans Runne?"

GG nodded.

"We got his dental records sent up to Umeå. They X-rayed his jaw as soon as the body arrived. It's him."

The dog was trying to sniff out something in her pockets, and she pushed him away. Why hadn't she recognized Hans Runne from the pictures she'd seen? The beard, she thought, his sunken cheeks. It all happened so quickly when a person went without food. The details came flooding back to her like a river in spring. The unmade bed, the junk mail on the floor in the hallway, the rubbish that hadn't been taken out. Over a week had passed since she visited his apartment. The man in the basement of the abandoned building had been dead for a few days at most. She felt a knot in her chest, the realization that she had made a terrible mistake. Paloma Runne's photographs of her father flickered by. Wearing a Santa hat, a Midsummer crown in his hair, playing Hamlet with a skull in one hand.

"They've only just got started up in Offer," said GG. "People have basically had free access to the house, so the only person who hasn't left prints is probably the perpetrator. This isn't something we're going to solve with forensic evidence. What a goddamn name for a crime scene, by the way."

"Have you spoken to his daughter?"

"Not yet. Luleå is tracking her down. She's a student at the university there."

"We didn't find anything illegal in his background, nothing to suggest there'd been any crime." She felt a powerful urge to defend her actions. "My sense when we went into his flat was that he'd just gone away for a while. Hans Runne seemed like a perfectly normal man. An actor. He'd been through a divorce, might've had a drinking problem, but there was nothing that stuck out."

"A normal man," GG repeated.

"I know," said Eira. "There's no such thing as a normal man."

"Or woman."

Not in our world, in any case, she thought. It was her job not to be deceived, to see through the falsehoods, to ask all the necessary questions.

"Take the old lady over there," said GG, nodding to a woman shuffling slowly along the road, hunched over a walking frame with bags from the supermarket in Kramfors swinging from the handles. She had probably just come on the bus. "What do you think we'd find if we dug into her past?"

"That she won big on a scratch card," said Eira. "It was on TV, must be ten or fifteen years ago now. No one knows what Bettan did with the money, but there are rumors. Some people claim she was the victim of some kind of romance scam."

GG laughed.

"You see, this is why I want you on board," he said, smiling in such a way that she couldn't help but do the same. "Or one of them, anyway. I can't think of anyone with better local knowledge than you. To be perfectly honest, I'm useless at finding my way in the woods, but don't tell anyone."

The sun was in Eira's eyes, the leaves on the trees glowing in burning splendor. If it weren't for her deep aversion to fishing for praise, she would have loved to ask what the other reasons were.

"Other than the odd break-in, I've barely spent any time up there," she said. "I don't know any more about the people in Boteå Parish than anyone else."

"You know it's called Boteå Parish, for a start."

"Well, technically it's a district now, but most people still say parish."

GG stubbed out his cigarette and flicked it neatly—and possibly dangerously—into a nearby bin.

"I know you've said no before," he said, "but I thought I'd swing by and see what it would take to convince you this time." Rabble began bouncing around his legs as he got up. Eira tugged on the lead, pulling the dog into her arms.

"There was a reason I couldn't then," she said.

"And now?" His body was blocking the sun.

Eira looked out at the hodgepodge of a community where she had grown up. The Ångerman River valley had never been subject to any town-planning laws, with new houses simply built on top of the old ones, no more than a jumble of shacks at one point in time. She could see the chimney and the ridge of the roof on her childhood home. Her thoughts turned to how quiet and lonely the house now felt, and to her brother, who was serving time for manslaughter in Umeå. The dead man in Offer wasn't someone she knew. Things would be different this time.

"I'll need to talk to my boss," she said.

"Already done," said GG. "It's not a problem. Or rather, it's always a problem, but we'll sort it out internally."

"OK," said Eira.

"Should I take that as a yes?"

The fields stretched out in an open landscape between the farms to the south of Sollefteå. In one of them, hundreds of whooper swans had gathered before their long journey south. They sounded like a chorus of untuned trumpets as Eira got out of the car.

A woman was standing by the ditch at the side of the road, watching the birds. She was casually dressed, the wind tugging at her blond hair. Few would have guessed that she was an investigator with the Violent Crimes Unit.

"So, you're back," Silje Andersson said with a smile. It was the first time they had spoken since Eira found herself on the wrong side of the table in an interview room, trying to navigate questions about her own brother.

"How far have you made it?" Eira asked.

Silje pointed to a couple of houses on the other side of the road.

"Three point eight kilometers from the crime scene. We'll be seriously lucky if anyone saw anything."

"People often see more than they think."

"Or less," said Silje.

They left their cars at the side of the road and trudged over to the nearest farm. The dilapidated, dirty gray barn seemed too far gone to save, but the main building looked freshly painted.

The woman who opened the door was wearing sweatpants and a hoodie. A toddler and a golden retriever peered out from around her legs.

"Shit," she said once they explained who they were. "I heard on the radio that they'd found someone dead outside of Sollefteå, but I didn't realize it was so close. Was he murdered? Is that why you're here?"

"We don't know much yet," said Silje.

The woman invited them in, clearing her laptop and papers from the table. "I try to work whenever I can, but Ester's home from nursery with a runny nose, so I haven't got much done today."

Her dialect didn't sound local, from somewhere farther south. The kitchen was messy, bordering on chaotic.

"You're going to catch whoever did it, right?" she asked, giving the child an anxious glance. The usual fears had set in.

"Have you lived here long?" asked Eira.

"Only a year. We don't know many people yet."

"Have you ever been out to the abandoned house up by the lake, by Offersjön?"

"I wish I had," she said. "I really love abandoned houses. I've often wondered whether it's OK to take the things no one else wants."

They told her the timeframe they were interested in, from the middle of September when Hans Runne first disappeared. It was now October 15. An entire month. Few people could sort between memories over such a long period. They forgot, got things mixed up—assuming they had even noticed anything in the first place.

The woman opened the lid of her laptop and brought up a calendar, not that it helped.

"Living out here in the countryside—and with young kids—it can be hard to tell one day from the next. That's what's so nice about escaping the rat race."

"No strange cars, anything like that?"

"I'm sorry, I have no idea who usually drives past."

There was probably no point asking her husband, either. He knew next to nothing about cars, had only just got his driving license. He'd had no choice now that they were living in the sticks. Fed up of their cramped lives in the suburbs, they had sold their small flat and bought all this, with money to spare. She could just as easily do her work as a copywriter from here, even if the internet connection left a lot to be desired.

"You haven't been out there picking berries or anything?"

"Why bother when we've got plenty at the edge of our property?"

"And I'm guessing neither of you are into elk hunting?"

The annual hunt had taken place a few weeks earlier. People would have been out in the woods then, if not otherwise.

"No, God, no. We're vegetarians."

They thanked her and tried another few houses, where no one was home. Knocked and knocked until a widower opened his door. He insisted on making them coffee and ham sandwiches. Police officers had to eat something, he said.

Silje made do with coffee, but Eira said yes to the sandwich. She got the impression that the man was lonely, cheered by their visit.

"Oh yes, I know the house," he said, taking out precut buns and butter, searching his fridge for the ham. "It's a disgrace it's been left empty like that. Agnes and Karl-Erik would be turning in their graves if they knew. If there's a life after this one, that is."

Which, he added, he didn't believe there was. Once you were dead and buried you returned to earth, and just as well. Eternity would be tedious, constantly repeating things. Better this way, when the days had a bit of variation, changes in the weather and visits from beautiful women.

Police officers, he corrected himself.

"Agnes and Karl-Erik?" asked Silje.

"No one's lived in that house since they died, must be over ten years ago now. They had four kids, I think, they must all be past sixty now, but none of them wanted to take over."

That was the sad truth.

"And the people who own it now," said Eira. "Have you ever met them?"

"No, who are they?"

"A forestry company, I think." She glanced down at her notes. A business by the name of High Woods Holdings had acquired the property from the estate four years ago.

"Aha," said the man. "So are they going to clear the trees up there now?"

He said it without much emotion, more a statement than a question. Logging was an everyday occurrence in the region.

"Does the name Hans Runne ring any bells?"

A frown, an attempt to rack his memory for people and acquaintances. In the end he shook his head. If his parents were still alive, they could have told the officers all about Karl-Erik and Agnes Bäcklund. He had never really known them himself, both would be over ninety now, but he knew that Kalle had been part of the regiment over in Sollefteå and that Agnes worked on the till at the grocery store, an awfully long time ago now.

"Jan must be the only one who stayed in the area," he said, topping up their cups from the coffeepot. "Worked at the council offices in Sollefteå before he retired, now he's one of those people who spend their time bickering about politics. Quite right, too. Don't have the energy for that myself, not these days. I seem to remember that Karl-Erik had another child, from his first marriage, not that I've ever met them. There was none of this every-other-week being ferried back and forth business, even if people could get divorced."

There had been rumors about his previous missus, who was known simply as "the first wife." That she was difficult, from somewhere up Nolaskogs way, you know what they're like. Rash, a bit too confident, but also inclined to feeblemindedness, if you were unlucky. He laughed at the stereotypes—they were nonsense, of course—but the general feeling was that Kalle Bäcklund had traded her in for a better model.

"People always said he was kind, not what you'd expect from a military man of that generation; Agnes was actually the stricter of the two. Always telling the kids off when they traipsed mud into the house, that kind of thing."

That was what his younger brother had said, in any case. He used to go over there to play. The widower himself fell between the two generations.

In the end, Eira interrupted him.

"What we're really interested in are any cars or people you might have seen over there. Anything that seemed out of the ordinary over the past month."

"Well, I can't see the road from here." He gestured to the window, slightly downcast not to be able to help them. "But I can always ask the neighbors."

"Did you take part in the elk hunt this year?" asked Eira.

"Oh yes, got some painkillers for the back, damned sciatica." He thought for a moment. "But over by the abandoned house, on that side of the lake . . . No, I don't think we went over there at all."

An hour later, they had ticked off another three houses and talked to as many hunters. All confirmed that the year's elks had been felled kilometers from the crime scene.

Slowly but surely, they began to compile a list of cars that had pulled over or been seen parked by gravel tracks, driving down turn-offs that didn't lead anywhere, details such as "a white Volvo earlier this autumn, I wondered who the hell it could be, but God knows when that was."

Silje left her car on the edge of the community and rode with Eira instead. She sat with her laptop open on her knee, typing up the scant, incredibly vague details as they drove north, past a mirror-still Offersjön, a hint of ice around its shore.

"Whoever it was, they knew where they were going," said Eira. "They hardly drove around the area on the off chance of finding an empty house."

"We still have to ask."

They drove right up to the former iron foundry in Gålsjö. Pulled over and turned around by the cabins the summer visitors had long since vacated for the season. The few year-round residents who were at home hadn't seen anything noteworthy. Yes, there might have been a car by the forest road, but you just assumed it was someone out foraging for mushrooms, it wasn't something you paid much notice to. There were chanterelles growing in various places around the lake, but no one wanted to say exactly where.

"That's the kind of thing you want to pass on to your kids, you know?" said a woman who was leaning on a walking stick after breaking her femur. "Not that they're especially interested, so obviously if you want to know . . ."

By the old iron foundry, Silje trudged off to find a toilet. Eira got out of the car and watched her disappear between the empty workers' barracks. Just a few years earlier, during the great influx of refugees, the place had been full of life.

"Had to make do with the woods," Silje said once she came back, rinsing her hands using a bottle of mineral water.

It was only once they were back in the car, heading south, that she finally brought up their last meeting, the old investigation.

"You're not your family, you know," she said. "Not your parents or your siblings."

"I know," said Eira.

"I just wanted to put that out there."

"OK."

"I don't have any contact with mine," said Silje. "That works too."

Her words ate away at Eira as they knocked on another few doors on the other side of the road. The thought of not having to worry about what other people needed, no longer feeling guilty. It gave her a sense of emptiness.

"Turn left, right here."

Eira hit the brake. Finally, someone out and about. The man came towards them in a pair of overalls, pushing back his face shield. He had a workshop on the farm, smelled like freshly cut spruce.

"Yeah, you know what, I have seen a car parked up in the woods there," he said once they told him who they were.

"Near Offersjön?" said Eira.

"Yeah, maybe one hundred meters away. No more than two hundred, in any case. A Fiat Punto. Gold, I think it was."

"And when was this?"

He waved his hand in the air. The timeframe was slightly hazy.

"Could you show us on the map?" asked Silje.

"Might be better if I come with you."

The man drove ahead of them in his van, Svenne's Carpentry printed on the side. He indicated in good time before the turn.

The road tapered off and was swallowed up by brushwood. There was a wide turning circle in one direction, likely an old storage site for timber. The Fiat was parked some way in, between the spruces. Its front seats had been removed and were set out on the ground, like armchairs in a living room. The hubcaps were missing, as was the registration plate, every window broken.

"I'm guessing this has been here longer than a month?" said Eira.

The man laughed.

"Oh, I can promise you that. Must've been a few years now."

"So what makes you think it's of interest to us?"

Eira couldn't help but peer in through the broken windows. The steering wheel was also missing, and there was a plastic bag full of water-damaged papers on the back seat. Old schoolwork, she saw. She could make out the year 1972 and a name written in pencil, Rosemarie Strindlund. It was the surname that caught her eye, all too familiar.

"I've tried calling the police and the council and God knows who else," said the carpenter. "But now you can arrange for the lump of junk to be taken away whenever it's convenient."

Once the carpenter had gone, irritated that the police couldn't do anything about the old car—thus confirming his suspicions about the direction society was heading in—they trudged through the forest on nonexistent trails.

The abandoned house wasn't far from the wreck, voices reaching them through the trees.

"They could have come in this way," said Eira.

"Not surprising no one saw the car if they did, considering how long the Fiat has been here."

In the glade around the crime scene, the technicians were busy wrapping up. Removing a spotlight, winding in cables. The police cordon would soon be taken down, the cars driving away.

"We've got plenty to work with," GG said as they approached. He moved away from the house and lit a cigarette. As far as Eira could remember, he was always on the verge of quitting, every drag his last. "Twenty-five different fingerprints—was that what you said?"

He turned to the forensic technician who had just emerged from the house in a pair of protective overalls.

"Twenty-three," said Costel Ardelean. "But we can probably rule out thirteen or fourteen of them as belonging to kids."

"Can we, really?" GG muttered. "Rule them out, I mean? How many cases have there been lately? Not here, but they could've read about them, taken inspiration from them. Teenagers holding other teenagers captive, forcing them to give up the PINs for their bank accounts, doing the kind of thing that gets people's attention on Instagram."

"Isn't the ATM a bit far away?" said Silje.

A few more technicians came out, carrying a bundle between them. Material of some kind. A rolled-up mattress, too small for a grown man. Was that what he had been lying on? Eira felt a sudden, intense sense of being alive. The smell of the chill in the air, the others' breath.

"Some of the people we talked to remembered the family who used to live here a long time ago," she said. "But no one knew the current owners."

"They don't seem to care about their property, in any case," said Costel. "The house could have been unlocked for years. Every single person who's been creeping around here could have left a trace, not to mention the people who lived here last." He sighed. "Their relatives. Playmates. Dinner guests. We might be able to pin our hopes on the blood—assuming it comes from someone other than the victim."

In addition to the blood that had soaked into the mattress and the blanket the man was wrapped up in, they had found traces on a set of garden shears. Aside from that, there was no sign of violence, no drag marks or anything of the sort. The man was wearing jeans, from one of the more expensive Swedish brands, a shirt, smart shoes, and a thin jacket.

Hans Runne was hardly dressed for a walk in the forest.

A flock of fieldfares landed in a row on the ridge of the roof, as though each had a predetermined spot. Their call almost sounded like rattling. Eira's thoughts drifted to the photographer who had raised the alarm, to the ravens mentioned in her report. She knew that they liked to feed on other creatures' prey, eating the last of any cadavers they found.

"The question is what kind of crime we're talking about here," said GG. "Kidnapping, that's clear, but is it murder? Did they plan to come back?"

One of the technicians closed a trunk lid. Someone else took down the police tape. They had no answers. Nothing but guesswork and hastily drawn conclusions that they would do best to avoid.

"Or did they leave him here to die?"

Eira drove home alone. As she passed the whooper swans' territory, she spotted another flock of birds off in the distance. Geese, from what she could see, hundreds of grayish-brown heads. This was clearly some sort of central station for all kinds of migratory birds, a junction between north and south. A man with a telescope on a tripod was standing by the side of the road.

She left the door open to avoid disturbing the birds and slowly made her way over to him.

"Canada geese," he said softly, without looking up. "Not what you come to see, of course, but the odd barnacle goose occasionally tags along with them. Geese aren't so picky. If a bird wants to join another flock, so be it. You see there, behind the main group? If you're really lucky, you might spot a pink-footed goose, but they're less common."

He let Eira peer through the telescope, though she couldn't tell one bird from the next.

"Are you interested in birds?" he asked.

"Not really." She held up her ID. "I'm actually investigating a serious crime that took place not far from here. Kidnapping, possibly murder."

"Ah, yes, I heard about that." Their eyes shifted up towards the forest, where there were a couple of houses by the edge of the trees. "I saw the white-tailed eagle set off from there yesterday morning, which usually means the ice is starting to form. Or that someone disturbed it. It has one of its nests right by there."

"Do you go up there often, to the lake?"

"It's been a while. At this time of year you want to follow the big migratory flocks."

"What about the middle of September?"

"Is that how long he was there? Lying dead?"

"Do you remember whether you were in the area at the time? Whether you noticed anything? A car, a person, anything that seemed out of place?"

The man took off his hat and ran a hand through his hair. A few more lines appeared on his forehead.

"I'm thinking about the woodpecker," he said, slowly searching his memory. "The three-toed woodpecker, I don't know whether you're familiar with it? No, probably not. I followed the trail north of the lake there, it pecks a ring around the trunks of spruce trees to get at the sap, but it took me a few days to actually spot it. There might have been someone out foraging for berries, you know, people from town come up here during the season, but so long as they keep quiet and there aren't too many of them I don't mind. When they're shouting into their phones and causing a fuss, that's the kind of thing that annoys you, but was it then? The memory's not what it used to be. I've got a diary at home, where I write all my observations—not that I keep track of people and cars, that kind of thing doesn't interest me."

Eira gave him her number and asked for his. They were interrupted by a sudden honking overhead, yet another flock of geese approaching.

The man hunched over his telescope again, turning it to the north.

The apartment in Nyland smelled clean and fresh. There was very little junk mail or other post on the hallway floor, likely only from the past couple of days.

"Someone has cleaned," said Eira. "I'm sorry, I should have stopped them."

With no suspicion of a crime, there had been no grounds to seal the apartment.

The floors in the dead man's home had been scrubbed, the kitchen counters wiped, the rubbish taken out. There were no longer any glasses on the table in the living room. It felt like the evidence had been swept away, like a breeze had blown through the apartment.

Eira closed her eyes to remember what it was like before. She was good at detail, at noticing things that seemed unimportant. No overturned furniture, no sign of a struggle; she would have reacted to that.

"He'd been drinking red wine," she said. "There was a bottle over there." She pointed. "I think it was empty. Only one wineglass out, plus a smaller one, possibly for whisky."

"Like he'd had guests?"

"Or drunk both himself. My sense was that he was alone."

She closed her eyes again to focus on her impressions of his lone-liness. Was that something she had actually seen, or was it a conclusion drawn from the musty air, the dirty dishes and empty bottles, reinforced by what his ex-wife had said about their divorce?

The duvet had been smoothed out in the bedroom, the throw folded neatly on top.

"I'm not sure whether the bedding has been changed, but it was unmade before, the duvet was half on the floor."

"Like he'd had sex?"

"Yeah, maybe . . . Or just in a hurry to leave."

"We'll take them just in case."

What else? The Ulf Lundell book had been open, now it was closed. That was hardly important. Or was it? Perhaps it signaled a cer-tain calmness, a man who took the time to read before going to sleep?

"If you're deliberately trying to get rid of evidence," said Eira, "why would you bother to close a book?"

"Maybe they were reading it together," said GG. "Before the killer decided they'd had enough."

Eira laughed. It was a quiet laugh, and didn't last long at all, but it felt liberating to actually allow herself to do it.

"There was something about his ex-wife," she said after a moment. "She denied he was in a new relationship, but she also tried to give the impression that she didn't care. I got the sense that she hadn't quite let him go."

"Anyone who claims they have is usually lying." GG sounded glum, as though he were speaking from experience. They peered into the bathroom. More clean surfaces, a hint of bleach in the air, a few lonely shaving products in the cabinet. There was a faint shadow inside her colleague, a darkness she hadn't noticed before. Last time they worked together, he had mentioned trying for a baby with his new girlfriend. Eira knew it hadn't exactly gone to plan.

"She painted a picture of Runne falling apart after the divorce," she continued. "Said he'd started drinking more, being careless with money. But she's hardly objective."

"No one is," said GG. "Especially not if they've been married."

They made way for the forensic technicians, GG holding the door open for her as they left the apartment.

"We want to be missed," he added. "And if that fails, remembered."

Down in the yard, they joined their colleagues, who were busy canvassing the neighbors. They went from building to building on Borgargatan, knocking on door after door. Like many of the other streets in Nyland—named after merchants, bishops, and captains—the name bore witness to the locals' sense of grandeur at one point in time. A century earlier, an investigation had determined that Nyland was home to the best spoken Swedish in the country. The community had competed with Kramfors to be granted a town charter, so confident of victory that they built a courthouse and grand streets worthy of a big city, but ultimately they lost. Opposite the building where Hans Runne had lived, dandelions now grew between the tracks of a disused rail line.

They had managed to keep his name out of the press, but it was surely only a matter of hours—a day, at most—until they would no longer be able to get spontaneous reactions out of people. The minute his name became common knowledge, people would start to talk. They would remember things they thought they had seen, or be so ashamed by how little they knew their neighbor that they tried to bend the truth.

It was just under two years since Hans Runne had bought his apartment for next to nothing, 35,000 kronor, and returned to Nyland, where he grew up.

An old woman living opposite had given him a spoonful of cumin; the man certainly seemed to like cooking. She knew he was an actor and that he'd had a part in the wildly popular series about an archipelago doctor some twenty years earlier. She had tracked it down on SVT Play, just for the sake of it.

They also spoke to a woman from Bosnia who worked as a carer. She left home early in the morning and rarely saw anyone. To a man who had just retired from the sawmill in Bollstabruk, the last in the area.

"Five weeks ago, you say? I hardly remember if I saw my own brother yesterday. Do you ever think about how the days merge together more and more? You trudge the same loop, ten thousand steps, that's what they say you should do. They've got us obsessed with counting our steps towards death. No surprise there's never any revolutions these days."

They had ticked off the first building and were back out in the yard. GG took the opportunity for a quick smoke.

"You have this idea that people must know their neighbors when they live out in the sticks," he said.

"Don't let them hear you calling Nyland the sticks," said Eira.

In the next stairwell, they were met by a shout that echoed and wrapped itself around her like a tight knitted sweater.

"Oh my God, Eira Sjödin, is that you?"

Eira racked her memory, peeling back a number of kilos from the woman's body. Her hair might have been darker back then, but those eyes, that laugh . . .

"Stina? I didn't know you lived here."

Her childhood pal, her best friend. Eira was immediately racked with guilt. She was the one who had moved away and returned, but she had never got in touch. For some reason the responsibility was always on the person who left. It came with a sense of betrayal, even if they had lost contact long before.

"My God, you look the same as ever," said Stina. "I heard you were a cop now, that you were back. I've been waiting for you to call."

Her eyes wandered over to GG, her smile changing.

"This is Georg Georgsson," said Eira. "Lead investigator with Violent Crimes." It sounded much too formal, as though she thought she belonged to that world and was taking a step back from the one she came from.

"Oh shit," said Stina.

"We're investigating a crime against someone who lives in the building next door."

"Here? Who? Seriously?"

They had been friends from the very first year of school. Stina was the one Eira had broken the rules with. Taking their bikes all the way to Kungsgården, for example, creeping around the house where Lina's killer lived.

"Do you know a man called Hans Runne?" asked GG.

"Yeah, God, yeah. The actor, right? I can't say I *know* him, but he seems nice. Not bad looking, either. What's going on, has he done something?"

"He was found dead."

"Come off it. Here?"

The floor in the hallway was littered with shoes of varying sizes. Eira remembered that Stina had got pregnant while they were still in high school, that she'd had to take a year out. How many more had she had since, two or three?

"I saw him with a girl once," she said. "Really young, actually. It made me do a double take."

Eira searched for a photograph of Paloma Runne on Facebook as her childhood friend recalled that Hans Runne had been playing loud music late one night, with his balcony doors open. Stina had shouted over to him, it must've been a few months ago, that was it, back when it was hot, but not to complain, she'd been hoping for an invite to the party.

"Was this the girl you saw?" Eira held up the image.

"Yeah, right, could've been."

"That's his daughter."

"OK, thought it might be. He must've been what, fifty?"

"Forty-seven."

"Right, still handsome though." Stina flashed GG an appreciative glance. Eira gave her card before they left, a call me if you think of anything, it would be good to catch up sometime.

They met the others for a debrief by the cars. The clouds were rolling in from the surrounding mountains, over the yard outside the dead man's building.

"His old classmate from junior school lives in the block at the far end," said a trainee from Sundsvall—they had brought in extra resources. "He claims they were best friends back then, but they didn't hang out."

"He could just as easily have bullied him," said GG. "No one ever has as many friends as someone who's just died."

"We've got a guy on the ground floor in number twelve," said Anja Larionova, a local investigator who typically dealt with petty crimes in Kramfors. She was in her sixties, but she often dyed her hair according to her moods and the season. It was currently a shade of pink. "Uno Harila," she said, flicking through her notes. "He used to stop and chat with Runne whenever he ran into him, even though they disagreed on most things."

"Such as?"

"The way the country is run. Runne was someone who, and I quote 'wants them to let in every Tom, Dick, and Harry, even though people like him are out of work.'"

"Was he talking about actors there?"

She gave GG a smile. "More generally, I should think. Anyway, Harila scrolled back on his phone and found a message from his wife that made him remember toilet paper."

"Toilet paper?"

"His wife sent him a message reminding him to buy some, so he's sure of the date. It was September 12, a little before dinner."

Two days before Hans Runne's phone last put out a signal.

Anja Larionova had recorded his statement. The others huddled around as the air grew cooler and the first raindrops began to fall.

"Yeah, it's coming back to me now," said a man's voice, a hint of a Finnish accent. "I was lugging a huge pack of toilet paper out of the car. I'd done a big shop at Willys in Kramfors, it must've been on sale—every roll's half the price that way. He came out and held the door open. On his way to Härnösand, he said, nicely dressed, heading to the pub. I remember that, because he was always complaining about having no work. That's probably why it stuck in my memory, that and because I was balancing sixty-four rolls on my shoulder."

"He starts getting a bit long-winded here," said Anja Larionova, switching off the recording. "But essentially he says that Runne was talkative, that he seemed in good spirits. The witness didn't want to talk shit, as he put it, but Runne could put on airs sometimes."

"And his clothes?" asked GG.

"A shirt and some sort of fancy jacket, possibly a blazer. No tie, that wasn't Runne's style, he was more the bohemian type—a bit of a do-gooder. Uno Harila's words. The elderly woman one floor up described him as terribly nice, a real man."

GG met Eira's eye.

A shirt, a fancy jacket of some sort.

That could fit the description of the clothes they had seen, filthy and oversized on the emaciated body in the basement.

They went their separate ways, and Eira headed back to her car outside the supermarket. She decided to do some shopping while she was there; the fridge had been in a sorry state ever since her mother moved out. Two grilled chicken thighs, a bag of chips, a quick lap around the vegetable aisles, frozen salmon.

There were many reasons she hadn't reached out to her old friends since she moved back home. Kerstin's dementia, above all, which had kept her on a relatively tight leash. There was the difficulty of answering any questions about Magnus, too. Did she have a single female friend who hadn't been in love with him at some point?

But that wasn't the whole truth.

Eira paid and left the supermarket, pausing when she reached her car. She heard the shopping trolleys rattling across the car park, acquaintances bumping into one another, shouting hello and making small talk for a moment or two.

It struck her that Hans Runne might have gone through the same thing. He had lived in Härnösand for almost twenty years before moving back to Nyland, and had also done a few brief stints in Stockholm.

There was a certain imbalance in being the person who returned. As though something had been upset, something to do with loyalty. Talking to your old classmate from the building at the end of the street could be harder than chatting to a complete stranger.

So who did he gravitate towards?

An actor, in a place like this. And one who was looking for work, at that.

Eira walked the short distance over to the old courthouse, where no courts had been in session for years. A composer from down south had bought the huge building around twenty years ago. She remembered he had been charged with environmental offenses after he threw a burning piano from the Hammar Bridge as part of a concert project.

"Bloody hell, yes," said the composer, who spoke with a thick Skåne accent. "He knocked on the door one day, asking if I had anything in the works, a role in a project or something. I gave him a glass of wine and we spent the evening chatting. Has something happened to him?"

He slumped down into a chair in the foyer when Eira broke the news. It was something she had done many times, being the messenger who turned people's worlds upside down.

The composer had been busy working on a piece for a Dutch violinist that would have its world premiere in Dusseldorf, but they had brainstormed the idea of putting on summer performances about the witch trials that took place in the area. It was so exciting to have an actor in the neighborhood, and Hasse would have been perfect in the role of the priest from Ytterlännä's old church, the one who condemned the women to death for witchcraft.

They had bumped into each other at the supermarket a few times since, chatted a little, but other things got in the way.

"I can't say I really knew him, but he seemed pretty harmless. Had a bit too much of a need to assert himself, maybe, but who doesn't?"

Eira took Rabble out that evening. Ran with him on a slack lead as she thought about the hunched body in the basement, letting everything she had seen and heard swirl through her head. Her brief meeting with Stina kept coming back to her, thoughts about where their paths had diverged, whether it was when Stina got pregnant and withdrew from the group, from school, or whether it was Eira who pulled away, afraid she might never leave. That she would end up getting pregnant, trapped. At the back of her mind, the question that had been bothering her since she was old enough to long for something she couldn't quite put her finger on reared its head: stay or leave, home or away? She still didn't have any answers. Eira had come home because her mother needed her, but now?

She heard the thudding of paws alongside her and thought about how invisible Hans Runne's life seemed to have been during his last few years. These streets were so full of memories, stories about people and events she had heard time and time again.

Eira Sjödin wouldn't leave any anecdotes behind. There was nothing about her that stuck out, that was worth sharing with others, nothing noteworthy. The air would simply fill in the gap she left, like the water closing in behind a foot on stepping out of the river.

When she reached the beach, she unclipped Rabble's lead. A few leaps and he was gone, sniffing around in the darkness somewhere. She became aware of the uncertainty beneath her, a terrain in which deep holes could open up. Some of the beaches flanking the Ångerman River were made of waste from the sawmill era rather than solid ground. The silence embraced her. Nothing but the odd car crossing the Sandö Bridge as it rose up into the heavens, driving away.

"Coincidences," said GG, closing the door. "Have I ever mentioned how much I hate coincidences?"

They were at the police station in Härnösand, in a meeting room with views out across the bay that cut between the islands on which the town was built. Outside, the blustery north wind whipped the last of the autumn leaves up into the air, some as high as the fourth floor.

Other than GG, Eira was the only other person physically in the room. Everyone else had joined remotely, from Sollefteå and Sundsvall. The investigation didn't have a fixed base, it stretched across the whole of southern Ångermanland, from the crime scene eighty kilometers inland, via Nyland where Hans Runne had lived, and out to Härnösand on the coast, where his phone had last connected to a mast on the evening of September 14.

"Either he was in Härnösand when his phone went off," said GG, "or his phone was here without him."

It was now October 18. The trail couldn't be much colder.

Silence, the clearing of a throat, the crackle of someone moving near their microphone. Five or six faces in squares on a screen, one person joined and another disappeared, a hoarse voice, an unfamiliar dialect. Eira knew a few of them in passing, but most were complete strangers.

"He spent a lot of time in the online casinos," said someone from Sundsvall, tasked with going through his bank accounts and other records. "No huge sums, just a few thousand kronor, not even into five figures. No sign of any big loans in his accounts, but no real assets either . . ."

The sound faded to a murmur, interrupted by a voice she recognized.

"We found thirty or so pieces of physical evidence in the house," said Costel Ardelean. "But only one fingerprint matching any of the databases. Belonging to a dead person. Shot with their own weapon."

"Recently?"

"Three years ago."

"Damn it."

GG was fiddling with a felt-tip pen on the table in front of him. In the past he might have started drawing lines and circles on the whiteboard at the front of the meeting room, adding dates and times, a structure that grew and gave the illusion of progress, but it was pointless when anyone who had joined remotely couldn't see.

Besides, it would soon be rubbed out.

Eira took a blank sheet of paper from a stack on the table and began sketching out the details for herself as various voices recapped what they knew.

Social media activity, call lists. Using his bank statements, they had been able to trace some of his movements, buying tickets, paying in bars, but the timeline was irritatingly vague and full of holes. It was like the life line on a palm with all its creases and folds, broken and diffuse. Either that or a river and its many tributaries.

Almost two days had passed between the last known sighting of Runne outside his apartment building and the point at which his phone signal vanished.

After that, a month of nothing.

"So, an unemployed actor leaves his home early in the evening on September 12 and uses his card for the last time that same evening . . ."

"At three different bars. The last one was Stadt in Härnösand," Silje spoke up. She was in Sundsvall. "And judging by the total sum, we can probably assume he was drunk."

There were no further transactions after that, just his phone connecting to various masts, moving back and forth along the river.

"But that doesn't tell us who actually had the phone," said GG. He got up and took a few steps, meaning the majority could only see his trousers. "It could have been the victim, but it could just as easily have been the perpetrator or some teenage kid who found it dumped somewhere. The key thing is that Hans Runne didn't make a single call after his night out in Härnösand."

"If he got drunk that evening," said Silje, "and then started wandering around Härnösand, he could've got into an argument with the wrong people?"

"What are we looking at in terms of overall criminal activity here?"

The answer was a long one, and came from an investigator focused on organized crime in the region. Sundsvall was a large city by Swedish standards, but it wasn't home to any of the family-based crime networks often debated in the press. Those gangs had started to branch out from the bigger cities in the south, however, extending their tentacles into Norrland and making sure there wasn't a single part of the country that was left wanting for narcotics. On top of that, the traditional motorcycle gangs were locked in increased competition in the drug trade.

"I spoke to the pathologist just before this call," Silje butted in. "The autopsy won't be finished until tomorrow at the earliest, but she gave me some tentative information about his mutilated hand."

The two missing fingers.

"The wounds hadn't healed when he died, and they were infected. Three to seven days old, that was her guess."

Eira heard multiple people take a deep breath. This was something concrete, violent. It was something to go on.

"OK," said GG, leaning forward over the table, towards the screen. "As soon as we have an exact timeframe, we'll start knocking on doors in the area again. This gives us at least two occasions when someone up there could have seen the person or persons responsible—when Runne was first taken to the house, and when the perp returned."

"Three," said Silje.

"What?"

"Three occasions," she clarified. "The two wounds were at different stages of healing. This is just preliminary, obviously, and not something the pathologist was willing to put down in writing, but . . ."

"What exactly are you trying to say?"

"That it looks like the perp went back twice, not once."

"Jesus Christ," someone blurted out.

"Why cut the fingers off someone who seems to have been broke?"

"I guess they thought he had money."

"So are we talking about one perpetrator, or multiple people?"

They had forgotten all about the etiquette governing digital meetings, one person speaking at a time, with clear beginnings and endings. Instead they began talking over one another, in both Sundsvall and Härnösand, even the local investigator in Sollefteå.

"Smartly dressed, isn't that what someone said? A fancy jacket or something? Even if the guy didn't have any money, he looked like he did."

"Are we really sure he's as clean as he seems? They must have been threatening him with something—blackmail, something shitty he'd done to someone."

Eira gave up trying to keep track of who was saying what.

"Could it have been over a close relative? I don't know if you remember the case we had in Sundsvall, a kidnapping, a whole family was held hostage to get at the son."

"Or maybe they just did it for fun."

"If that's the case, why stop at the fingers?" said Silje. "According to the pathologist there was no other sign of violence."

"Torture doesn't always leave a mark. There are methods, I seem to remember the junta in Argentina using them, for example. They focused on electricity, waterboarding . . ."

"And where do you think they got the electricity from, in an abandoned house?"

"Thanks everyone, that's enough," said GG, quickly recapping everyone's tasks. Once the scraping of chairs had faded and everyone had disconnected, he turned to Eira.

"What do you think, shall we pay the ex-wife another visit?"

• • •

Cecilia Runne seemed to have won the lottery in the divorce. Even the stairwell of her building was flooded with light from the tall bay windows. Eira had always thought that Härnösand had a certain arrogance, as though the town itself was looking down on her with its grand buildings and pompous parks. Perhaps it was because it had always been the seat of power in the region, home to the county administrative board that gave the orders to bring in the military against the striking workers in Lunde in the 1930s. An inherited sense that it was the kind of place where you were supposed to doff your hat, curtsey or get down on hands and knees.

"Sorry, I don't know what I was thinking," said Cecilia Runne. "Just that our daughter shouldn't have to deal with it. I asked her to send the key." She was perched on the very edge of the sofa, the mug of green tea in her hand shaking slightly. She put it down without taking a single sip.

"So you went in and cleaned three days before we found him," said GG. "Why? Did you have reason to suspect that your ex-husband was dead?"

"No, no. I kept thinking that he'd run off or got caught up in something; it wouldn't be the first time." Her eyes drifted to a piece of art above the TV. Abstract, geometric shapes. GG waited for her to go on. The woman poked at her cuticles. Her nails were perfect, pale pink. The color actually matched the sofa. Eira felt a sting of unease when she noticed that. Someone has to keep it together, she thought. There's always someone who can't afford to give in to the chaos.

"I didn't think he'd been murdered," Cecilia Runne eventually said. "If anything, I thought . . ."

"What?"

"Hasse came across as happy, but there was another side to him, the darkness overwhelmed him sometimes. That probably goes hand in hand with a sense of grandeur, doesn't it? The idea that you're worthless if no one actually sees you. All eyes on me, you know?" She rubbed something from her eye, blinked, a tear or an eyelash. "I saw that it's in the evening papers now. They're calling him a famous actor. Why didn't they ever write that while he was alive?"

The police had released his name that morning. Hans Runne's relatives had been informed, and there was no real reason to try to keep it from the papers. If anything, they were hoping for tips from the general public. There were trainee officers manning the phones in Sundsvall, attempting to sort the cranks from the reliable callers.

"He would treat complete strangers to a round of drinks at the pub, people he'd just met, even though we could barely afford the rent and the bills. I'm earning well these days, but back then . . . And all so he could be the center of attention for a while. He did get acting jobs, he'd be away for months at a time, but then he stopped getting them. He started talking about them instead, telling anecdotes about famous actors he'd worked with, making grand gestures to show that he could."

She took a tissue from a box on the coffee table and discreetly blew her nose, then hid it in her hand.

"Sometimes I think the only reason he moved back to Nyland was so he could blame everything on Nyland. Anyone could see that, if he didn't get any parts there."

"Have you met anyone else since your divorce?" asked GG.

"What does that have to do with anything?" She laughed and pushed her fringe to one side in a girlish way, crossing one leg over the other. "If you really want to know, no, I haven't. Falling in love would obviously be nice, but I'm not sure I ever want to get married again."

"Do you still love him?"

A strained laugh, a glance in GG's direction that was, perhaps, slightly flirtier than appropriate.

"What a question," she said. "Do I have to answer that?"

"Is it a difficult question?"

"No, it's just a bit private."

The officers tasked with scouring Hans Runne's social media presence had established that he liked his friends' posts but rarely shared anything about himself. His last post was from June, when one of his films was repeated on TV. Cecilia Runne had given that particular post a heart.

"It was me who left him," she continued. "He'd barely looked at me for years, but then he decided that he couldn't live without me, that he'd go under if I left."

"Was he jealous?"

"Yes, actually, but this has nothing to do with me, does it?"

The questions continued. Who Hans Runne associated with, what he usually got up to in Härnösand, whether they were in the habit of meeting. None of Cecilia's answers gave them anything concrete to go on. He seemed to have done what many people do after a divorce: found new friends. Or perhaps it was his old friends who had rejected him. Hans had taken her surname when they got married, and he had chosen to keep it after the divorce. Rather that than go back to being a Svensson again.

"I have no idea who he hung out with," she said. "Hasse would've tagged along with anyone willing to pay him attention for a while."

Bittens Rockbar was only two blocks away, on the corner of Storgatan. It was quiet that afternoon, Dylan playing over the speakers. A poster on the wall revealed that there had been an Oktoberfest party the weekend before, with half-price drinks for anyone in lederhosen.

"Damn it," said GG. "I should've dusted mine off."

Hans Runne had likely come straight to the bar from the train station that evening in September. He had settled up less than an hour later, meaning he couldn't have drunk more than one beer.

The man behind the bar recognized him from the photograph.

"Yeah, God, I was reading about this online a few hours ago. We were talking about it, how he used to come here sometimes, but as for who he chatted to . . . Sorry, as long as people are behaving, I don't pay much attention to what they're up to. They order a beer, they get a beer. I know he usually wanted a pint of bitter, that's the kind of thing you notice in this line of work. We once got talking about how Ulf Lundell has started sounding more and more like Tom Waits over the years, that same slowness and a different kind of depth, you can't hear as much Springsteen in him anymore. Your man said that might just be what happens with age, as the final darkness approaches. Or that maybe it's a different kind of calm. Either way, it was beautifully said, but I don't know whether it's true."

"Was this in September?"

"No, no, it must've been over the summer, maybe even last summer."

They made their way over one of the bridges, where the inlet was no wider than a canal. Hans Runne could have taken the same route when he moved on at around eight that evening, going for a dinner that cost him 275 kronor.

GG walked with his eyes on his phone, muttering something about hundreds of tips that had come in.

"Who's going to remember someone quietly drinking a beer? A poor sod on their last walk?"

The town's streetlamps rippled in the dark water, bursting into cascades of light. Eira remembered a story that had been passed down through the generations, about the day the first electric streetlamps were switched on in Härnösand. It was the second place in Europe to get them, long before Paris and Rome and Berlin. Someone had cried out for the sinners to be forgiven, but most had celebrated the remarkable invention. Pushing a button and creating light, just like in the Bible. It was hard to grasp just how wealthy the town had once been.

The restaurant was down by the quay, in a building that looked like a small cabin with round windows. It was dinnertime when they arrived, and they decided to eat. Salmon pasta and sirloin steak. GG ordered a glass of red wine.

"I don't have to drive," he said. "There's a police apartment I can use a few blocks from here."

A quick glance at the prices on the menu was all it took to establish that Hans Runne had only paid for one person. His bill covered a main meal and, at most, a glass of the house wine.

"Sorry, I wasn't working that evening," said the restaurant manager. She was around Eira's age, a little over thirty, her fair hair tied up in a ponytail.

"The question is how much you have to spend for someone to remember you existed," GG said once she had gone. "What's the limit? Dessert, a coffee, and a shot of brandy?"

The waitress who brought their food remembered Hans Runne.

"I don't really know why," she said, studying the photograph. "Maybe because he flirted a bit, but not in a creepy way. More, you know, to cheer me up. He said he hoped I had big dreams."

"And you're sure he was alone?"

"Yeah, that's why I stayed a bit longer than usual, because he was by himself. You want to give people a bit more attention then, you know?"

"Did you see him leave?"

"No . . . I don't think he left a tip . . ."

The food gave them the illusion of being off the clock, a shadowland at the edge of their professional lives. Swampy ground, one might call it, a place where it was easy to sink into the private sphere—particularly if, like GG, you lacked all boundaries.

"So, what's your living situation these days?" he asked once the waitress was gone. "You married, in a relationship?"

"Nope, I'm alone," said Eira. She immediately wanted to correct herself. Single, she should have said. That sounded much more positive, hopeful, and self-confident.

"Is it your childhood home you've taken over in Lunde?"

"Yes. Well, no, it's still my mum's house, but someone has to look after it." Did he really think this was a simple conversation for her? The truth was that Eira couldn't make a single decision about the house without talking to her brother. GG knew that Magnus was serving a six-year sentence for manslaughter, of course. He had led the investigation.

"And you're happy there?" he asked, cutting off a big chunk of steak. "Among the stones where, as a child, you used to play?"

"Yes, of course I'm happy." Eira ate a forkful of tagliatelle and wished she didn't have to drive home, that she could drink wine and get lost in a discussion about all those things, really get drunk.

"It's cheap, in any case," she said. "They finished paying off the mortgage years ago. If you owe money you're not free, that's what my dad would've said, launching into a story about how the mill shackled its workers with debt."

"Well, cheers to that," said GG, draining his glass.

Eira went to the toilet before they left. GG's words about stones had stuck in her mind. The line came from an old Swedish poem: *I long for home. I seek where'er I go—not men-folk, but the fields where I would stray. The stones where as a child I used to play.*

She had moved back to Ådalen for her mother's sake, but was that the whole story, or did the place mean more to her than she realized?

They cut over the street to Stadshotellet. GG peered up at the windows, to where the infamous dance hall had once been, one floor up.

"Hotel bars," he said. "People drift through them, often only staying one night."

"You never know," said Eira.

"And he spent . . . how much?"

"Eighty-nine kronor."

"One beer, then."

"An expensive beer."

"Unless our man got into a fight or started stripping on a table, we're not going to learn anything new here tonight," said GG. "We've requested the names of all the paying guests from that evening, so that'll be plenty for us to go through over the next few days. On top of the hundred"—he took out his phone—"the 149 tips from the public. Go home and get some rest."

"OK."

"Umeå tomorrow."

"See you there."

• • •

He felt pleased with himself as he climbed the steps to the bar in Stadt. Towards the murmur of voices, the music, the clinking of glasses, and the illusion that anything could happen.

It had been the right decision to let her go. The chances of finding out anything new were minimal, and she had been working as hard as ever, police assistant Eira Sjödin.

There had been moments when he wanted to ask her to come with him, and they weren't entirely for professional reasons.

The thought of her caused something unsettling to spread through him, something that was best washed away with something else.

GG sat down at the bar and ordered a gin and tonic from the town's own distillery. It was strange how popular luxury spirits had become in the area. Whatever happened to the proud Norrland tradition of making moonshine in the basement or the outhouse? It had become increasingly rare to catch a whiff of the solvent-like smell of fusel alcohol during raids.

GG had a brief conversation about it with the barman, and decided to put off flashing his ID.

He would rather avoid giving his title, would prefer just to sit there, scanning the bar. Letting the sense of drunken expectation fill him, even if the place wasn't what it had once been. When he was growing up, the bar had a reputation as a den of debauchery—it had even been immortalized in a hit song from the eighties about the heat and sweat at Stadt in Härnösand.

Not this time, GG thought as he sipped his drink, drumming up the necessary energy to do his job. Exactly how long had he been avoiding the women who might do real damage to him?

Almost two years now.

"So, what do you think?"

GG looked up. At first he didn't understand what the bartender was asking him. Everyone was expected to have an opinion on everything these days.

The man pointed down at his drink.

"Ah. Good," said GG.

"Hernö Gin beats almost anything else in the gin world right now, and I'm not just saying that because we're in Härnösand."

GG dug out his phone and brought up the image of Hans Runne. "Do you recognize this man?"

No reaction. The bartender really was trying. GG gave him the date, the evening when they knew Runne had been to the bar, but no.

"Let me see if I was working then." He checked his calendar. "Nope, sorry. Do you want me to ask my colleagues?"

GG had managed to make the switch to whisky by the time all the other members of staff had studied the photograph. One of the waiters recognized him, but couldn't pin him down to a particular evening, and not with any particular company either.

A single evening, remembered by no one. *What're you doing here, brother?* That was what GG would have asked him if they were sitting at the same bar together. *Why did you take the bus to Kramfors and then catch the train to Härnösand? All that way. What were you hoping for?*

Out of habit, his eyes began wandering the bar, entirely of their own volition. They latched on to one woman for a second or two, then another.

They all seemed young, which set his warning bells ringing. If there was one thing he couldn't allow himself to do again, it was get close to a younger woman.

One of them happened to meet his eye, but she quickly looked away. The fleeting glances of hotel bars.

Another drink, and that would be it for the evening.

His last girlfriend had been around their age. It was probably just the dim lighting and the alcohol, but he could actually see her sitting over there, laughing with the others. The attraction had nothing to do with their bodies, that was such a superficial cliché. It was the sense of curiosity they woke in him. Seeing the world in a new light, through eyes that hadn't already seen everything, being fundamentally shaken up. Ensuring that the rest of his life wouldn't be more or less the same.

A minefield.

She had packed her toothbrush and everything else that was scattered around the apartment, told him she had to put herself first. She was right about that.

GG had talked about it with an old friend he saw from time to time. The friend had been loyal and really let loose on her, said she was clearly only out to get knocked up, that she had dumped him as soon as that plan went off the rails. But GG had stood up for her. It was the other way around, he said. He was the one who had duped her, giving her the impression that he was a man who could provide everything she needed, the way people always do in the first glow of love, when nothing is quite real but we tell ourselves that everything is truer than before.

He had been lying low ever since, as best he could.

His pocket buzzed with a message. GG realized he was struggling to focus. A slight nausea when he tried, his eyes a little hazy.

"I've been thinking," he read. "There are a few things I'd like to talk to you about."

The message was from Cecilia Runne, the victim's ex-wife. Had he really given her his number? Maybe he had. Her fate had really struck a chord with him, the fact that she was mourning without quite counting as one of the mourners.

GG tried to focus on the tiny clock in the top corner of his screen. The numbers were so damned small, but surely it wasn't so late yet?

One tunnel led into another, a never-ending tunnel, farther and farther away. She was going the wrong way, but she couldn't turn back. An alarm started blaring and Eira ran, ducking down, she had to make it, that was her alarm, she had forgotten she was working and now she was late, someone would die, there was a way out, it led to the basement beneath her own house, the crawl space where she sometimes hid as a child, that was somewhere no one would ever look. The sound grew louder, dragging her back to reality.

The voice mail took over before Eira managed to reach her phone. It was just after five in the morning.

She was wide awake the minute she heard GG's voice. Something had come up, he said, she would have to go to Umeå on her own.

Eira downed her glass of water and opened the blind. It didn't make much difference; the darkness outside was compact. She felt an anxiety in her body, the dream still lingering. It was both familiar and new. She often dreamed she was running late, in the wrong place, but never in basements or tunnels. It didn't exactly take a dream reader to work out what it meant. The case had encroached into her sleep, she was powerless against it.

A psychologist might have said that she needed to establish clearer boundaries between her work and her private life, but what would be left of her sense of self then, if she didn't care, didn't allow herself to get involved?

She set the coffee brewing and checked the train times from Kramfors. There was one that left for Umeå in an hour, meaning she could avoid the roads. The ice could arrive without warning at this time of year.

The air smelled like snow, a delicate layer of frost on the car windows.

Eira parked outside the station and ran inside to print a few documents so that she could make the most of her time on the train. She bumped into August in the stairwell on her way back down.

He blocked her way, a smile on his face.

"Haven't see much of you lately," he said.

"Busy with the case," said Eira. She couldn't help but smile back. It was easier when they weren't sent out on patrol together, standing a little too close, her eyes lingering on his. She hadn't seen him in days, and wanted to stay in that warmth, the slight nervousness. He was taller than her, even though he was standing one step below.

"You going to catch the bastards, then?" he asked.

"We'll get them. Though we don't actually know if there's more than one." She checked her phone. Ten minutes until the train left. "I have to go." She deliberately brushed his hand as she passed. He gripped it for a brief moment.

"I've missed you," he said.

It was rare for anyone to board or leave the train at Västeraspby. The new station to the north of Kramfors was in the middle of nowhere, surrounded by nothing but forest. A small waiting room that had been burnt down not long after it opened, only to be rebuilt. Strange that they had chosen to put the station there and not in Nyland, just a few kilometers away. It could have given the community an opportunity to flourish. But the vision had been to link the Bothnia Line with the airport, even deeper in the forests, thereby creating some sort of transport hub.

As the train pulled in to the near-deserted platform, it didn't feel like anything of the sort.

A single older man boarded the train, taking a seat at the very end of the carriage. There was something familiar about him. He smiled and nodded, but it wasn't until he had taken off his rucksack and put it down on the seat beside him that Eira realized who he was. The telescope case.

The ornithologist.

Geese stopping over, whooper swans. She wondered whether they had left now that November was approaching, whether Offersjön had already frozen.

The birdwatcher got up and slowly made his way towards her, gripping the backs of the seats as he walked. The train rocked as it sped through the forests, over fields that glittered with frost in the rising sun.

De Vahl, that was his surname. That or something like it, she had jotted it down somewhere. Devall? The name wasn't uncommon in the area, it could be traced right back to one of the Walloon blacksmiths who had arrived in the eighteenth century. There were some ten or so different spellings, many had tried to make it sound more

Swedish in an attempt to fit in. She knew one person whose ancestors had actually changed their name to Larsson.

Bengt Devall, that was it!

"Sorry to bother you, but you're the police officer, aren't you?" The man gestured to the seat opposite her.

Eira confirmed that she was and instinctively shuffled slightly closer to the window. Had the pandemic forever altered the natural distance between people?

"I've been thinking about giving you a ring, you see," he said. "But then I thought you were probably busy enough as it was. Terrible thing, what happened. And in the same woods we're always trudging about in. Keep an eye out for bears, everyone knows that, but people? Well, you don't give much thought to them when you're out walking, that they might be a threat. That's more a city thing."

And the home, Eira felt like adding, though she held her tongue. For an elderly man in the region, the real dangers often came from within: loneliness, the urge to drink. If a male from Norrland died of a gunshot wound, the chances were he had fired the weapon himself.

"Did you think of anything else?" She wasn't looking for small talk or company, had already taken out the printouts and was planning to delve into the other cases of kidnapping that had occurred in recent years. Someone in Sundsvall had compiled a long list.

"I checked my logbook after we met," said Devall. "And it was as I thought: I was out and about looking for the three-toed woodpecker on the fourth and fifth of October. I've seen my fair share of them already, mind you, but this was before the migratory birds started to arrive . . ."

The train slowed into Örnsköldsvik as he told Eira all about the woodpecker's habits. The hill and its ski-jump track loomed over the town like a giant, slumbering as it waited for snow.

"Numbers are actually going down, so we shouldn't take them for granted, they're disappearing like so many other species with the old forests, they live off insects on dead trees."

"What did this make you remember?" Eira asked once the train set off again, avoiding the debate about whether they should be protecting the birds or supporting the forestry industry. It was a hot topic. The forests meant jobs, money. Most people she knew in Ådalen wouldn't exactly be manning the barricades for the three-toed woodpecker.

"A terrible scream," said Devall. "I don't know how I could have forgotten it, but I suppose my mind was elsewhere. I get completely lost in the birds' world when I'm out there, as though I could fly off with them. I often do, in spirit."

"Which direction did this scream come from?"

"It was definitely over that way, though you can never quite say for sure. I must have been around ninety, one hundred meters from the old house. The strangest thing was the silence afterwards. I listened closely—I've got a highly tuned ear, as you can imagine—but I didn't hear anything else. No shouting, no footsteps, no car starting. Nothing. I suppose that's why I forgot all about it, I told myself it must have been an animal after all."

"You didn't go and look?"

"I should have, but . . ."

"But?"

"The white-tailed eagle," he said with an apologetic smile. "It has a nest nearby, and if you spot one of them . . . Well, you know."

The University Hospital in Umeå provided specialist care to half the country, from Sundsvall in the south to Karesuando on the Finnish border, some 900 kilometers north. It was the size of a small town, a jumble of buildings in every possible style and size, built over the span of a hundred years; there were alleys leading this way and that between the units, veering off and coming to a dead end, and Eira got lost several times before she eventually managed to find the 1960s building housing the Department of Forensic Medicine. As a responding officer, she had never had reason to come up here before—particularly not considering it involved a journey of 170 kilometers. They could have asked for the results of the autopsy over the phone, of course, but GG had insisted on doing it face-to-face.

"You ask different questions when you've got the person right in front of you. Grab a coffee, catch any vague impressions, anything they're not sure about." He used that special instructive tone on her sometimes, as though there were some sort of secret plan in which her temporary role change was expected to lead to something else. "Never underestimate the power of doubt, Eira."

The pathologist was Eira's age, somewhere around thirty-five, and she introduced herself with her given name. Janina. They had already spoken over email, her surname was Lyckow. It struck Eira that people in management positions were increasingly the same age as her.

"I'm so glad you could come. Really, it's great the train was on time." She had a warm handshake, her tone like they were enjoying a morning coffee break together. "Did you manage to get any breakfast?"

"I had a Polar bread wrap on the train. Two, actually."

"What about coffee?"

Eira had grabbed a cup in the café carriage, where she had gone to get away from the ornithologist as they pulled into Västerbotten, but she didn't want to say no.

She helped herself to half a cheese roll too, given they had already been bought.

"Good," said the pathologist, studying her. "You might find your appetite is a bit so-so later."

"It's OK," said Eira. "I'm used to most of it."

"Mmm, that's what I thought too." Janina smiled and loaded her cup into the dishwasher. "Shall we?"

The corridor smelled clean and fresh, chemical. Stainless-steel furniture, disinfectant. Eira remembered the almost macabre feeling from her training, when they were taught how to read wounds. The thrill of discovery stirred up by the breakdown of stomach contents and the extent to which the insects had taken over, the way she had to remind herself: this was a person.

"I don't know if you want to see him . . . ?"

"Do I need to?"

"Technically, no. Some police want to see the victims with their own eyes, others don't."

Eira wondered which category GG fell into. The kind who wanted to see, she suspected. He wouldn't be satisfied with anything less.

Janina Lyckow grabbed a stack of papers and a bunch of keys from her office. She picked up a glass jar from the windowsill and held it up to the sunlight.

"Look at this poor thing," she said. "It was still alive when we went in."

The worm writhed listlessly against the inside of the glass.

"Was that in his . . . ?"

"In his stomach, yes. He must have ingested quite a few. We talked about letting it go, but I wanted to wait for the investigating officer."

"I don't think we need it," Eira said, swallowing.

"We had to call in an entomologist to ask how long a worm could survive in that kind of environment. A pretty long time, that was his qualified guess. They need food, moisture, and oxygen, but there's plenty of those in a human body—just like in loose soil."

Eira swallowed again.

"Though on the other hand, it would've come out pretty quickly the natural way, so he likely only ate it a day or two before he died."

They had also found traces of flies and other insects, parts of a beetle.

"But this is probably the most interesting thing, speaking of stomach contents."

She switched on her computer, brought up an image. Eira stared at the mushy mess, unable to make out a single thing.

"Parts of a bird." The pathologist moved the cursor across the screen. "The air sacs here suggest it was a larger species, from the crow family. You can even see fragments of feathers and bone, probably pneumatic bones, you can recognize them by the fact that they're full of little pockets, so they can fill up with air. Every part of a bird's body works in harmony to make it possible to fly. I'd never really considered how ingenious they are." Janina Lyckow chatted away with the enthusiasm of someone who had just learned something new. Eira remembered the ravens, how they had been flying around the house, caught on film by the photographer, what people said about them. She wondered whether the scent of death was present before it actually occurred. Whether that was why the bird had made its way inside.

Scavengers.

The pathologist took her through a series of locked doors, an airlock, into a cooler room. Polished doors hiding the recently deceased, people who had been found dead.

"Dehydration," she said. "That's the primary cause of death. Generally speaking, a person can't survive much longer than forty-eight hours without water, so he must have managed to trap the rain somehow, until that was no longer enough."

They hadn't quite managed to straighten him out, his spine stiffened into a hunched position. Eira could now see just how thin he was, naked in the glare of the bright lights, nothing but skin and bone.

"Unless he just gave up," said Janina, "and crawled into the corner to wait."

"Like an animal going away to die?"

"It's probably more that they can sense their own weakness, and then they hide away to prevent any other animals from getting at them. They probably don't have much concept of death."

"How long had he been dead?"

"Around two days, no less than thirty-six hours."

They had been able to determine that by measuring the levels of potassium in his vitreous humor. The question of how long he had been locked in the basement was harder to gauge, but the amount of time he had been living on next to nothing likely corresponded with what they already knew about Hans Runne's disappearance.

Around four weeks, give or take.

Janina Lyckow gently took his left hand in her own glove-clad palm.

"Injuries to his fingers, broken nails, probably from trying to prize the door open. We can see that on both hands. I understand the door was reinforced?"

"Rebuilt in the fifties, to air-raid shelter standards," said Eira. "I think people could claim grants for that kind of thing back then." It was a time when people were still preparing for the arrival of war, when the decree went out to the nation. She pictured the small window. It let in air, rainwater; it would have been little protection against the atomic bomb, but it had prevented Hans Runne from escaping.

"Other than that, there's no sign of physical violence, aside from what you already know," the pathologist continued. "Which isn't to say that there wasn't any. A professional can achieve a lot without leaving any clear marks, and after almost a month . . ."

Eira couldn't tear her eyes away from the man's left hand. The wounds had turned black. He was missing his ring and little fingers.

"A pretty strange procedure," said Janina, stroking the back of his hand as though he still had sensation in it. "First they broke his little finger, then they hacked away at the skin and muscle with a dull blade of some sort."

"Could it have been a pair of garden shears?" asked Eira.

They had found Hans Runne's blood on a pair in the basement.

"If they weren't too sharp, yes," said Janina Lyckow. "It could be possible."

They would examine the blades, it wouldn't take long to determine whether or not they had been used. Eira had seen a photograph of the shears. They were rusty. It must have been slow going. She had used her mother's secateurs from the sixties to attack the weeds in the garden that summer.

They stopped off in the break room for a quick cup of coffee.

"Did they use the same type of tool the second time? On his ring finger, I mean."

"Looks that way, yes."

"If that was the plan, why didn't they take something better suited to the job?"

Janina Lyckow finished off her double espresso and smiled.
"That's where I hand it over to you."

She was surrounded by black birds. One had been captured just before it landed, wings outstretched. Another was glaring at her with jet-black eyes. Behind them the wall of the house was visible in all its many shades of gray, the grain of the wood and flakes of paint that had likely once been a rusty red.

There were other details she recognized. The rotten porch. A ripped net curtain. The enlargements were hanging from lengths of washing line that had been strung across the room. They felt fateful, beautiful, and deeply unsettling.

"The hardest part is choosing between them," said Tone Elvin, the photographer. She was a little under thirty and had an unusual beauty, her mouth slightly too large for the rest of her face, one of her eyes a slightly paler shade of blue than the other. "It's like deleting a chapter from a book, if you see what I mean. Everything is part of the story."

Tone Elvin's simple studio was in the basement of an ordinary apartment building in the area of Umeå known as East of Town. On her way over there, Eira had noticed new vegan restaurants and cafés working hard to look cozy, students sprawled in armchairs with their laptops on their knees. She always felt like the future was much closer than the past whenever she came to Umeå.

Back home in Ådalen it was the other way around.

Tone Elvin apologized for the mess in her cramped kitchen and closed the door to the room off to one side. Eira managed to catch a brief glimpse of an unmade bed and a bag on the floor. The air smelled slightly musty, mixed with the usual darkroom chemicals.

"It's not like I live here," the woman hurried to point out. "But I often work late, and sometimes I just need to lie down. My photographs provoke strong emotions, too."

"What are you planning to do with them?"

"I've been talking to a gallery, and they might have space as soon as January." Her eyes shone, her hands busy tidying smaller copies of the images. Eira noticed a few printouts, a draft ad. *The Abandoned*, that was what she was calling her exhibition, *photographs by Tone Elvin.*

Eira felt a sudden dizziness. Perhaps it was down to too much coffee or to the close proximity to death, both earlier at the hospital and again now, looking at photographs from the scene. She braced herself against the draining board, flecked with paint.

"You know he has a daughter, don't you?" she said.

"Yeah, yes."

"Are you going to invite her?"

"Do you think I should? Yes . . . I probably should, that's a good idea."

Eira filled a glass with water—it seemed to take forever—and drank it down.

"His name was Hans Runne," she said.

"I know, I've read about him."

"Then you might also know how long he was locked in the basement, in the house you photographed. I've just come from the Department of Forensic Medicine. He ate worms and spiders to survive, but ultimately he died of dehydration."

"Do you think that hasn't been on my mind?" Tone was close to tears. "I can barely sleep at night because I can't stop thinking about it, that I could've helped him if I'd realized."

Eira took a couple of deep breaths. Going too far could be risky, particularly when she was alone with a witness. That was one of the reasons they were supposed to work in pairs. She couldn't understand why GG had bailed on her, today of all days. Though on the other hand, this visit hadn't been planned, it had been her own idea to track down the photographer while she was in Umeå.

"And have you remembered anything else," she asked, managing to sound softer than a moment ago, "while you've been thinking about it? Any sounds, anything that didn't seem right, that caught your eye?"

Tone looked down at the floor, seemed to retreat.

"I felt uneasy," she said. "I don't know whether I actually heard anything. I thought it was just the house. Old places like that often make noises."

"We now know that the perpetrator returned to the house, at roughly the same time you were there."

A wild look appeared in the photographer's eye.

"Seriously? Could he have been there then? Could he have seen me?"

"Did you see anything to suggest that? A car, a shadow, anything?"

"No. Nothing. I swear I didn't see or hear anything. Nothing that sounded like a person, anyway. Why would I lie?"

Because the guilt would be too much to bear, thought Eira, if you suspected something wasn't right and still walked away. She chose not to press the photographer any further.

"I'd like to look at the rest of the pictures," she said instead. "We only have one of them so far."

"Sure." Tone's face lit up slightly. "Of course you can. They're far from finished yet, but you're welcome to look."

"I mean I'd like to take them with me."

"Now?"

"So that we can examine them on a computer, enlarge them if necessary. They're evidence in a murder inquiry. I'm sure you understand."

"But I don't have copies of everything, and some of them aren't very good, I'd really rather avoid showing . . ."

"Then I can borrow the negatives and sort it out myself."

"But I can't just give you the negatives. I've sublet my apartment to be able to afford all this, I can't just . . ."

Eira left the studio with a sense of guilt over how she had acted, that and a coerced promise from the photographer that the images would be available in the morning.

Whatever she was going to do with them.

Study the grain of the wood, the movements of the birds?

Demanding the negatives had been a spur-of-the-moment decision, and she probably didn't have any legal grounds to have done so. If she was perfectly honest, it was because she had been furious, but that was a poor justification. Eira could only hope that the photographer didn't post about it all over social media.

She also hoped Tone wouldn't google the name Sjödin and discover the real reason Eira had chosen to extend her trip to Umeå by a few more hours.

In the past, prisons were often situated centrally, likely with the aim of deterring the country's subjects from breaking the law. Umeå's old prison was right in the heart of the city, and had been transformed into a hotel under the name the Old Jail. Its replacement was on the very edge of town, in a concrete bunker hidden behind high fences that the locals could ignore unless they had reason to visit.

Magnus had cut his hair. That was the first thing she noticed when they led him into the visitors' room. A cropped style that made him look tough, or possibly well brought up, she couldn't decide which.

Different, in any case.

"How are you?" she asked once the guard had stepped back.

Her brother shrugged. His shoulders seemed broader than usual. He looked healthy, fit, and for some reason she felt shy.

"I'm OK," he said. "The grub's not too bad. I'm working in the woodshop, making chairs. And I've started studying philosophy."

"That's great," she said. "I've heard there's a real shortage of philosophers in the job market."

"Just what Kramfors needs."

A moment of smiles.

"Mum's in the home now," said Eira.

Magnus took her hand. His touch made her feel like crying.

"Thank you for sorting everything out," he said. "For being there for her."

Eira pulled away.

"You shouldn't be in here," she said. "You could retract your confession. We'll get you a good lawyer and petition for a new trial, you could say . . ."

"Stop."

"Mum is always asking after you, every time I go to see her."

This time it was Magnus who pulled away, clasping his hands behind his head and leaning back, rocking on his chair as though to increase the distance between them in the cramped room.

"I've told you why I did what I did," he said, his voice firm. That tone always made her anxious, its roots going deeper than she could remember. "We agreed that we wouldn't bring it up again. If you're just going to keep nagging me about it then there's no point you coming out here."

You agreed, thought Eira. My opinion didn't count. Magnus had told her what really happened the evening Lina Stavred disappeared, why he was taking the blame for a murder he didn't commit. He had threatened to confess to worse if she didn't keep her mouth shut, and despite her better judgment, despite being a police officer, Eira had done as he asked.

Every night since had involved an endless monologue, thoughts of what she should have said and how she could have acted, but those were words she never actually said aloud.

"Mum might be completely lost in the fog by the time you get out of here, Magnus. You might not be able to get through to her. She's going to forget who you are."

"I've been on my best behavior," he said, running a hand through his short hair, making it look a little messier, more like the brother she knew. "They'll give me day release soon. I'll go down and see her then."

"OK."

He had children, too. Two sons who lived with their mother in Gothenburg. Eira was on the verge of mentioning them, but she knew it would only make him angry.

"What kind of philosophy are you studying?" she asked instead. He spent the rest of her visit explaining that while we *think* we are seeing the real world, it is in fact nothing but a shadow.

• • •

Before she caught the early-evening train home from Umeå, Eira had time to speak to the friend Hans Runne had called just a few days before he disappeared. They met over soup in a cozy book café in one of the grand wooden buildings in the same area of town as the photographer's studio. When Eira arrived, the man—Göran, an old acting buddy—was busy flicking through Lars Norén's last diary, and he immediately began telling her what a talent Hasse had been.

"Though to be honest with you he sometimes flinched at the real depths, the sore points in himself."

Who doesn't, thought Eira, struggling to concentrate. Lina Stavred was still on her mind. It was over twenty years since she vanished, at just sixteen years of age, and everyone was convinced she had been murdered. Her own parents had had her declared dead once enough time had passed.

But Eira had discovered that she was still alive. Magnus didn't want to know, and when she tried to bring it up with GG, he had told her that the case was closed. The whole thing had been a mess, with her trying to protect her brother, crossing the line.

But who was she if she didn't protect her own brother?

"Hasse had no idea, I would've noticed if he had," the friend continued. "He didn't seem down or anything like that. He was actually on good form. Had a job on the go in Umeå, asked if he could crash at my place. When he didn't get in touch I assumed it was all just talk, that he hadn't got the part after all. That kind of thing happens so often, the film industry's a jungle."

He grabbed a napkin from the table and blew his nose.

"But he was already dead. I mean, Christ."

Hasse Runne, who had always been such a survivor, constantly pushing forward. They had joked like always on the phone. He'd started dating again, his friend laughed at the memory; Hasse had never had any problems as far as women were concerned—not in getting them interested, anyway. It was hanging on to them he struggled with.

"There was something flighty about him, like it was himself he couldn't keep hold of. I don't really know where that came from. A sense of abandonment, maybe? An absent father?"

"Do you know if he was seeing anyone in particular?"

"I doubt it. Hasse was a romantic. If he'd fallen in love he would've been shouting her name from the rooftops."

As the train carried Eira south along the Norrland coast, speeding into the bluish-black dusk, she attempted to summarize the meeting. But it was as though her notes seemed to lose all meaning. She closed the document and took out the list of earlier kidnappings instead.

They needed to make the perpetrator their starting point, she thought, not the victim. She was increasingly convinced that Hans Runne had bumped into the wrong people after staggering out of the bar in Härnösand. There was simply nothing in his life or his character that pointed to anything like this. Not unless he was an incredibly skilled actor.

Thanks to an electrical failure just south of Örnsköldsvik, it was after nine by the time Eira arrived in Kramfors. Too late to pop in and see her mother as planned. She would just have to wrestle with her guilty conscience until tomorrow. She had off-loaded all responsibility onto the local authorities, there had been no other option. But it wasn't just that, it was the relief she felt. Days that passed without her finding the time to visit Kerstin. Eira's stomach ached when she thought about it.

Getting into the car and driving home to the quiet, half-empty house in Lunde didn't feel like an option right now. Her trip to Umeå had dredged up something inside her; the palpable closeness of death, the sheer scale of the loneliness that preceded it.

Magnus, returning to his cell.

She desperately wanted a glass of something alcoholic, anything would do. Ideally three or four. Good old-fashioned drunkenness, laughing and forgetting for a while.

There was only one person who came to mind.

"Fancy a beer at Kramm?" she wrote.

"Come over instead," he replied.

During August's last posting in Kramfors, he had rented one of the many empty apartments in the public-housing blocks on Hällgumsgatan. He had moved up in the world now, she thought as she walked through the private homes by the railway, beautiful old 1930s villas with neat piles of raked autumn leaves on their lawns.

He pulled her into the hallway, no need for any artifice, no explanations. Eira found it liberating not to have to say anything. They both knew what "a beer at Kramm" really meant, that was how it had all started. August paused as they backed into the bedroom, Eira's hands fumbling with the knot on his sweatpants.

"I've got a sauna," he said.

"You're not serious?"

"Just switched it on . . . if you . . . what do you think?"

And so they drew it out until every last cell was crying for release. Eira probably wouldn't recommend a sauna in that context, particularly not one that had been heated to almost 100 degrees. She had thought she was about to fall back onto the red-hot rocks at one point, but August's grip had tightened. Her body felt slightly tender where his hands had been. A heat that didn't want to fade.

They slumped onto the tired old sofa in the lounge afterwards.

"Nice place," she said.

"I'm renting it cheap over the winter. The owner's kids haven't decided whether to sell or not."

Strange how easy it was to slip back into old habits. To rediscover the contours of his body. The simplicity, the lightness she remembered.

"Do you ever think about anyone else?" she asked.

"What do you mean?"

"When you're having sex."

He had a girlfriend, she knew that, just as she knew they had a liberal attitude to love, that they were allowed to sleep with other people, to fall in love if it happened.

"Of course I do," he said. "But I didn't just now, if that's what you're asking. I was only thinking of you."

"That's not what I meant, I mean more generally."

His hair tickled her skin.

"So who do you think about, Eira? When you're not thinking about me?"

"Do I really have to tell you?"

"No, only if you want to."

Eira clambered out of his arms and into the shower, let the water run cold. The cramped sauna must have been built sometime during the seventies. She could tell from the plastic floor and the brown wet-room wallpaper that had started to come loose at the joins, revealing the chipboard beneath.

She checked that the ancient heater was properly switched off before wrapping a towel around herself and heading back upstairs. They drank beer in the kitchen and she told August about her day, about the autopsy and how she imagined those four weeks in the basement must have been. It felt good to get it out of her system.

August had been sent out to deal with a shoplifter at Willys. A six-pack of lager.

"Just another day in Kramfors."

It wasn't until they were getting into the old woman's narrow bed and August reached for something from the nightstand that she noticed his ring. Thin and golden.

"Did you get married?"

"No, not yet, we're just engaged."

"You and Johanna?" Eira had met his girlfriend once, over coffee, when she came up to visit. Johanna sold beauty products and drank green smoothies; she was warm and enthusiastic and likable. "Are you going to keep . . . ?"

"Sleeping with other people?"

August fiddled with the ring. Strange she hadn't noticed it at the station or while they were in the car together. Maybe he took it off at work, like he had taken it off earlier. Was it so that it didn't burn his finger in the sauna, or because she was coming over?

"It doesn't change our approach to love," he continued. "I do what I want and so does she. It just means we've decided to stick together. I felt like it was probably time. A fixed point, you know? Something that isn't changing all the time."

"Well, congratulations," said Eira.

She lay awake for some time after he dozed off.

Twice in her life she had believed in a love that might last, if not forever then at least for the foreseeable future.

The first was her foolish, immature love for Ricken, her brother's friend. He probably could have convinced her to stay in Strinne for the rest of her life, surrounded by junk cars, if he hadn't broken up with her instead.

The second was a man she had met in a bar during her time in Stockholm, just after she finished her police training. After their third night together—an experience that surpassed almost anything else—Eira had decided that he really *saw* her, that he liked what he saw, and she had started to dream about the future. The fact that he wanted to see her again was proof that he felt the same way. Surely there was no way emotions could be quite so overwhelming if they weren't mutual? Whenever he canceled a date or failed to get in touch, she always made excuses for him. He was afraid of making the leap, unsure of himself, and that meant she needed to be more open with her love, to make him feel safe. Or maybe he was struggling to process the fact that she was a police officer, and she would have to be softer and more vulnerable around him. When he told her he couldn't get into a relationship right now, she had thought that "right now" was relative, what did it really mean? A week, a month, six? She could wait, no problem; she was from Norrland, stubbornness was in her blood.

In the end he told her that he liked her, she was a nice girl, but that it was all a bit much. As far as he was concerned, it had never been love.

The darkness she found herself falling into then, the jet-blackness enveloping her. It was a bottomless pit, no light whatsoever. How stupid, to imagine that someone loved you. She became more cautious when it came to her feelings—they only made her see things that weren't really there. In her next relationship, she was the one who hadn't been in love.

She curled up against August's body and gave herself over to the calmness of sleep. He was getting married, and that was well and good. She didn't need to worry about him.

There were no messages waiting for Eira when she got to the station the next morning, no particular tasks for her to do. Nothing but a group email from GG, saying that they could have their meeting later, unclear when.

She sat down at a free computer and continued where she had left off the day before. Her body was tender after her night with August, a slight headache from too little sleep.

The list of kidnappings was much longer than she had expected. The trainee officer in Sundsvall who compiled it had included every case from across the country over the past year, painstakingly and in chronological order, both those that had led to charges and others that had been dropped.

Eira skimmed through the summaries, filtering and ruling out as she went.

Kidnapping was a crime that had become increasingly common in recent years. The motive could be to scare someone into silence or to squeeze money out of the victims' relatives over an unpaid debt. Some of the more sadistic cases involved grievous bodily harm and humiliation, often carried out by younger perpetrators who uploaded the footage to social media. Most common of all were the robberies, however. Thieves adapting to an era in which people no longer walked around with wallets full of cash. There were gangs that systematically kidnapped their victims, driving them around or taking them to a bike storage facility, abusing and threatening them until they gave up the PIN for their bank cards or transferred money online. In a handful of cases, the victims had actually been forced to go to the bank and withdraw the money themselves.

An unsettling development, but hardly relevant in this particular case. Not a single attempt had been made to rinse Hans Runne's paltry accounts.

Then there were the sexual motives, of course. Eira skipped over a kidnapped girl and a raid on an apartment brothel in which kidnapping was one of several charges. No, there was no sign of sexual violence in Hans Runne's case.

She had worked her way back a whole year in time when a strange case from Norrbotten caught her eye. A forty-three-year-old man found locked in a basement, badly traumatized and in need of medical attention.

Eira was in the process of searching for more details when Anja Larionova, the local investigator, appeared in the doorway.

"Do you know where George Clooney is?"

"Who?"

"The hottie from Sundsvall, your new boss."

"They don't look alike, do they?"

"I think I've found something."

There was a general consensus that Anja Larionova was the sharpest mind in the Kramfors Police District and that she would be in charge if she weren't quite so uninterested in climbing the career ladder. Focusing on the minor crimes in the area was her own choice. "That's where the rift in society stems from," she always said. "Granny's stolen dinner service."

The two women grabbed a coffee and went through to her office. Things were pretty quiet at the moment, Anja explained. Winter was coming, which meant the local thieves had started checking in to rehab centers. Not a single summerhouse had been raided all week.

"So I offered to do some digging into this." Anja Larionova

pushed a document from the National Land Survey towards Eira, her long fingernail pointing to the name. High Woods Holdings, the company that had bought the abandoned house in Offer four years earlier. "Judging by the name, you'd think they were after the felling rights."

"Yeah, well, it was hardly the house they wanted. The place had been empty for over a decade, since the old Bäcklund couple died."

"At the same time?"

"Three months apart," said Eira. "She followed him."

"A lot of people can't handle the loneliness."

"Or maybe she'd been clinging on because she had someone who needed her."

Eira found herself thinking about the trees growing around the old house, how close they were, practically wound around one another. She had heard that trees could actually communicate via their roots, sharing water and nutrients, choosing closeness over more light.

"And then it took six years for the kids to sell up," said Anja Larionova. "Sounds like an inheritance dispute. If people could just make a bit more of an effort to get on, we wouldn't have all these places left to crumble everywhere."

"So why did someone pay"—Eira peered down at the sheet of paper—"ninety-two thousand for it if they didn't want to move in or cut down the trees?"

"I'd say that's a pretty good price for an address where you can register a company that then goes on to rent it out to another fifteen or so other businesses."

Eira flicked through the sheets, printouts of articles and excerpts from various registers. Her eye was drawn to words like Russian organized crime, barons, dummy companies.

"What is this?"

Anja Larionova got up and closed the door. She stood quietly for a moment with her hand on the handle. Eira hesitated. Whenever a conversation petered out suddenly, her grandmother always used to say that an angel had just walked through the room—this felt like it could be an entire army of them.

"Do you know how I got the surname Larionova?" Anja asked.

"I heard you were married to a Russian," said Eira. "And that you may or may not have killed him."

"If he ever turned up again, I might."

Anja leaned back against the windowsill. The sun was high in the sky, flooding into the room through a haze of exhaust fumes and dusty glass.

"We met at Stora Hotellet in Umeå, I was there for a conference. I know, I was an idiot. This was around the same time I invested my pension fund in a scam."

Eira laughed. "I thought you were supposed to be a police officer?"

"Let's just say I take my professional hat off when I get home—and when I fall in love, though don't mention that to anyone else." A wry smile, a flicker of sadness. "He was so handsome, and he was in a real rush to get married—so he could get citizenship. He grew up in the Soviet Union, which meant he knew how quickly borders and laws could change. We got married in secret, a private ceremony. I didn't even tell my parents beforehand."

Her gut told her something was wrong, but she had chosen to ignore her suspicions, wanted to believe in love. He traveled a lot. On business, he said. Currency, investments. That should have been enough to raise her suspicions, to make her put on her police officer's hat, but as she said, love . . .

"Not long after our third anniversary, he vanished."

"Once he was a Swedish citizen."

"He was only ever after the papers, documents that made him someone other than who he really was."

"Who was he?"

"Well, he wasn't called Larionov, that's for sure. Once I found out it was a fake name I decided it would be OK to keep it. Why go back to being an Andersson when I could be a Larionova? Like the ice hockey player, you know, the guy who played for the Soviet national team?"

Eira tried to remember what she knew about ice hockey from the time when she was born and wondered why they had strayed so far from the topic at hand.

"I appreciate you telling me, but I'm not sure I really understand what this has to do with the case."

"Appearances and illusions," said Anja Larionova. She straightened a flowering plant on the windowsill and then moved back over to her desk. "In a world where no one knows anyone else, the right papers are as good as cash, and having Swedish papers carries a lot of weight. They make you seem trustworthy."

"Like your ex," said Eira.

"I'd be grateful if you didn't mention him. He doesn't have anything to do with this, it just made me think of him."

"Who?"

Anja smiled.

"In the same way you-know-who came on to women in hotel bars to get Swedish paperwork—God knows what he needed it for—international criminals, and especially those with roots in Russia, started buying houses in inland Norrland a few years back, and we all know where you can find cheap houses."

"But no one ever moves in?"

"Have you heard of the Barons from Èze?"

"I have now," said Eira. It was in the paperwork on the desk in front of her.

Anja Larionova emphasized that she was far from an expert in Russian organized crime—"putting aside my own highly personal experience of it, ha-ha"—but that she had run a few searches, and one name had led to another.

From High Woods Holdings to Saint Petersburg and a man with prior convictions for serious fraud and pyramid schemes. In addition to the house in Offer, he owned a number of companies in the Seychelles. High Woods Holdings had a homepage boasting that it could help businesses avoid tax. *Send material support to private individuals in complete confidence, without leaving a paper trail.*

"It's probably supposed to sound incomprehensible," said Anja, describing how High Woods Holdings set up a form of company for hiding money, which was then sold on. A picture began to emerge, of a man posing by a sports car outside a casino in Monaco. Several of the people involved had houses on the French Riviera, hence the name Èze, which was between Nice and Cannes.

"Money laundering, in other words."

Eira remembered the painted daybed in the kitchen, the net curtains. The thick floorboards made from Norrland pine that had grown slowly, over a century or more.

"The house can come crashing down, but it still serves its purpose."

Kerstin Sjödin was balancing on a chair, trying to unhook a picture from the wall, when Eira came into the room. The floor around her was littered with books.

"What are you doing, Mum?" Eira gripped her arm in an attempt to make her come down. She immediately began thinking about broken hips, how quickly a person could be left bedbound.

"Oh good, you're here." Kerstin gripped the frame, tugging it so hard that the hook came loose. "This shouldn't be here, it's not mine."

"You had that hanging in the living room for years, Mum. I thought you liked it."

"I've never liked this thing. It was his, he can have it back."

She finally got down from the chair, clutching the frame tight. The etching of the river and the logs.

"Shall we sit down and have some coffee?" Eira unpacked the small princess cakes she had bought from the supermarket. "If you want to move things around in here, I can help you. I don't have time to do it today, but we can go over to the house together sometime and pick up anything you'd like."

Kerstin turned the frame over in her hands.

"What did I tell you, it's got his name on it, so don't come in here telling me I'm wrong."

Sure enough, there was a printed sticker reading Veine Sjödin on the back. Eira's father had always stuck labels on absolutely everything, his books, his lunch box, inside his boots. Growing up, nothing was given, none of his possessions could be taken for granted, and he had tried to impress that on his own children whenever they asked why anyone would want to steal his old junk.

"Dad's dead, you know that, it's been more than ten years. I don't think he cares about the etching."

"Then she should have it," said Kerstin. "She's the one who inherited everything. Laid claim to the whole lot, leaving the two of you with nothing."

"Forget all that, Mum. It doesn't matter."

Forgetting was the last thing she should be telling her mother to do. Before long everything would be forgotten, her memories, the present, all gone. Kerstin had seemed a little clearer since she moved into the home. She no longer had to fight to keep things together, rattling around inside that big house, forgetting where she was going. Her world had shrunk to her bedroom and a shared dining room.

"Those aren't mine either, so you can take them with you when you go."

Eira picked up the books from the floor, beautiful old editions, classics by Vilhelm Moberg and crime novels by Sjöwall and Wahlöö. She had done a lot of guessing when she packed those, hadn't checked them for name tags.

"And there are some of mine I can't find," said Kerstin. "That's the worst part. I think someone has been coming in here and stealing them."

"You still have a lot of books at home," said Eira. "We can make a list next time I'm here, all the ones you'd like to reread."

A memory exercise, she thought, that was a good idea. Something to talk about as their conversations petered out. So much of what they used to talk about was linked to their everyday lives, to objects and memories in the house, things that needed doing and had always been done.

"They just come in and out whenever they feel like it. I know some of the old ladies, but I don't know the others."

"Come on, no one has stolen any of your books." Eira made a mental note to check whether paranoia was part of her diagnosis, whether it was a consequence of everything growing hazier. Her mother had never been like this in the past.

"Is it just us today?" Kerstin looked down at the cups on the table, the plates and their half-eaten cakes. "Isn't Magnus coming?"

"You know he isn't, Mum."

"Did he say that?"

The usual anguish. Should Eira remind her that Magnus, the golden child, was currently locked up in Umeå and likely wouldn't be granted leave for some time? Did she really have to bring it up every time, to upset her so much? In that sense, forgetting might actually be a blessing. Though on the other hand, it was Eira's responsibility to cling on to reality. The burden was on her shoulders now. That conversation often ended with Kerstin in tears, over everything that had gone wrong and how badly she had failed as a mother.

Look at me, Eira wanted to say, one out of two isn't so bad, but that was the kind of thing she never said. It wouldn't help. Magnus was, and always would be, the one she missed.

Her phone broke the silence before she got round to making any decisions, ringing in double time. A special ringtone she had selected so that she never missed a call from GG.

"I need to take this."

She went out into the corridor so that she could talk to him in peace. Not the best idea in a home for people with dementia. Old women trudged back and forth, one rocking in an armchair; there were shouts for help and muttering to no one in particular.

"Sorry, what did you say?"

"The National Operations Department's intelligence unit," GG repeated. "They've taken over the Russian line of inquiry, and the Economic Crime Authority is involved in the money laundering side of things. There's not much we can help with at the moment."

"So what should we do?"

An old lady in a raincoat was tugging on the handle of the main door, shouting that she wanted to go home. Eira turned around and went back into her mother's room, out onto the small balcony.

". . . an inmate we're waiting for permission to interview in Salt-vik, with links to the east. But I doubt we'll be able to get him to talk."

Her mother seemed to have nodded off in her armchair. Eira closed the door behind her. They had also received a couple of tips that were worth following up.

"One from a group of people who saw him at Stadt that evening. There was a bit of an argument over a chair, Runne claimed it was his."

"Finally," said Eira.

Since Hans Runne's name and photograph were released, along with an appeal for information, they had been overwhelmed with tips, some more reliable than others. It would have been strange if no one had seen him in the busy bar that evening. Someone always saw something; no one went completely unnoticed.

"And the woman has been in touch, too," said GG.

"Which woman?"

"The one he met there, apparently."

"Seriously?"

"I'm going to interview her tomorrow."

Eira waited for him to go on, but he didn't say any more. She heard crackling, noise in the background. He was probably outside too.

"Do you want me to come down to Härnösand?" she asked.

"No, no need, I can do it."

His tone was curt, and she felt a sudden flicker of uncertainty. The autumn chill seeped into her, she watched the ferry docking in the distance.

"What do you think about me taking a trip up to Norrbotten?" she asked.

"What was that?"

"Norrbotten," Eira repeated. "Malmberget, specifically."

"What's there?"

Eira recapped what she had found in the list of kidnappings, the case that seemed to differ from the others. A man who had been found locked in the basement of an evacuated building in the mining community just over a year ago. There was no suspect, the preliminary investigation still open.

"That's what, eight hundred kilometers away?"

"Seven hundred."

"And you can't do it over the phone?"

"I want to see the crime scene," said Eira. "Really capture the vague impressions, the doubts. Who was it that said that?"

"Must've been someone smart," said GG.

"I'd like to talk to the victim, too."

"He's still alive?"

"He is. Traumatized, apparently. Practically psychotic when they found him. I don't know what kind of state he's in now, but it might be worth a try."

Kerstin flinched as Eira closed the balcony door.

"Is that you?"

"I have to go now, Mum. We already had coffee. I'll ask the staff to clear the cups away."

"No, no, I can do that."

A quick hug, a pat on Eira's cheek, an expression of tenderness that was never over the top.

A shout from behind her back once she set off.

"You've forgotten everything." The etching, the stack of books. "I want you to give it all back. No one's going to come in here and accuse me of stealing."

"Come on, Mum, she doesn't care about his old prints."

"Right is right," said Kerstin Sjödin, getting to her feet. Eira realized just how crooked she had become over the past year. "Otherwise I'll have to do it myself."

There was snow on the ground when she arrived in Gällivare, the sun nothing but a suggestion of brightness beyond the mountains. Flying north would have taken her thirteen hours and three transfers, going down to Stockholm and then back up again. On the night train, the journey took only eight hours, and she would be asleep for most of it anyway.

Eira bought two croissants and looked up the directions to the police station. The snow crunched underfoot.

The man who came out to meet her introduced himself as Heikki, though his name badge read Henrik Niva.

"Welcome to Gällivare," he said, making coffee as he explained that he was a community police officer and had only been assisting Violent Crimes on the case.

"Same," said Eira, telling him that she was usually a responding officer in Kramfors. That was how you introduced yourself in Norrland, particularly if you came from farther south. *I'm no better than you.* "It's been a long time since I was last here," she added. *I'm not a complete stranger; I am aware you exist up here.*

She had been eight at the time, keeping her father company on the road. They slept behind the seats in his lorry, saw the mountains get higher and higher, the trees increasingly gnarled the farther north they drove.

"I remember him lifting me up onto his shoulders by the fence so that I could see the Pit."

"You probably won't recognize much," said Heikki Niva. "Most of Malmberget's gone now. Before long, the Pit'll be all that's left."

He had printed out sections of the investigation, and Eira skimmed through them as the flakes of pastry fell from her croissant.

"I think we followed every lead as far as we could," he said. "'Til there were no roads left, you might say. Can't think of many cases that were as much of a dead end as this one."

A photograph of an oblong face, thin glasses, a high hairline. Eira looked for similarities with Hans Runne, but she drew a blank. The man's name was Karl Mikael Ingmarsson, he was forty-four years old, and he lived in Börjelslandet near Luleå. Mikael, as he was known, had been on a business trip to Gällivare in September last year. He was a consultant in the building trade, and had booked an overnight stay at the Grand Hotel Lapland.

"We've got the hottest construction boom in the country right now," Heikki explained. "Aside from Kiruna, that is. They're better at marketing themselves up there, a huge hoo-ha in the world press and all sorts of architecture competitions the minute they have to move the town a few meters. We've been at it fifty years here, but like I said, we're almost done."

Mikael Ingmarsson's company worked for a number of subcontractors, he was the link to the big construction firms who had enough muscle to win contracts. That was where dirty money often came into the picture, apparently. Heikki Niva had learned all about corruption and bribes in the building trade.

"We looked into it, of course. Well, Luleå did, they're the ones who know more about financial crimes. But ultimately, we need to be able to link someone to the scene."

"And you still don't have any suspects?"

A glum shake of the head.

Mikael Ingmarsson had eaten a late dinner at the hotel and was on his way back to his room, head slightly fuzzy from the wine, when he realized he had left his briefcase in the car. He hadn't seen whoever attacked him from behind, barely knew what was happening before he woke up in a basement in Malmberget.

"Would you like to take a look at the hotel?"

"I'm not sure it'll tell me much." Eira had been past the Hotel Lapland, a mishmash of building styles from different eras, the latest resembling a glass skyscraper. "A hotel's a hotel."

"Places like that make me anxious, personally," said Heikki Niva. "The way they're so anonymous, all the rooms the same."

"But I would like to see the place where he was locked up."

Her colleague laughed as though she had said something funny.

"Which one?"

They drove the five kilometers from Gällivare to Malmberget in his private car. Rows of prefabricated villas had been set up in a field along the way. It was known as the Mid-Area and was where many of the residents of Malmberget had been given replacement homes, either there or on the hillside where other new houses had sprung up. A community was being torn down, and the people, preschools, and companies had to be moved elsewhere. Eira could see cranes virtually everywhere she looked. Heikki Niva explained that the old rivalry between the twin communities made it difficult for Malmberget natives like himself to make the move to Gällivare. It hurt their pride, they had to swallow their sadness over everything that would be lost.

"Not everyone can handle it, mind you," he said, pointing to an abandoned tower block as they drove into Malmberget. A dystopia of dark windows, tattered curtains, a broken blind. Several guys he knew had jumped in the nineties, part of a wave of suicides. No one could say whether it had anything to do with the sense of loss, but he thought it was probably harder to imagine a future when they were literally tearing it down around you, trickier for a lost young man to work out who he was supposed to be.

The vein of ore ran directly beneath Malmberget, and the tremors from the mine could cause a house to come crashing down at any moment, a hole opening up beneath it. It was a ghost town. The shops were boarded up, signs hanging crooked; a number of buildings had collapsed, others left empty while they waited to be demolished. It felt strange, given how modern the place was. Most of Malmberget had probably been built during the sixties.

Heikki took a detour along Kaptensvägen, his childhood street—or what was left of it, anyway. The road came to an abrupt end at the fence marking the area at risk of collapse, and then the Pit took over, the huge crater splitting the community straight down the middle. Eira could make out rooftops in the distance on the other side, where the street continued under the same name.

"It's the sports hall's turn next," said Heikki Niva, pointing out the window as they drove. "The soul of the place, that."

He pulled over on the crown of a small hill and got out by a fence that looped off towards the edge of the forest. The views over the mountains were incredible, stretching for miles.

"This was where they found him, locked in the basement of one of the multifamily buildings on Långa Raden over there. Sheer luck they got to him in time. If it wasn't for the quake that night, God knows what might've happened."

"OK . . ." Eira peered in through the fence. There was nothing but heaped earth left on the other side. She could see tarmac beneath the thin covering of snow, a road leading to nowhere.

"One of the nicest areas in Malmberget, this," he continued. "Wooden houses that've been standing since the mine first opened."

"So they tore the house down?" It had been stupid to come here, Eira realized, a huge waste of time, traveling seven hundred kilometers to look at a scrap of wasteland.

"Christ, no," said Heikki Niva. "It's in a glade outside of Koskull-skulle."

Eira felt a certain sense of relief once they left Malmberget, putting the empty houses and deserted streets behind them.

"Ingmarsson's mother lived in the apartment until she died a year or two back," Heikki Niva said as they pulled out onto Mellanvägen and the forest grew thicker around them. "That's why he had the key. He wanted to swing by while he was up here, he said, to see whether there was anything left. To say goodbye to his childhood, once and for all."

"But if someone attacked him from behind . . ."

"Exactly. How could they know about the building, where it was, that it was empty?" Her colleague's hands drummed the wheel in time with the eighties disco tune that was playing on the radio. "Believe me, we looked into it. Did Ingmarsson take them out there and make up the attack afterwards? Were they associates of some sort? Did they know him from before, were they locals?"

After eight kilometers, he turned off at a sign bearing the area's old name, Hermelin, and pulled up at the start of the new Långa Raden. The houses weren't the only thing that had been moved; the street names had also upped sticks.

"And what did you find?"

"Nothing that explained it. Ingmarsson said he might've woken up and given them the address, though he didn't remember anything like that. The psychologist said it wasn't impossible. Maybe he did remember, but felt threatened. We followed that line of inquiry too, in interview after interview. He was in a bad way."

With their elaborate woodwork and small-paned windows, the hundred-year-old buildings looked a little out of place on the freshly leveled ground, where nothing had yet grown.

They got out of the car.

"I called the family to let them know we were coming. They weren't too happy about it. Not exactly what you want to be reminded of when you've just got married and moved into a new home. They would've preferred for those ghosts to stay back in Malmberget."

The couple that had taken over the apartment were in their early twenties, the man holding a baby in one arm. The place smelled like fresh paint, and the hallway was cluttered with ski equipment.

"I never go down to the basement," said the woman, taking the baby from the man as he followed them and unlocked the door.

Like the rest of the apartment, it had also been renovated. Heikki Niva went first, showing Eira where they had found the man. Bare walls, a Ping-Pong table. The windows were larger than in the basement in Offer, but still too small for a grown man to be able to squeeze out of.

"Are you treating it as attempted murder?" she asked.

"Unclear," he said. "But the perp can't have been banking on someone finding him in time."

In Mikael Ingmarsson's case, it wasn't a lack of food and drink that had left him on the verge of madness.

There had been a chest freezer in the basement with him, her colleague pointed to the corner, that was how he had survived. The place still had power, possibly because there was a good deal of elk meat and a couple of grouse inside. The police suspected that some of the construction workers had been making use of the freezer while they still could.

Ice he could melt for water, meat he could eat raw.

"So, what do you think?" Heikki Niva asked once they were sitting in the pizzeria in Koskullskulle afterwards.

He had wanted to make the detour purely for the pizzas, and was busy wolfing down the house special, with cold-smoked reindeer meat and orient dressing, a Norrland specialty.

"I don't know," said Eira.

They discussed the obvious, that seven hundred kilometers was a huge distance. That aside from being close in age, there were no immediate similarities between the two victims. The approach. None of Mikael Ingmarsson's fingers had been severed, but was that relevant?

Eira chewed and swallowed in an attempt to find words for what was really little other than a hunch. What wasn't there, an absence of logic.

"Do you think I could speak to him?" she asked.

Most people felt the need to be helpful, to be at the center of events. To fight evil in society, to become heroes or to feel, for a moment at least, like their life served some higher purpose.

Add to that the urge to solve mysteries that made virtually every child stare up at the stars, wondering what lay beyond them.

GG had been such a child. He had once spent half the summer break sitting by a junction, carefully noting down every single registration plate on the off chance that the police might need to track someone down, and as a result he felt a certain understanding for all the tips that came flooding in. He just wished, as he got into his car to drive home to Sundsvall, that he had achieved something useful that day.

Something that had led them even a millimeter closer to the person who had taken a man's life in the worst way imaginable.

Slowly, and alone.

He had two missed calls and a message from his brother, which didn't help his mood.

"The estate inventory, Jojje. We really do need to get it done."

There wasn't another person on earth who called him Jojje. Not since their father died in early July.

That hot, damn summer.

GG wasn't entirely sure how his brother spent his seventy-hour working week, but he knew it was something to do with finance and that it paid enough for a beachside plot in one of those Stockholm suburbs that liked to send their benefit claimants to Norrland.

They'd had that discussion, too. Possibly not the best timing, over beers and schnapps at the wake.

That was three and a half months ago, and they now had just two weeks—TWO WEEKS, his brother's voice echoed in his ears—before they had to submit the inventory. "And then there's the matter of the archipelago property," he shouted, his name for the family summerhouse and its outhouse. "We need to decide what to do with it." He then mentioned the figures plots like that were commanding now that everyone was desperate to escape to the countryside, adding that a South Korean company also had plans to build ten hotels along the High Coast.

GG missed his turnoff at the next roundabout and found himself back on the road to Härnösand. May as well keep going; he had forgotten to give back the keys to the apartment there. He also had zero desire to go home. Dust and dirt, unopened mail, almost certainly nothing to eat in the fridge. He would need a change of clothes, but the shops were still open, he could always buy something new in Härnösand. Take the rest to the dry cleaner's.

The temporary nature of the police apartment embraced him. It made no demands of him, nothing calling for him to *deal with* anything.

GG threw the bag of new clothes onto the bed and opened a bottle of wine.

He had two missed calls from a lawyer, too. Right, the inmate he was supposed to be interviewing at Saltvik. It was too late now. He opened his laptop in an attempt to get a better overview of everything that had happened during the day and to summarize his own contributions, which were nonexistent.

A tipsy group of middle-aged men who claimed to have spoken to Hans Runne, but couldn't remember what had been said. A woman who had exchanged no more than a few words with him at the bar.

"Was he alone?"

"I think so. I didn't see him talking to anyone else."

"Did the two of you speak again?"

"No, I think that was all."

GG topped up his glass. He didn't have the energy to dig out the woman's name, or to go back to his notes from the group of men. Instead he typed the words "estate inventory" and began searching for ways to request an extension.

The investigator with Sweden's most northerly Violent Crimes Unit was called Anders Anttila, and he met Eira at the station, grateful for any information that could lead the case forward.

"Call me Double-Antti," he said. "Everyone else does."

At first Eira thought it must be because of his build—the man was both tall and wide—but then she remembered that the same thing had happened with Heikki Niva in Gällivare, that it was common for people with Swedish names to be given Finnish nicknames in the bilingual area.

Anders Anttila became Antti Anttila, aka Double-Antti.

He had racked his brain and couldn't see that they had made any obvious mistakes, but he hated leaving things unresolved.

"It's like having chapped hands in winter," he said. "An itch you just can't shake."

The last hint of sunlight faded behind them as they drove east from Luleå. Mikael Ingmarsson lived in a grand Norrbotten farm-stead in a rich old farming community, a traditional wooden building painted red.

He had insisted on them coming to him, didn't want to see the inside of another police station.

"I thought I was done with all this," he said when they arrived. "All I want is to wake up one morning and feel a sense of confidence."

"We really do appreciate you talking to us," said Double-Antti. "As I said on the phone, it's entirely voluntary, but we could use your help."

"I just don't know what else I can tell you."

The three children were home from school and nursery, and the house hummed with electronic tunes. His wife, wearing a pale linen shirt, was sitting at her computer in the kitchen, and she closed the lid with unnecessary force. Double-Antti took care of the introductions; he and Petra had clearly met before.

"I really hope you have some news for us," she said. "Or are we just supposed to accept that they've got away with it? What they did wasn't just to Mikael, you know. It affected the entire family."

"We're doing everything we can," said Double-Antti, turning to the man. "What do you say, shall we go somewhere quiet, where we're not in the way?"

"We can talk here," he said, shouting for the children to go up to their rooms. "So long as it doesn't take too long. I promised my son I'd help him with his math homework."

Eira's immediate impression was that he had recovered, nothing she could see suggested otherwise. In good shape, she noticed; he had a certain physicality about him, his movements quick and efficient, possibly slightly forced. He had changed his glasses since the photograph in the case files was taken, round with black frames, and had also shaved off his hair. He had nothing but a short fuzz on top of his head now, light blond or graying.

"I'd like my wife to stay," he said, sitting down beside her, dragging his chair slightly closer. "This is something we're processing and going through together."

Double-Antti sat down at the other end of the table, and Eira followed his example. The couple showed no intention of offering them anything to eat or drink, which was unusual for northern Norrland. Not offering someone coffee was broadly equivalent to telling them to go to hell.

"There's a case farther south that resembles yours in several ways," Double-Antti began. "Involving a dead man near Sollefteå. You might have read about it in the papers?"

"What does that have to do with Mikael?"

"We don't know. We're wondering whether there could be a connection. That's what we're trying to establish."

He let Eira take over. She spoke briefly about the abandoned house in Offer, showed them a photograph of Hans Runne. Mikael Ingmarsson gripped his wife's hand. Perhaps he was imagining how things might have ended for him, reliving his period in captivity anew.

"But I still don't understand," said the woman. "This was . . . where did you say?"

"Just outside of Sollefteå."

"So these idiots are on some sort of Norrland tour, are they? What do you think they're after?"

"One of the things the two cases have in common," said Eira, "is that they don't seem to be ordinary robberies, that we can't see any clear motive."

"Crazy people don't need a motive, do they?" said the wife. "Why would anyone have a single reason to go after Mikael?"

The man still hadn't said a word about anything Eira had told them. He wasn't even looking at her, his eyes focused on some point behind her.

"As I'm sure you can understand, we're looking for a connection," said Double-Antti. "I wonder if anything Eira has told you about this person sounds familiar, whether you could have had anything in common . . . ?"

Mikael stood up so abruptly that his chair almost tipped over behind him. He went over to the sink and filled a glass, then paused. Leaned over the counter, his muscles tense. When he turned around, he was still gripping the counter tight, as though his world risked turning upside down.

"An unemployed actor," he said. "What could I possibly have in common with him?"

"I don't know," Double-Antti replied calmly. "What do you think?"

The man stared out through the window. The raindrops glittered in one of the trees, frozen pearls of ice on the branches.

"I think you're desperate," he said. "You'd do anything to make it look like you're doing your jobs, but you know what? I don't care whether you catch them. I want to move on with my life, that's all I want, so you can go now. I need to help my son with his homework."

He barked out the last part. His wife got to her feet and put an arm around him.

"I think we're done here."

They were driving straight into the moonlight. The heavens seemed so close you could reach out and touch them.

"Do you believe him?" asked Eira.

"I'm not much one for belief." Double-Antti chewed a piece of gum as he gripped the wheel. "I'm the kind of detective who needs facts on the table."

He seemed to be apologizing for the lack of progress, given how far she had traveled.

"You always like to think the breakthrough is just around the corner. Maybe that makes me an idiot for never giving up."

They sat in the car for a while once they reached the hotel by Luleå's northern harbor. Double-Antti shook out a new piece of gum from the pack and offered it to Eira.

"I had a mentor when I first joined the force," he said. "A proper old-school type. He died ten years ago, but I can still hear his thick Tornedalen accent—almost like it gets clearer with time. He always said that police work wasn't about sitting at a desk, mulling things over. The answers are in the facts, observations, physical evidence, in what we see and don't see. No one is invisible, not even the criminals; they always leave a trace."

"And yet it seems like whoever was responsible here vanished into thin air," said Eira. She recognized what he was saying. She too had worked with an older officer who tried to teach her everything he knew, and Eira had gladly soaked up his experience—right up until she discovered the serious mistakes he had made in a murder inquiry some twenty years earlier, when he was so convinced he could see the truth that he pressured a fourteen-year-old boy into confessing to something he hadn't done.

But those were different times, she thought. I might have done the same thing.

Double-Antti hit the wheel in frustration.

"The evidence is out there," he said. "But no matter how hard I dig, I just can't see it. Maybe I've been looking in the wrong place. We all have our blind spots. That's something else he used to say."

His approach appealed to Eira. She liked facts, things that were definite and clear. You started at the bottom, and if everything went well, you added one piece to the next. It was her brother who was drawn to the big ideas, all vague and incomprehensible, about the meaning of life and our place on earth.

"But what those blind spots are . . . ," Double-Antti muttered. "I turned fifty last year, and I still don't know."

The room was slightly too exclusive, and hardly within police budget guidelines. Eira paid for that luxury with her own money. She probably could have caught the sleeper train, getting home in the middle of the night, but her need for a shower had won out. Besides, she liked staying in hotels. Their anonymity appealed to her. She opened the curtains and looked out over the flat rooftops, a haze of lights from the harbor in the distance. She took a long shower and then flopped naked onto the huge bed, an abundance of fluffy pillows. Eira turned on the wide-screen TV as her hair dried, an absurd program in which people who had never met before got married.

Around nine, she got dressed and made her way down to the bar. Paloma Runne was already waiting for her, slumped in a low armchair. The ceiling lights looked like planets, drapes dampening the sound of voices.

"Get a drink if you want one," said Eira. "Or something to eat." She ordered a hamburger for herself. "I'm glad you could come."

She had sent a message to the young woman on the train from

Gällivare, less because she had questions than because she wanted to explain. Why, almost a week after they found her father, nothing seemed to be happening.

"You're never going to catch whoever did it, are you?" Paloma had ordered a Cosmopolitan, and was drinking it through a straw.

"You can't give up yet. It's only been a few days, we're following several leads."

Her words became empty clichés under the girl's critical gaze, sooty black lines around her eyes.

"How are you?" Eira asked instead.

Paloma pulled a face.

"In some ways it's like nothing has changed," she said, so quietly that Eira had to lean in to hear her. "I almost never had my dad close by. But now that he's gone, it feels like he's here. Inside me, if you see what I mean."

"I think I do."

"I chose to study engineering physics so I could show him what I was capable of, but now I don't know. Maybe I'd rather work in theater. Behind the scenes, on the lighting or something."

Eira's burger arrived, as did Paloma's Feta salad. She poked at it as she finished her cocktail at worrying speed.

"Dad never really said anything real," she continued. "When I asked him if he'd met anyone, he told me I was the most important person in his life. When I asked him how he was, everything was always fine. I know he just wanted me to be happy and not worry—I'm always worrying—but now I'm sitting here and I can't answer any of your questions. He left me without any answers."

The gravel crunched beneath his new running shoes, his pace steady and even. For a short while, his headlamp was the only source of light. He was alone.

Mikael Ingmarsson darted through the underpass and turned west, along the road that ran parallel to the E4.

Away from the panic that had been dredged up again, worse than ever. He pushed himself towards his maximum heart rate as he ran up the incline.

He wasn't supposed to wake up feeling like he was suffocating every night. He thought he had put it all behind him. If he didn't look back, it would fade away. Not completely, he was under no illusions about that, but in the same way as grief after someone dies; time would help to dilute and disperse the event, everything else good in his life would help too. The kids, the house, the garden kitchen that would be ready by the time summer came round.

The lactic acid made his legs burn. That was where his willpower came in. If he just pushed on a bit further, there would be no room for thoughts.

If he got his pulse a little higher, his heart wouldn't stop.

The fact that the police kept showing up from time to time was something he had learned to live with. Follow-up questions, hopes that he might have remembered something else.

But Mikael Ingmarsson never remembered anything else.

There was no alternative. If he didn't think about what he had done, it didn't exist.

The cars raced by on their way towards Luleå and Haparanda. No one could see him in the darkness; he was nothing but a sudden flash of brightness when their headlights hit his reflective jacket.

He had googled the dead man in Sollefteå once the police left, read everything there was to read as his son reeled off his eight times tables.

A man around his own age, locked in a basement and left to die. The police were appealing for tips, fumbling in the dark, wanted to know whether anyone had seen him at Stadt in Härnösand on a particular evening in September.

Mikael Ingmarsson reached the petrol station where the Finnish and Russian lorry drivers were settling down for the night. He could hear Finnish country music streaming from one of the cabs.

If he had told them everything, as it actually happened, would the man still be alive now? If he had made a different decision when he came round in the hospital.

He paused for a moment to set his heart-rate monitor to intervals.

One minute at a fast pace, followed by thirty seconds' jogging. The watch, which measured every step he took with pinpoint accuracy, was a birthday present from Petra. *I thought it might do you good to get back in shape.*

That meant she couldn't object to his runs getting longer and longer, two hours, two and a half. He did intervals on the tarmac, along the whole straight stretch towards Ängesbyn, chasing an endorphin kick that reminded him of happiness. His blood pumping through his veins, reminding himself that he was still alive.

It was too late to change anything now.

What would he say?

Sorry, I might've bent the truth a bit, would you mind telling the man's daughter I'm sorry?

The road was pitch black. A single streetlamp by the fork up ahead, it got closer, lighting up his path for a moment. His heart-rate monitor screamed for him to speed up.

By the time the train pulled in to Kramfors, the morning meeting was long over. Eira had managed to join remotely during the brief windows when she had enough signal. Much of the focus had been on the Russian links to the house in Offer, the formation of companies and money laundering. GG wanted a report on her trip to Norrbotten, but he didn't ask any questions.

The room at the station where the visiting investigators usually worked was empty, so Eira laid claim to it. She sat at the computer for a while, trying to get her thoughts in order, before eventually getting up to make a cup of coffee and chat to a colleague who had just returned from an arrest. They had received a tip-off about a man who had been writing abusive messages online. He was in possession of at least three weapons he didn't have a license for and, from his grandparents' house in Lugnvik, had been surfing the web for instructions on how to make a bomb.

"I guess there have always been people like him round here, angry loners lurking on the fringes," said her colleague, patting the coffee machine as though that might make it grind the beans faster. "But they hardly ever used to do anything about it. The question is whether they're happier now."

"They find kindred spirits online," said Eira. "A sense of community."

"And somewhere to point the gun—other than at themselves."

Eira took a bucket of warm, soapy water back to the office with her, dampened a bone-dry sponge. She cleaned the old notes from the whiteboard and then began trying to piece together an overview of the case.

The man who had been locked up in Malmberget was still on her mind. She had actually dreamed about him in her soft hotel bed. Nothing to do with his nightmarish experience, nor anything sexual; she was late picking up his children from nursery, trying to find their boots. Incredibly strange.

Eira worked methodically, listing everything that linked the two cases and everything that separated them. By the time she was done, the two columns were roughly the same length.

The victims were men, that was the obvious link. Both might have been attacked at hotels in small or medium-size towns in Norrland, though as far as Hans Runne was concerned there was still a huge question mark there. Eira had tried to find GG's reports from his interviews with the people at Stadt that evening, but she couldn't find them. If they had led to any useful information, she assumed he would have mentioned something.

The construction industry also came up in both cases. Mikael Ingmarsson had worked in a landscape full of gray zones, in which subcontractors occasionally paid to win contracts. Hans Runne had found work as a painter on various building sites. Dirty money wasn't uncommon in that industry, of course, but as a lead it felt incredibly weak.

Eira found herself thinking about the blind spots her colleague in Luleå had mentioned as she continued to add information to the whiteboard. She heated up a ready meal of meatballs and mashed potato that she had bought from the shop at the train station, then ate it straight from the carton, standing in front of her scribbles and lines.

There was one detail that stuck out. It stood all alone, without a single connection to Malmberget or anything else from Hans Runne's case.

His fingers.

The perpetrator had gone back twice to sever his fingers with a pair of rusty gardening shears. In an attempt to force him to do what, pressure him into what? As Eira stared at the board, she suddenly realized why it made no sense.

Everything she knew about Hans Runne told her that he was a man who chose the easy route in life. He wanted to be seen and admired, he bent the truth to keep his daughter happy, frittered away money, and avoided everything he found difficult.

Would that same man really have withstood weeks of isolation? Would he have been willing to give up a finger instead of bending to whoever had locked him up?

Eira wrote up a few supporting words in an attempt to follow the thought to its conclusion.

"I didn't know you were left-handed," said someone behind her. His voice gave her a rush of adrenaline. She hadn't heard August come in.

"It's not something I ever think about," she said. That was the truth. She wrote by hand so rarely these days that she had almost forgotten the feeling that had taken root through her left hand during her schooldays: that she was slightly awkward and wrong.

August studied the scribbles on the board.

"Makes me think of one of those American films," he said. "You know, where the misunderstood genius writes out all these impossible equations on the blackboard and ends up winning the Nobel Prize."

Eira tried to rub some ink from her fingers. It was like she was seeing her handwriting through August's eyes, and she realized just how childish it was. There were some words even she couldn't read.

"Do you have time to help me with something?" she asked.

"Sure, as long as this doesn't start ringing." He patted his mobile phone. For a split second, Eira wished she could tag along with him, responding to a reported shoplifter at Nylands Järn or a drunk in Bollsta, picking up some speed on the tarmac.

She hunched over her computer and brought up the files the photographer in Umeå had sent, searching through the countless images.

"There's supposed to be a program for improving the image quality . . ."

"Do I look like the IT guy?" August was right behind her; she could feel his breath, the speed at which his heart was beating. "Just because I'm young and handsome and come from Stockholm, everyone thinks I must be good with computers."

He placed a hand on hers and moved it somewhere else entirely.

"I'll do it myself," Eira said with a laugh.

The sound of his phone ringing saved them from doing something stupid. She gripped his hand before he left.

"But speaking of handsome," she said. "Are you doing anything tonight?"

"Sorry," said August. "I'm getting the night train to Stockholm."

"OK," said Eira, opening an image labeled HAND.

"But I'll be back the day after tomorrow."

"Sorry, but I really need to look at this." She couldn't quite focus until he had left the room, until the sound of his footsteps had faded.

The black ravens were back in front of her again.

Hans Runne's hand, enlarged, at an increasingly high resolution. She could make out a streak of something pale just in front of the window. This was one of the images the photographer had rejected, possibly because it looked like a piece of rubbish, something ruining the shot.

Eira managed to wrap her head around the program, making the picture even sharper than before, until there was no longer any doubt.

/

GG picked up on the third ring. He sounded short of breath.

"I'm in the lift," he said. "On my way to a meeting with HR, some sort of incredibly urgent staff survey."

"We were wrong," said Eira. "We've been wrong the whole time."

"You'll have to keep it brief, I'm afraid."

She heard the ping as the image came through to his phone.

"And my glasses are in my office, unfortunately," said GG. "What am I supposed to be looking at here?"

Eira had closed the door and was pacing back and forth across the room.

"I'm assuming Hans Runne was right-handed," she said. "Because I haven't seen it mentioned anywhere. If he was left-handed there'd be some mention of it, that's the kind of thing people always notice."

"What are you getting at?"

"His fingers."

"Yes, I can see that it's a picture of his hand," said GG. "But that's about it."

There was another ping as the lift reached the right floor. The ambient sounds changed, voices in the background.

"It wasn't the perpetrator," said Eira. "He did it himself."

"What?"

Eira swallowed. She had seen a lot on the job and rarely felt queasy, but this was really getting to her.

"Ravens are scavengers," she said. "They didn't land there by chance. Hans Runne had traces of bird in his stomach, and it seems pretty unlikely that he would've managed to catch one in the basement."

There were a few seconds of silence.

"Are you saying he sawed his own finger off?"

"Yeah, either that or he cut or chopped it, however you do it. Probably using the shears, in any case. I just spoke to the pathologist, she said it could be possible."

Perhaps it was the pain—the madness—that had prevented Hans Runne from noticing the photographer, from being able to make his presence known.

Or had he tried? Was that what had made her hurry away, something frightening and nonhuman?

Eira's thoughts turned to the ornithologist, who had heard a terrible scream and then nothing more. The timing could fit. She could barely even imagine that kind of pain.

"It would also explain why the two injuries occurred four days apart," she continued. "He lured his food towards him, and then he tried again."

GG was quiet. It sounded like he had stopped walking. Eira could practically hear his thoughts whirring, their previous assumptions crashing down. The exact same thing that had happened to her a few hours ago.

The darkness that came creeping in.

"So there wasn't any blackmail," GG eventually spoke up, clearing his throat. "Left to die, like a rat in a trap."

She heard the hopelessness in his voice. A door opening, a woman saying it was good he had come, even if he was a day late.

"Great work," he said. "I'll be in touch again soon."

If anyone—a trainee officer or a reporter, for example—had asked GG why he was driving inland that afternoon, he would have said something wise and evidence based about the crime scene.

About how the prosecutor on the Olof Palme case, attempting to do what the Swedish police had failed to do for thirty-four years—namely solve the murder of the country's prime minister—went back to the crime scene. Scrutinizing every last detail, every single discovery and witness statement, until a picture of the killer began to emerge.

Not everyone had been happy. The accused gunman was a pitiful figure who had managed to die before the case could ever be tried in court, but that wasn't the point. The crime scene was.

It didn't matter if it had been two months or thirty-four years, there were still clues to be found. Nothing could be entirely erased. Something was always left behind, in the walls, in the grass and the ground a person has trod, in the memories and everything else we think we've forgotten, but which rise back to the surface if we stubbornly continue to ask questions for long enough.

GG was particularly fond of that approach, not that anyone had asked. As he turned off towards Offer, the only person he was trying to convince was himself.

Northwards, then deep into the sparsest of sparsely populated areas, forests stretching up towards the mountains.

The sky was heavy above the treetops. GG left the car by the side of the road and made his way to the abandoned house on foot. A scrap of police tape was still hanging from a branch, he reached for it and stepped into a swampy hole, his foot sinking to his ankle. When he pulled it out, the bottom of his trouser leg was wet. He aimed for the remnants of a wooden floor to survey the area, so quiet this time.

There had been a shed there once. A life lived.

The birds' chirping seemed so insensitive.

GG wouldn't admit it publicly, because he worked in an area of the country that was dominated by forests and bodies of water bound together in an intricate ecosystem, a place where a man's worth could be measured in the value of the elks he had felled or his past victories on the ice hockey team, but he felt unwelcome in nature.

It was uninviting. It never took him by the hand and said *Georg, my son, shall I show you the mosses and lichens and teach you how to survive out here?*

The door had been secured with a provisional lock. He opened it and stepped inside just as the rain began to fall. A soft pattering on the tin roof that quickly grew in strength, trickling down the windowpanes.

The effect was strangely vivid, providing movement in a space where everything had ground to a halt. He made his way down to the basement. The murky afternoon light barely made it in through the small window, but he didn't bother to turn on his torch.

He watched the space darken as he sat there. A realization that grew in strength, that they had been following the wrong lead. The severed fingers had overshadowed everything else.

GG tried to picture Hans Runne before him, living. No sign of violence, he had voluntarily gone down the stairs and then he was trapped.

Why?

His eyes adjusted to the darkness.

The basement had changed, of course, cleared of all objects, which had been analyzed without providing any real answers. That was just how it was. At some point it would all be needed, once they had a suspect and could tie them to the case. GG knew there was nothing else for him to find here. It was the twists and turns in his own brain he wanted to get at, the natural confidence in his professional abilities, which, combined with a certain arrogance, usually meant he could trust his gut and lead a preliminary investigation in the right direction.

Instead he found himself mulling over the same questions that he had when he first came to the house, with the key difference that the nameless man now had a name. He could feel his presence in the darkest corners of the basement, a loneliness that overpowered all else.

What were you doing here, Hans? And who were you thinking of when you carved your name into the wall?

Eira's trip to Malmberget had rewarded her with a day off, preventing her from tipping over into too many hours for the week. That meant she had no excuses not to get to grips with the cleaning. She had been ignoring it for far too long, a fact that left her with a vague sense of guilt—not that she had ever been particularly bothered about that kind of thing. The battle against filth and decay was a mother's lot, the generation of women responsible for raising living standards, literally cleaning up the Sweden of old, fleck of dust by fleck of dust; it was inherited, carved into their genes.

But now her mother was no longer around. She was all alone, in a house that had been robbed of its warmth and its heart. That sense of loss made itself felt in every room. In the pale rectangle where a frame had once hung, the darkness left by a missing lamp. She had taken down the curtains in the living room, rail and all, only for Kerstin to change her mind and ask for a different set. They were now lying in a heap on the sofa, a thin layer of dust encroaching on them. She needed to do a load of washing, but there was something wrong with the machine, and she would probably have to buy a new one.

As Eira picked up a sack of clothes and material she was planning to take to the charity shop in Kramfors, she managed to knock over a couple of bags in the hallway. Out spilled empty bottles, junk mail, a stack of local newspapers from the past month. The sight made her think about Hans Runne's apartment and how one day someone would come into her home and study everything Eira Sjödin had left behind, everything she had never got round to doing.

There was the bag of books, too. The ones her mother had rejected from the care home. The etching belonging to her father.

Eira threw everything into the trunk of the car. She pulled over by the bins and got rid of the rubbish, then continued up onto the Sandö Bridge. Roughly halfway across, she turned off towards the islands and had to hold back behind two all-terrain vehicles full of troops. Making their way out into the wild, no doubt, to simulate a terror attack or a kidnapping. Peacekeeping forces from all over the world came to Sandö to train, and the police occasionally received reports of strange goings-on in the woods ahead of missions to places like Mali or Colombia.

The road continued straight out into the river, an embankment linking the two islands. The forest on Svanö was much thicker than Eira remembered it, nature reclaiming lost ground. The logging industry was now nothing but a ghost in people's memories, something they felt obliged to mention and point out: this is where so and so was, this is where fifteen hundred people used to work. Her father always used to talk about the workers' barracks down by the old ferry berth whenever they came out to the island, not to mention the girl whose name Eira had inherited, an innocent bystander hit by the army's bullets during the workers' strike of 1931—that was where she once lived.

You could see the barracks from the yellow-brick villa where Veine Sjödin had moved after the divorce. Gone were the trampoline and the goalposts that had kept her stepbrothers entertained.

Marie-Louise still dyed her hair mahogany red.

"Goodness, is that you, Eira? I hope I haven't done anything wrong."

She laughed at her own joke.

"I just wanted to say hello," said Eira, avoiding a hug. "And I've been having a bit of a clear-out, I found a few of Dad's things."

"Oh, that's nice of you."

Marie-Louise took the bag and invited Eira inside, come in, come in, you should feel at home here.

The old tension reared its head the minute the front door closed behind them. The house smelled the same as ever, with the same floral décor, the same sense that she needed to be on her best behavior. Marie-Louise was fragile, sickly. Eira always had to remember that, so that it didn't become too stressful having another child around.

"You should have called ahead," said Marie-Louise, searching the cupboards. "I don't have anything to offer you."

"Don't worry," said Eira. "I just ate, it's OK."

It was so easy to fall into old habits, taking pains not to be a burden. Eira could see her father tiptoeing around them, watching. She knew how hard he found it if they didn't get on.

She'd had her own room for the first year, but then the boys got bigger and needed their own space, and she was given a sofa bed in the TV room on the first floor. Magnus had left home by that point, never set foot there. Not even during the wake after their father's funeral.

"What am I supposed to do with all this?" asked Marie-Louise, pulling a few books from the bag and studying them with a look of skepticism. "I only ever listen to audiobooks."

"They've got his name inside," said Eira. "So legally speaking, they're yours."

"That's no way to look at it. We're family, there's no need to be worrying about that."

"I've got more than enough stuff, and I doubt Magnus cares."

"No, of course," said Marie-Louise, her eyes drifting away. "Not where he is."

Eira's teenage hackles were raised. On the few occasions she had raised her voice in this house, it was to defend Magnus, not herself.

"He mostly just reads philosophy," she said.

"One of the boys might want them, though they don't have much interest in art." Marie-Louise turned the etching over, trying to decipher the artist's name.

Their father had asked them to renounce any claims to his estate before he died. He knew where he was heading months in advance, and said he didn't want his wife to be left homeless. Eira understood that, didn't have it in her to think of herself at the time. And Magnus had signed too. He was a free man; he didn't care about material possessions.

"Are they both OK?" asked Eira.

"The boys?" Marie-Louise's face lit up whenever she talked about her sons. One was studying in Umeå, the other working as an electrician in Ånge. Eira listened, slightly ashamed that she didn't take more of an interest in their lives.

"I should go," she said, getting to her feet.

"Already?"

"I've got a lot on at work. I'm helping Violent Crimes in Sundsvall, investigating the murder up in Offer, I don't know whether you've heard about it?"

She felt a childish urge to brag, though she knew that nothing she achieved would ever come close to being an electrician in Ånge.

"At the old Bäcklund place?" Marie-Louise's eyes widened. "My God, those poor people, of course I've heard about it. The idea that something like that could happen in their house—everything always had to be just so there."

"Did you know them?"

"Oh yes, I was good friends with one of their sons." The memory made her adjust her hair. "We were actually together for a while, so I've been up there. To the house, I mean. It was a while ago now, I can't have been much older than seventeen."

"What was his name?"

"Per," she replied without hesitation. "No, hang on, maybe it was

Jan? He was head over heels for me, in any case. Wanted to take me home to meet his parents, good grief."

"What were they like?"

"I was only there a few times." Marie-Louise had slumped onto one of the kitchen chairs with the etching in her lap, stroking the image as she spoke. It bothered Eira that she was so comfortable taking it as her own. "I remember he had an annoying little sister who really clung to him, she was so jealous. His mother too, she was one of those women with a real penetrating gaze. Like no one was good enough for her son, even though he was the one who'd made a catch. There was a lot of talk about becoming part of the family, that we do things this way or that way. I mean, my God, I was only seventeen, I had no plans to get married. Janne was good looking, but I told him he could keep his mum for himself."

"Do you know why the house was left empty?"

Marie-Louise shrugged.

"No one wanted it, I guess. There was nothing special about it, right out in the middle of the woods. And I had other offers, if I can put it like that."

Eira considered asking another few questions, but none seemed important enough. A brief affair some fifty years ago, children who had long since sold their parents' house. Marie-Louise had a tendency to take all the attention, to make everything about her.

Eira began putting on her shoes.

"I'm glad to see you're doing well," she said.

"You know you're always welcome here."

The silver Audi was blocking access to her driveway when she got home. Eira got out of the car with the sense that something big must have happened. Why else would GG be standing by the fence, talking to her neighbor as Rabble nuzzled his hand?

"The inspector has just been telling me what a good job you're doing," said Allan Westin, standing tall and smiling as though Eira was his own daughter, his pride and joy.

"I tried to call," said GG. "But then I realized I was passing by anyway."

"Has something happened?" Eira checked her phone. It was dead, the screen dark. "Sorry, the battery must've run out."

GG gestured to the front door.

"Shall we?"

Only then did Eira notice that his coat was wet. She hadn't been caught in the passing showers herself. October was drawing to a close, November approaching with its dampness and its dull gray chill.

GG took off his muddy shoes in the hallway.

"I drove up there," he said. "I thought I might see something if I could just look at it through different eyes."

Eira put the kettle on, asked if he wanted tea or coffee. Having him in her kitchen felt both uncomfortable and interesting. He was too tall for her grandmother's wooden chairs, and she became aware of just how old fashioned the big pine table was, the dust clinging to the layers of grease around the extractor fan.

His phone pinged stubbornly in his hand, but he hesitated before looking down, as though he wanted to avoid it.

"Risk and impact assessments relating to the restructuring propos- als," he read, practically spitting the words out, "must be submitted by Monday at the latest, typed, checked, and signed, blah, blah, blah . . . This job would be a lot fucking easier if they would just leave us to get on with it." He threw his phone down. "Could I use your toilet?"

Eira rummaged through the packs of tea for something reason- ably fresh, wiped down the kitchen table, and felt slightly excited that he was actually there. It wasn't so strange, the road really did pass by the house. She was grateful he had ignored the fact that she was on a mandatory day off, or maybe he just needed her so badly that it was worth the intrusion.

She felt warm when he came back into the kitchen. GG stood by the oven, leaning back. He smelled like the forest, a hint of sweat mixed with her mother's never-ending supply of lavender soap.

"So, did you get anywhere?" asked Eira, pouring water into two cups. She never usually drank tea, but was making an exception for him.

"What do you mean?"

"In Offer, while you were up at the house." She sat down to avoid standing too close to him, but quickly got back to her feet. "Do you take milk?"

The fridge was right by the oven, and she had no choice but to brush past him.

"No, I didn't have any sudden insights," said GG. "Didn't see the light. I wanted to go up there on my own so I could sit in the basement and try to imagine what it was like. Having to mutilate your own body to survive, for a few more days of that life. Was it worth it?"

"Have you dropped the Russian angle?"

"I'm leaning that way," said GG. "It's not against the law to buy a house. It's not against the law to register a company. None of those barons or their cronies have been in or out of the country. It's all consultancy firms here, loopholes there. Just show me someone who has actually been in Boteå Parish."

"Maybe we should go through everything again," Eira suggested, without much enthusiasm. "There must be something we've missed. No one doesn't leave a trace."

GG smiled.

"That," he said, "was a double negative, which, according to the laws of mathematics, should be a positive. Though sadly that doesn't apply in this case."

Eira had never thought about it before—no, she had, just not like that, she really had tried to avoid thinking about it—but he was so attractive when he smiled.

"I found it hard to leave," GG continued. "The rain just kept coming down, so I sat on the daybed for a while. I read through everything, thought the silence might help me see things more clearly. But do you know what I realized?"

Why was he looking at her like that, so closely, as though she had an answer for him?

"No," said Eira.

"That I'm glad we've got you on the case."

He put down his cup. The tea bag was still inside. Had he even taken a sip? Eira searched for something to say.

"I should probably get going," said GG, though he didn't move. For almost an entire minute, he didn't move, but then he cleared his throat. "I was going to say see you tomorrow, but I'm not actually working."

Breathing wasn't the problem, it was doing it at a normal pace.

"I'm off too," said Eira. "But I can come in if you need me."

She watched through the window as he walked across the garden *where as a child she used to play* and wished she had been able to say something else, something inspiring or appreciative, something that had cheered him up or made him feel good about himself; he was a good man, a very good man . . . She saw his car pull away behind the bushes and garage.

GG was twenty years older than her, he was her boss. He appreciated her work, that was all.

Eira realized that her own car was parked badly on the road, and she grabbed her keys to move it. The logic that followed wasn't the clearest, but it was there all the same. She had another plastic bag in the back seat. Why not deliver that too, while she was at it? Then she would scrub the entire house, get rid of the old, and take charge of her life.

She drove back up onto the Sandö Bridge and continued some ten or so kilometers north, following the river.

The yard was bathed in darkness, the only light in one of the basement windows. As ever, the door was unlocked, so Eira let herself in. She heard Ricken drumming along with a Queen track, Freddie Mercury's voice filling the house.

"Fuck, you scared me," he said, turning down the stereo and putting his sticks to one side as she came down. His instruments jostled for space with two wood-frame sofas, the kind found in almost every

Swedish home at one point in time, a symbol of modernity. Eira thought she could remember how the hard armrests felt against her back.

"Have any of your relatives had a Fiat Punto stolen?" she asked, tossing the plastic bag to him.

"What the hell is this?" Ricken pulled out a stack of water-damaged school assignments from 1972, the ones from the back of the abandoned car in the woods. Eira had recognized the surname on the labels, of course. Ricken had been her brother's best friend for as long as she could remember, her first true love. She had come to see him from time to time even before Magnus was arrested, and had been back on a few occasions since. She liked spending time with Ricken. There were days when she could ignore all the wrecked cars in his yard, the fact that she didn't really know how he made a living, and just sprawl out on his sofa and talk about life. He was still one of the most handsome people she had ever met, possibly because she saw him as he was back then—though no longer quite as wild or dangerous. She had stayed over a few times, too. His body was still as familiar as her childhood haunts. Lying on his sofa, Eira had a fit of laughter as GG's words came back to her, the lines from the old poem: *I long for home . . . the fields where I would stray, the stones where as a child I used to play.*

She hadn't been a child then, of course, but nor was she an adult. Ricken represented the period in between, when everything had taken shape, when her dreams of love were formed.

"Rosemarie Strindlund," he read, carefully peeling the crisp sheets of paper apart. "They must be my aunt's. She upped sticks to Skövde after my cousin moved there—have I ever mentioned that he makes a ton of money developing computer games? He's the family genius. Where did you find these?"

Eira told him about the stripped-bare vehicle, the reason they had found it. Ricken remembered his relatives being upset over a car being stolen, but it must have been four or five years ago, back when they were emptying his grandparents' house.

"That was where this stuff had been all these years," he said, opening an exercise book and reading aloud from an essay about an underground world opening up in the middle of the river, at one hundred meters' depth. "Aunt Rosemarie should've been a writer. Thanks, honey. What can I do for you?"

"Stop calling me honey."

Eira got up to grab a beer from the fridge. That meant she would have to sleep over.

"You could do some asking around," she said. "Find out who dumped the car, whether anyone hangs around up there."

"Sure, so long as I'm allowed to give them a beating once I get hold of them."

"No, you're not."

"Fucking cop." He pulled her close and kissed her on top of her head. "Are you staying over?"

GG threw off his coat in the kitchen and saw that he had brought the mud in on his shoes. He took them off and used a cloth to wipe up the worst of it.

He couldn't shake off the dirt from the house in the woods, almost as though death itself was clinging to his back. Stop being so goddamn melodramatic, he muttered to himself.

Pathetic.

His phone was dead, too. He plugged it in and took the bottle of whisky and carton of noodles over to the sofa. The police apartment he had borrowed was full of things that meant nothing to him: bare tabletops, a medium-firm bed, all bought from IKEA. There was something nice about spending time there, a sense of not quite being fully present.

The truth was that he hadn't slept in his own bed since the night he dragged Eira Sjödin around the bars and restaurants of Härnösand.

It had been idiotic to track her down on her day off. How could he justify it, on work grounds? Personnel grounds?

He couldn't. He had stood there like an idiot in her kitchen, unable to give her anything concrete. The only thing he had done right was to resist the urge.

GG filled his glass and stared at the picture on the wall, a framed photograph above the TV. For some inexplicable reason, it was of a bridge in New York.

He remembered a conversation he and Eira had once had in the car, back when they first started working together. He had asked the police assistant, a complete stranger at the time, about children— and he had done it pretty abruptly, he now realized. His first impressions of her were still clear in his mind. Integrity and warmth, a rare understanding that he perceived as mutual. She looked straight into him while she listened to him talk, as though the words mattered less than where they were coming from.

But how had she answered his question that day?

GG tried his best to remember. Yes or no or maybe? It made no difference. What mattered was that he never ended up there again, particularly not with a colleague. That was a road he had already been down.

A road to hell, he thought, an old song he couldn't quite remember popping into his head. He ate some of his cooling noodles and felt his blood surging, or maybe it was the whisky galloping through his veins, making him change into one of his new pairs of trousers, a shirt that smelled like chemicals.

GG regretted his decision the minute he climbed the stairs to Stadt.

The bar was already packed, far too many people. He should have gone to bed, or at least somewhere else, someplace where the hunt wasn't quite so obvious.

He was sick of pulling himself together and showing off the best version of himself. Just last week he had made a huge blunder, one he hoped no one would ever find out about. But despite all that, his damn gaze began to wander.

What about her, pretty but boring, or her, far too young, stay away from her, *Jojje*, you'll only end up on your own again. He spotted another woman, plainly pretty in a way he thought he could like, no artifice, she actually looked vaguely familiar. She smiled at him. GG turned around to see whether there was anyone else around him. He couldn't remember where he had seen her before, but he desperately hoped she wasn't someone he had slept with during a particularly irresponsible period of his life. There had been times when he gave himself over to love, others when he fell into self-loathing.

He knew exactly what time it was now.

Time to support a local business and alternate between whisky and gin, time to think about what loneliness could do to a man.

The least he could do was smile back when someone noticed him in the crowd.

NOVEMBER

Lugnvik was still home to the low background hum of powerful engines and other noises, heavy industry clinging on. The sawmill had been closed for years, but hulking great tin sheds still hugged the shoreline, and the dock was still in use. An enormous cargo ship was currently moored there, stacks of timber from the mill in Bollsta waiting to be shipped.

"So, what do you think?" asked Silje, rummaging through her bag with one hand as she checked her messages with the other. "Is he someone you'd hire if you wanted your house painted?"

Eira gazed over to the old wooden shed that the painting and decorating company had taken over and tried to come up with something that didn't feel right.

Some sort of dissonance, something false or evasive.

It had been her idea to visit to the company Hans Runne occasionally worked for. She would have liked to discuss it with GG first, but he had a few days off. Instead she had sat down with an investigator from the Corruption Unit, who took her through the way the construction industry worked—and above all its dark underbelly. She had read reports and scrolled through documents about bribes and buying contracts. Subcontractors who paid to win jobs could fly beneath the radar when it came to certain checks, making it easier for them to use undeclared labor and make money at the other end. The painting firm in Lugnvik seemed too small for that type of corruption, though there were, of course, plenty of small firms that operated on the fringes. A summerhouse owner in the area had been given an invoice for three hundred thousand kronor, covering work that hadn't actually been carried out, including an antique hand-planed floor that didn't even exist.

There was no sign of anything like that going on at the painting firm in Lugnvik, but Eira also wasn't the type to let something go too soon. In that sense, she realized, she was just like the dog, sinking her teeth into a stick and refusing to give it up.

The wind was coming from the east, carrying salt and sea air.

"I don't think they're involved in bribes or dirty money," she said after a moment. "Or not in any serious way, at least."

"What about locking their employees in abandoned buildings?"

"None of that either."

"Damn it," said Silje. "I must've left my snus at home."

She excused herself and went over to the minimarket to buy more. To deal with her missed calls, too.

Eira stayed where she was by the cars, trying to summarize everything they had learned.

The painter was a man approaching pension age. His business partner had moved north a year earlier, to Arjeplog. It was the snow that appealed to him, because you could no longer be sure there'd be enough to go skiing in Ångermanland, even in December. The painter had put an ad in the local paper, and Hans Runne was one of the people who got in touch.

"He didn't know how to do much, but he was a good listener and he was willing to get stuck in. Nice bloke, too. Plus he could come in at short notice. Terrible thing, what happened to him. Awful. Lock up the bastards who did it, will you promise me that?"

Someone from the unit had already spoken to him over the phone, just after Runne's body was found. A nice young man who wanted to know about Hasse's state of mind, whether he had any personal issues. But he didn't know about anything like that. That officer had been polite, thanked him; he hadn't started casting suspicions and implying things like these two.

"We pay what we're meant to pay, and you can be damn sure not everyone does that. Taxes and statements of income, the whole lot. I got into a bit of trouble when I was younger, but I promised my wife it'd never happen again. Lost my driving license and everything. That's the kind of thing you can never shake off. It's always there, festering away on your record. Did you sniff that out? Is that why you're here? Why don't you pay this much attention to the real criminals taking over out there?"

When he offered to ask his wife to come down and show them the books for the last five years, so they could see how easy it was to run a business in the sticks, they had thanked him and left.

Silje was back, a pouch of tobacco beneath her lip. It made her even more beautiful, strangely enough. A subtle disharmony that emphasized her perfect face.

"Have you heard from GG?" she asked.

"Isn't he off today?"

"That never usually stops him from picking up," said Silje, waving her phone in the air. "That was the third time the switchboard has directed people to me, and I'm left standing here like an idiot with no idea what they're talking about."

A timber lorry sounded its horn behind them, and they waited until it had passed and the rumbling had faded. Eira hadn't spoken to GG since he showed up in Lunde two days ago.

"What were the calls about?"

"There's a defense lawyer who's been calling and leaving messages. GG was supposed to talk to his client in Saltvik, apparently. Do you know anything about that?"

Saltvik was the prison on the outskirts of Härnösand, one of three highest-security facilities in the country. GG had mentioned it, Eira was sure of that, while she was visiting her mother. Standing in the noisy corridor with the confused old women, trying to hear what he was saying.

"He'd found someone there he thought might talk," she said. "I thought it had something to do with money laundering, but then he seemed to have dropped that angle."

"This is just so fucking typical of him, isn't it?" Silje was clearly angry, and Eira subconsciously took half a step back. "Why doesn't the idiot write these things down? He roams around like a lone wolf, not reporting to anyone, but this job just doesn't work when the lead investigator thinks he's smarter than everyone else. We should have a prosecutor actively leading the case—I know, I know, there's no need for that when we don't have a suspect, but everyone knows that GG wants all the power for himself, and they just let him get away with it."

"I saw him the day before yesterday," said Eira. "In the evening. He came over."

"To your house?"

Another lorry wanted to squeeze down to the dock, trailer after trailer as she tried to remember what GG had actually said.

"He'd been up to Offer, to the crime scene," she said once she could make herself heard. "But he didn't mention Saltvik, he didn't say anything specific about the case."

All he said, she thought, was that he was glad I was involved.

What else?

He had been sitting in the abandoned house, in silence, asking himself . . . what?

Whether it was worth it?

"I'm not the kind of person who cleans up after others," said Silje, opening the car door. "GG can deal with this himself once he's back."

She picked up her mother just before dinner. The carers had helped Kerstin get ready, and her hair was curled in a way Eira wasn't used to. Her mother had always worn it straighter, tougher, different.

"I bought some food from the deli counter," said Eira, "so we don't have to worry about cooking anything."

Kerstin fastened her seat belt, an anxious smile on her face.

"That must have been expensive?"

"I didn't buy the most expensive things, you know that."

This anxiety about money had been one of the first signs of her illness, long before any forgetfulness became obvious. Eira was living
in Stockholm at the time, which was one of the reasons it had taken
her so long to realize that her mother hadn't just become stingy, an
obsession with the price of everything that drove her to madness,
cut-out coupons and tablecloths Kerstin would force onto Eira because she had got such a good deal through the book club. It was
a trait that had always been there, an undercurrent of anxiety that
simply got worse over time. Kerstin was more than comfortable living on her pension, as she had been on her librarian's salary before
that; they had never wanted for anything at home. But it wasn't
about the figures in her bank account. It made no difference how
often Eira reassured her that they could afford things, that it wasn't
an issue, Kerstin became increasingly anxious because she saw it as
proof that her daughter couldn't be trusted. There was the future to
worry about, no one knew what that had in store. The fear of becoming dependent, of having to beg and borrow and get into debt.
And then there was the fact that it was rude to ignore the cost of
things, to forget where you came from, to take your comfortable life
for granted.

They drove under the road bridge where an artist had installed a
pink neon sign reading MY DREAMS, YOUR LONGING.

"You can start going through the books," said Eira, "while I get
dinner ready."

"Why would I do that?"

"To see whether you want to take any of them with you. We've
talked about this."

"No, I don't think there's any need for that."

Eira put the potatoes on to boil and mixed the salad, opening the
salmon and preparing a starter plate—antipasto, ham and salami,
the shaved parmesan she knew her mother loved. She also dished
out the shop-bought chocolate mousse into bowls, rather than leaving them in their plastic pots. She had been slightly shocked when
she saw the price of a piece of smoked salmon—the river was full
of fish.

It's in me too, she thought as she went through to the living room to bring her mother to the table. Remnants and traces, of you.

Kerstin was busy flicking through a poetry collection by Birger Norman. Poetry, thought Eira. Of course! Short lines, space between the words. You didn't even need to remember the start of the poem as the end approached. She had been bathed in poetry since she was a baby. Her mother couldn't sing, but she was a firm believer in exposing children to rich language and melodies, particularly in a place whose impoverished past was just a few generations back, and so she had read poems instead of singing nursery rhymes.

That was just the kind of thing Kerstin should take back to the home. Perhaps Eira could read to her, whenever her mother stopped reading herself, a rhythm that carried a certain comfort in it.

She felt an overwhelming sense of weariness at the thought of everything hidden away in the attic and the basement of the house, remnants of so many lives. How was she ever supposed to be able to clear it out without Magnus, deciding what to keep or throw away, what was worth something or not?

She left the radio on while they ate. The silences could get so long otherwise. Once they had finished eating, she switched on the TV, though she regretted it the minute the news started, reports of a man who had been murdered in a villa in Täby, an earthquake somewhere, scores of people killed. As Eira searched for something more enjoyable on SVT Play, she realized she was doing the very thing her mother had when she was younger: protecting her from the awful news out there, choosing the good. She found a quiz show, that could work; they always used to compete to recognize places from every corner of the world, to know the names of French Nobel Prize winners and Chinese delicacies. Kerstin was usually the winner, but she now sat quietly. Eira tried to get her into the spirit of the game, to search her memory for the answers, things she had heard once or knew she was supposed to know, but instead her mother's eyelids drooped, her head growing heavy, a jolt passing through her body. Confusion when she realized where she was.

"Where's Magnus? Did he go out?"

"He's not here, Mum."

"He's never been any good at keeping time. I don't know what I'm going to do with that boy."

Eira topped up her wineglass a little, though it only seemed to make her sleepy.

Everything you were afraid of has already happened, she thought.

"Magnus is fine." That was the response she chose this time, for the sake of calm, for the unfamiliar feeling of having done something nice for her mother. "He's just a bit busy at the moment."

She helped Kerstin to the bathroom, up the stairs, to her bedroom. Nothing had changed in there. Eira had been extra thorough with her cleaning, carrying in a couple of potted plants she hadn't yet managed to kill.

A pat on the cheek goodnight. She was surprised, touched, and a little concerned when Kerstin gave her a long hug.

Have you forgotten that we're not huggers, Mum?

Eira had left both doors open, and she lay awake for a long time, listening to the sound of snoring from the next room. She dozed fitfully, then got up to check on her mother, almost as though she were a new parent. Is she still breathing, has she fallen out of bed? She wished there was a formula she could use to calculate how much more the disease would have taken from her in a year's time, in four, by the time her darling child had served his sentence. Eira tossed and turned, sweating. She got up to open the window, saw a few veils of cloud illuminated by the moon.

Come home, you bastard, she muttered into the darkness, as though Magnus could hear her behind the prison walls 250 kilometers away. Come home.

She woke to noises from the ground floor. It wasn't yet six a.m., but Kerstin was already up, rattling around in the kitchen.

The percolator was on, bubbling and hissing. Eira resisted the urge to check if her mother had added enough coffee. She didn't say anything about her bed either, the sheets damp with urine. She just crept down to the utility room with the bedding and dumped it in a heap on the floor. She would buy a new washing machine today, she decided, trying not to rush her mother with her breakfast. Kerstin kept pausing midchew, a half-eaten sandwich in her hand for a full minute or two.

On their way out to the car, Kerstin spotted their neighbor. They stopped to chat over the fence, as they always had, and Rabble began jumping up and down with excitement.

"Have you got yourself another dog, Allan?"

"He's lovely, isn't he," said Allan Westin, keen not to embarrass her.

Eira stepped to one side when her phone started buzzing in her pocket. A message from Silje.

Where are you?

Eira replied that she was on her way to Kramfors, glancing back over to her mother, who was still chatting away.

Has something happened?

She tried to work out how long it would take her to drop off Kerstin at the home and felt her conscience tugging at her. Hours and minutes and her responsibilities at work; a man was dead, and it was down to her—well, not just her—to get justice for him. She would have to deliver if she ever wanted to get out of this place *where as a child she used to play,* a microcosm where time dragged on as two old people chatted about things that would be forgotten by morning.

"I'm really sorry, Mum, but I have to get to work, we need to go."

"But aren't we going to have a coffee?"

Silje's reply vibrated in her hand: Could you come to Sundsvall?

Eira opened the car door and took her mother by the arm. Allan Westin backed her up.

"Go with your daughter, Kerstin. You know what these young people are like, all we can do is try to keep up. Come over another day."

Sure, what is it? Eira wrote as she started the engine.

The reply came through almost immediately.

Explain later.

• • •

Silje had sent an address, but that was all. Eira tried calling her after she dropped off her mother in Kramfors, but the line was busy every time.

She turned off onto Esplanaden, Sundsvall's grandest street, an hour later. It was only then, as she slowly passed the descending odd numbers, that she realized the significance of the address.

An apartment in a turn-of-the-century building, a balcony that looked out across the avenue of trees below. She had sat on that balcony once, between trains, and GG had opened a bottle of red wine. They had talked about the Lina case, and he had declared it closed.

Silje was waiting on the steps outside.

"Why did you want to meet here?" Eira asked as she got out of the car. Despite the NO PARKING signs, she had pulled half onto the pavement.

"None of this is official," she said. "Just so you know. I haven't spoken to any superiors, no one else at work knows."

"What are you talking about? Has something happened?"

"I don't know, I don't have a fucking clue."

Silje unlocked the heavy door using a key. The stairwell was grand, just as Eira remembered it. Dark and quiet. Stone flooring laid in a pattern, an iron gate on the lift.

She suddenly found it hard to breathe.

"I couldn't get hold of GG, so eventually I phoned his son in Oslo, late last night. He called me again early this morning and asked me to go in. GG always keeps a spare key in his desk drawer at work. We're doing this as a favor to the family, so to speak."

The lift screeched upwards.

"Why isn't it official?"

"Let's call it consideration."

Eira stared into the mirror on the wall of the lift where their faces, hers pale and anxious, were endlessly multiplied.

Silje tugged at the iron gate before they had quite reached the fourth floor, making the lift stop around twenty centimeters short. Despite that, the gate opened and they climbed out.

"I'm not so stupid that I'd go in alone," said Silje, "but you might be wondering why I called you."

"Surely there must be others, here in Sundsvall."

"I got the impression you don't talk unnecessarily. I'm trusting you not to start gossiping at the station."

"Of course I won't," said Eira. She was flattered, but she also wished that Silje had chosen someone else.

She didn't want to be standing outside this door, unofficially. Carved from an unspecified type of wood, a brass nameplate.

G. GEORGSSON.

Watching her colleague turn the keys in both locks, reaching for the handle. No gloves, she realized, should we be wearing gloves?

"It has happened before," Silje said quietly. "Him going under."

The junk mail spilled out onto their feet as the door swung open, white envelopes, the local paper, a sense of déjà vu from another apartment Eira had entered recently. Similar smells, the same musty air.

"Isn't this a bit much mail for just a few days?" she asked, kicking the pile. A flicker of hope that he was staying elsewhere, maybe that was it.

"Lots of people just don't want to deal with the post," said Silje. "They don't bother opening it, close their eyes whenever they see a bill."

She stepped inside, seemingly without hesitating and still wearing her shoes, heading straight through the living room to the other end of the apartment. Eira's reluctance to go after her was purely physical, barging into his private sphere. They shouldn't be doing this, they should have a prosecutor's backing, a real suspicion.

The apartment had high ceilings, stucco, the kind of furniture you might see in an interiors magazine. Curved wood, Swedish and Danish design, light and airy.

Silje paused outside the bedroom. The door was ajar, and she nudged it open with her elbow.

"He's not here."

"Thank God."

Eira gripped the doorframe, dizzy once the worst of the tension faded. The room was a mess, the bedding a chaotic tangle. Withered potted plants in the window.

"I honestly thought . . ." Silje didn't need to finish her sentence, Eira knew what she was going to say. Every police officer had been to their fair share of apartments where someone had stopped answering the phone, where the mailbox was full, the stench seeping out. It was their job to go where no one else would. More often than not, there was no crime involved. A heart attack, a stroke, someone who had drunk until their internal organs gave up; overdoses, depressions that ended in the worst way imaginable. All those possibilities had flooded through her.

Eira had to sit down in the first chair she could find, a deep armchair with a fluffy lambswool seat. She looked down into the overflowing ashtray on the soft rug beside her, ash scattered all around it, a half-empty pack of GG's favorite brand. She seemed to be the last person who had seen him. He had got into his car and driven away from her house in Lunde three evenings ago, but where had he gone?

It seemed unlikely that anything had happened to GG. He was a tall man, over fifty, and she was pretty sure he worked out—it definitely looked that way. He had a certain vigor, a wiriness that reminded her of long-distance runners. It also wasn't down to luck that he had become the lead investigator with Violent Crimes. He was smart, good at his job, highly experienced. Eira had never thought of him as the kind of officer who leapt into things headfirst, taking unnecessary risks.

The days raced through her mind, tripping over one another. Things had been intense, she had been focused on the investigation, but she had also spent time with both Ricken and August, that felt distant now; she had been to Umeå and Malmberget, but before that they had interviewed several witnesses together, gone to see the victim's ex-wife, to the pubs and restaurants of Härnösand.

That evening, she realized, when they ate together, GG had ordered a glass of wine, said he wouldn't be driving home. How long ago was that?

Eight, nine days?

She leapt up and the room began spinning again, low blood pressure, delayed shock, perhaps. She went out into the hallway and carefully picked up the stack of newspapers. Checked the dates. From the kitchen, she could hear the thudding of cupboard doors being opened and closed, Silje mumbling to herself. "Didn't I say something was up, didn't I know something wasn't right? That fucking idiot. How long has this cheese been here, exactly?"

Eira straightened up and took in the bottles on the counter behind her, fruit flies feasting on the dried red wine.

"I think he might have borrowed an apartment in Härnösand."

There was a parking ticket on the windscreen when they came out. Eira tore it off without even looking at it.

"We need to call this in," she said. "Anything could have happened to him. We need the prosecutor on board."

Silje looked up at the sky, which was almost the exact same shade as the tarmac.

"Last time," she said slowly, "after his divorce—something GG claimed was a mutual decision, reached by consensus—he boarded one of the ferries to Finland. And we all know what people do on those."

"Drink," said Eira. "Play on the slot machines." She had been on a few teenage booze cruises herself, but that was all a long time ago now.

"Yeah, well, he was gone for several days, and it definitely wasn't because of the dinner buffet."

Eira thought back to their evening in Härnösand. Had GG ordered a glass of wine because he was staying over, or was it the other way around? Did he stay over so that he could drink? Another occasion came back to her, a morning when he had seemed particularly under the weather and she thought she could smell it on him, but she had never thought any more of it. Everyone drank from time to time, especially when they were out of town. What else was there to do in the evening?

"He spent several days going back and forth over the Bothnian Sea," Silje continued. "Checked in to a hotel over there for a few nights, too. He needed to see the horizon, that's what he said when he eventually came back and got his life in order. A hell of a reason to go on a bender like that."

She gazed past Eira, towards the sea, which stretched out somewhere beyond the stone buildings flanking the central boulevard.

"He's not an alcoholic, that's not what I'm saying. Not that I know of, anyway, I really don't think he is. But when GG hits rock bottom, that's what he does. So long as he does his job, it's none of my business."

Her colleague sounded angry, looked angry, but she had also gone to the effort of getting his keys. Why? To protect him? So that no one else would work out what was going on?

"We can't go into any more apartments as a favor to the family," said Eira.

"You're right, of course."

"Do you want to do it, or should I?"

"I'll call the prosecutor from the road."

They drove separately, neither sure where they would end up later. Eira had one of the commercial radio stations turned up high, jingles about instant wins and everything you could ever wish for at a DIY store in Birsta.

The retail parks on the outskirts of town raced by, the traffic thinning out when they reached the E4. Eira kept her eyes on the road. Not in the broad, natural sense, to spot turnoffs and fellow road users, but staring down at the tarmac disappearing beneath the hood, kilometer after kilometer of hard, rough surface.

There could be plenty of perfectly innocent reasons why GG wasn't answering his phone. At least three or four, all plausible. He might have met someone, dozed off in a drunken haze somewhere,

gone out to the edge of the archipelago and switched his phone to
silent.

That was what she would be thinking if it were anyone else. Eira
didn't want to believe that GG would simply drop everything, but
then again she didn't really know him. The picture she had of him
was falling to pieces. She had only ever seen a talented detective she
admired, wanted to impress.

He's a police officer, she told herself, involved not only in this
case but in countless others, ongoing and closed; cases in which the
perpetrators had been sent down and others where they had walked
free.

It was highly likely he had been threatened at least once.

But he really should be answering his phone.

The gulls screeched above the harbor in Härnösand. Eira got out of
the car for some fresh air while she waited. When Silje reemerged
from the police station, she was carrying the keys in one hand.

"Officially, I'm the one borrowing the apartment tonight," she
said.

The prosecutor had wanted to hold off on formally opening an
investigation. The apartment was police property, and by signing
it out in her name Silje had legally also made it hers, meaning they
could avoid all the paperwork and the risk of any leaks.

The disappearance of a murder detective, whatever the reason,
midinvestigation . . . No one wanted to think about what would
happen once the press found out.

"They had to give me the spare key, because GG never returned
his. The woman I spoke to was annoyed, to put it mildly. She said
she'd emailed to remind him, but he never replied."

They walked the short distance to the apartment. That was quicker
than driving down one-way streets, looking for somewhere to park.
The sea breeze found its way in between the buildings.

When they reached the door, Silje paused and pulled on a pair of
plastic gloves.

"Never hurts," she said.

Eira rummaged through her pockets for the gloves she always kept there, whether she was in uniform or in plain clothes, as she was now; it was so routine that she barely even thought about it. She felt the sweat collecting inside the tight plastic.

Neither woman said a word as Silje unlocked the door.

There was no post inside. Just a few flyers from firms that had ignored the signs announcing they weren't welcome.

It didn't smell, either. The place smelled of practically nothing at all.

A low hum from the fridge. Their soft footsteps on the linoleum floor. It was an anonymous studio flat with a sleeping alcove and a tiny kitchen, easy to get a quick overview. Silje bent down towards a carton on the coffee table, a few noodles still inside.

"These aren't from yesterday."

The curtain in the sleeping alcove was open. The sheets were crumpled, the duvet thrown back to the foot of the bed, a dent in the pillow. A shirt draped over a chair, a pair of underpants.

"Doesn't look like he's moved out," said Eira.

"Or maybe he just expects someone else to tidy up after him. That would be so typical of GG, wouldn't it?"

Perhaps she had meant it as a joke, a bit of sarcastic banter, but neither woman laughed.

The door to the bathroom creaked.

Eira stared at his toothbrush, left on the side of the sink. A tube of toothpaste that had been crumpled to squeeze out the very last drop.

The void left behind him, everything that remained.

"Hey, Eira." She heard Silje's voice from the kitchen. "Could you come here?"

There it was, his phone. Behind a whisky bottle and a couple of cups and glasses, fully visible on the worktop. It was plugged in to charge.

Silje poked it with a breadknife, making the screen light up. He had a laughing baby as his wallpaper, a gummy smile.

"Is it his?" said Eira.

"The kid?"

"I meant the phone."

"Could be his grandchild," said Silje.

GG's number was among the first in Eira's contacts list, and she hit dial. The screen flashed, the ringtone blaring a few seconds later. Drums first, then guitar, one of Bruce Springsteen's most famous tracks, she had heard that intro countless times before, in the car, wherever they were.

They both stared mutely at the screen where her name had flashed up.

Eira Sjödin.

"He can't just leave his fucking phone behind," said Silje.

"Maybe he plugged it in to charge and forgot it," said Eira. "It's easily done."

"For three days?"

"He doesn't have another phone, does he? One for work and one for his private life?"

Eira tried to remember GG talking on the phone. It wasn't hard, because he was constantly doing it, but she struggled to picture the phone itself. All she could see was how he looked in profile, when he turned away, his straight neck, his smile when it broke through.

"If I know GG," said Silje, "he wouldn't be able to manage two phones at once. He's the lead investigator. No one can keep on top of who he's ringing."

She hit the worktop so hard that the phone jumped.

"So where the hell has he gone this time?"

They ate a pasta dish, green peas glowing through the nondescript cream sauce, as they waited for Prosecutor Nora Berents to drive up to Härnösand. When her message came through to say that she had just passed Älandsbro, they left the restaurant before they finished eating.

"I've booked us a room where we can talk in peace," Berents said when they met outside the station eleven minutes later. She was new to the area, but experienced in the job. Rumor had it that a fractious divorce and a possible conflict at work were behind her decision to leave Stockholm.

She closed the door.

"Do you have any idea at all where Georgsson could be?"

Either she didn't know him well enough to say GG, or she was simply keen not to sound too familiar.

"Not a hint of a fucking clue," said Silje.

She recapped what they had seen in the two apartments, how long GG had been out of contact. Eira glanced up at the clock as her colleague talked, an old analog thing that had survived the digitalization drive, the hand jolting forward every minute.

It was 5:07 p.m., which meant it had been almost three days since she last saw him.

"And the investigation he's in charge of," said Nora Berents. "If we start there. Is there anything that leads your thoughts in that direction, aside from the fact that the victim was a male around the same age?"

"Forty-seven," Eira stuttered. "Hans Runne, that is. But GG is a bit older, isn't he . . . ?"

"Fifty-five," said Silje.

Eira pictured the actor in a different light, old-fashioned theatrical shots flickering by as the prosecutor waited for them to go on.

All the parts he had played. Some of them reminded her of GG, she realized. Not Hamlet, of course, but Macbeth. The only line she could remember from her schooldays was the one about life being a tale, told by an idiot. There was something of the sect leader from Selma Lagerlöf's *Jerusalem* in him, too. The man who convinced an entire community to up sticks for the Holy Land.

Something about his gaze, something powerful and luminous.

The minute hand jumped forward again.

5:08.

"How has he been lately?"

A moment's silence.

"Distant," said Silje. "There are things he said he was going to do that have fallen between the cracks. There might be aspects of the case that we don't know about."

"And his private life?"

There was a tension in the air, like the electricity in faulty wiring. Eira reached for a jug of water that could easily have been standing there for some time. Her mouth was dry.

"I don't know much," said Silje. "He got divorced five years back, two adult children. Lives alone now, if that's what you're getting at."

"I think you know what I'm getting at," said Nora Berents. "Has Georgsson seemed depressed, does he drink too much, is he struggling financially? You know the kind of questions you should be asking, as police officers."

The prosecutor had a couple of small planets floating beneath her ears, silver with multicolored stones that clashed with her sober clothing. Eira found herself watching them instead of meeting her eye.

"He seemed a bit down last time I saw him," she said after a moment. "Three days ago, around eight in the evening. He stopped off at my house after visiting the crime scene in Offer. I live on his route away from there."

The prosecutor looked down at her iPad, her notes.

"And that was the last time either of you saw him?"

"Yes," said Silje.

"You said he was down? In what way?"

Eira took a few deep gulps of water. It tasted stale, dusty. Talking about her boss like this felt dirty, wrong; his private life was his own business.

"He spoke about the case a bit," she said. "About the owners of the property, that it didn't seem to be leading anywhere, but also about things that . . ." She had to pause to catch her breath, swallow, her throat was burning. "What life is worth."

The prosecutor's gaze was sharp, boring into her.

"And if I ask you straight out . . ."

"The answer is no," said Silje. "GG isn't the kind of person who'd take his own life."

"I know this is hard for you, but you must realize that it's something we have to consider, just like you would for anyone else."

"People who die by suicide often think the world would be a better place without them," said Silje. "They're under the delusion that they're a burden. But GG thinks the world would be a better place if more people were like him."

"That can change if a person is depressed or suffering some sort of crisis," said the prosecutor, moving on to questions about other cases, any possible threats. That was the kind of thing they would have to investigate more closely if he didn't turn up within the next few hours: who had been released from prison, who had relatives that might want revenge? Berents said she would request his bank transactions, phone records, and so on in the morning.

After making a few calls, she announced that she had now officially stepped in as the leader of the preliminary investigation in the case of the man found in the abandoned house.

"So you'll both report directly to me," she said.

"And GG?" asked Silje. "Who's in charge of that?"

"You're both too close, surely you can see that?" said the prosecutor. "You have certain loyalties. You'll just have to trust the others to do their job."

He thought he had experienced real darkness so many times before, but it was nothing but a lack of light. Something his eyes could get used to, making out shadows and shifts in the gloom.

But this is something else entirely.

His hand disappears when he holds it out in front of him. The pain is still there, the throbbing from his attempts to prize the door open, from banging and roaring at the top of his lungs. He should be furious with the person who did this, but he can no longer access his anger. He remembers that saliva is supposed to be cleansing, and he sucks on his fingers, tastes blood.

The night has passed, but what about the day? Is it over yet, is he into his third full day now?

He sits hunched over, practically bent double on the bottom shelf in the earth cellar. The wood feels hard against his tailbone and his spine. The floor is softer, tightly packed earth, but that is also where the bugs are. He doesn't want the insects to feed on his body, to crawl in if he falls asleep. He knows a little about bats and earth cellars, that they feel at home there. There was some concern that they were disappearing as the old earth cellars were being torn down, but doesn't there need to be some sort of hole for them to get in?

His fingers explore the ceiling again.

Could they really live their whole lives in this darkness, this jet-blackness?

There is a hole, smaller than his hand, letting air in. That's all. He gropes for some sort of object in the darkness and finds the tins. There's a bottle too, an empty bottle. He smashes it against the iron door. Uses it to hack at the hole, causing earth and shards of glass to rain down on him. The bottle shatters when it hits rock. The hole is no bigger than it was before.

Think, he tells himself. Your thoughts are all you have, your common sense.

He tried to keep track of time at first, but eventually dozed off. When he woke he didn't know how long he had slept. He has screamed himself hoarse, even though he knows no one can hear him.

The bottle of water in his pocket was almost full when they climbed the hill.

He can't see exactly how much of it is left, but he can feel how light it is. That is the only time that means anything now: how long he can hold out until the next sip of water.

It was a jet-black morning when Eira drove into Kramfors, practically still night. Empty streets, the station bathed in darkness.

The clock on the dashboard read 5:23. She had managed to get a few hours' sleep on the sofa, a sleep so chaotic that it didn't count as rest. Certain details from the investigation kept swirling around in her head, mixing with panicked dreams about running out of time.

She sat down at the desk at the back of the station and logged in to the computer. A work laptop was being delivered for her at some point during the day, meaning she could finally log in to the preliminary investigation wherever she was, working through the night if she wanted to—something that was otherwise the privilege of the permanent members of the team.

It had taken her a lot to drum up the courage to ask the question the day before. Growing up, Eira had always been taught not to make demands; you were supposed to adapt to the circumstances, however shitty they might be. It was a question of perseverance, not being a weakling who lay down and whined. Either that, or you went out to protest. Demands were something people made as a collective.

"Of course," the prosecutor had told her. "You're one of the people who knows the case best. I'll get them to send you a police computer in the morning. They can update your contract if necessary."

A slightly dizzying feeling. So this was how easy it was, to ask and receive.

The computer was slow, trying to install an update. Eira felt time rushing through her, pulsing like the blood in her veins. It had been four days now since anyone had heard from GG.

She had decided to go through everything again, searching for links. There was no reason to suspect that one thing related to the other, but the shadow of him seemed to loom on every single page. What had GG done, what had he been thinking, which paths had he taken?

She knew large chunks of the investigation by heart, but there were also nooks and crannies where she had never set foot. Everything that had been brushed aside, barely mentioned.

That included the stacks of tips from the public. The bank transactions and call lists from further back in time. Peripheral interviews with possible witnesses whose names she had never even heard, hundreds of routine checks that had been carried out from Sundsvall.

She searched for the witness interviews GG had mentioned the day he brought up the prisoner in Saltvik on the phone. A group of men who had seen Hans Runne at Stadt, a woman who had spoken to him. It was the same thing there: Eira had only caught a fraction of what GG was saying, her mind elsewhere. She eventually managed to find one of the tips, a middle-aged man had called it in, and realized that GG had never followed up on it. The other one was nowhere to be seen. She couldn't find a single mention of the woman who had met Hans Runne at Stadt among the general tips, nor in any of the reports.

Maybe she was just misremembering what he said.

Eira paced around the room. A gray haze spilled down over the river and mountains, erasing the boundary between the sky and solid ground. The day had begun at the station, and with it the usual slamming of doors, phones ringing, voices in different parts of the building. Since her desk was at the very end of the corridor, she didn't see another soul until she got up to grab a coffee and make herself a sandwich around ten.

"Have you been avoiding me?"

August's voice behind her, full of laughter, like a brook in spring, frisky in a reckless way. His sheer presence made her smile.

Eira ran a hand through her hair, couldn't remember when she had last looked in a mirror.

"Aren't you supposed to be in Stockholm?"

"That was just over the weekend."

"OK."

She had lost track of how many days it had been since she last saw him, since they slept together. A week, ten days?

"Of course I'm not avoiding you," she said. "Things are just crazy right now."

"How's it all going?"

"What?"

The hum of the coffee machine stood between them, along with everything else lurking within. The kind of thing you couldn't bring up in a pantry, a workplace corridor, while colleagues called out hello in passing. The fact that something had changed between them, the balance. Eira had never laid any claims to August—the free nature of their love had been exciting—but now he was getting married. He had chosen someone else after all.

"The investigation," August clarified. "The man in the abandoned house. Or are you working on something else now?"

"Oh no, I mean yeah, it's going well." The machine spat out a filter coffee, extra strong.

"I can't stop thinking about it," he said. "Being locked up like that, completely powerless. Do you think there's any worse way to die?"

"I have to go," said Eira. "I have to get back."

Away from the temptation to confide in him and accidentally say something about GG. The prosecutor had been clear that they needed to keep the news within a tight circle for as long as possible.

She closed the door behind her.

Heavy, wet snow hit the windowpane. It would melt during the course of the day; the forecast was promising 41 degrees that afternoon. More or less subconsciously, Eira registered that as a positive.

It meant less chance of freezing to death.

She continued to delve into the investigation. The last thing she remembered GG talking about was the owners of the property, money laundering. He had sounded resigned, disappointed even.

Eira scrolled through page after page and realized just how much weight that lead had been given. If a man was found dead in a house owned by someone with links to organized crime, it would be misconduct not to look into it, of course. One theory was that Hans Runne had been used, or possibly just got in the way somehow.

Some thirty or so names had cropped up, and there was information about luxury cars and exclusive properties all over the world.

Eira thought back to the house in Offer, on the edge of the wilderness. The place didn't even have a letter box. But wasn't that the point? Its remoteness, the fact that no one would care or ask any questions?

If its only value was on paper, then why would these people get their shoes dirty and risk everything by going out there?

It was 10:43 when her phone finally interrupted her focus.

"The prosecutor was just here," said Silje.

Eira could hear that she was on her feet, her breathing quick.

"Have they found him?"

"No."

The melting snowflakes ran down the windowpane, blurring the town beyond.

"So what did she say?"

"They got GG's phone records from the network operator." Eira heard a car door slam, a certain distance in Silje's voice once she switched her to loudspeaker. "She wanted to know how important Cecilia Runne was to the investigation."

"His ex-wife? Not important at all, aside from the fact that she went into his apartment and got rid of possible evidence. But she had an explanation for that, she did it for her daughter."

"So why has GG been in close contact with her over the past week?"

"Has he?"

"He didn't mention anything to you?"

They tracked down Cecilia Runne at work, at the communications agency where she was a senior copywriter.

Pale walls, open plan, the only doors made from glass.

"Do you know who did it? Is that why you're here?"

"Is there somewhere we could sit down and talk?"

Eyes followed them as they moved through the office. Cecilia closed the door behind them in a room with two bright-red sofas. The glass walls made the space feel like an aquarium.

"Who was it?"

"We don't know," said Silje.

The woman glanced at the clock and mumbled something about a client meeting in fifteen minutes. She was as thoughtfully dressed as she had been during their previous meetings, in shades of green this time.

"I know this is tough," said Eira. "But we need you to take us through everything one more time."

"Why I went into the apartment? I've already explained. You were there, you and Georg."

"Georg?"

"Yes, Inspector Georgsson. You and he came over to my house, I told you everything. Don't you take notes?"

Eira saw people moving on the other side of the glass walls, heads turning towards them. It was the kind of environment in which you couldn't even pick your nose without being seen. They needed to ask questions without revealing why, ideally without alluding to GG's disappearance; the news could spread in no time at all.

"You've had some contact with our colleague since that meeting," Silje continued, in her friendliest voice. "The problem is that we're in the middle of a complex investigation involving a large number of people. That means things sometimes fall between the cracks, and unfortunately we've lost those particular notes. It's important for us to have everything in place to be able to compare and assess the different statements relating to your ex-husband. I'm sure you understand."

"Yes, I . . ."

"So I'm afraid we need you to take us through everything again."

Silje and Eira were sitting on one of the sofas, but Cecilia Runne was still on her feet, hovering by the door, as though she wanted to make sure she could be first out if the room caught fire.

"Well, I got in touch with him," she eventually said. "I felt like I hadn't really conveyed who Hasse was."

"In what sense?"

"I don't really remember all the details." Her hair was short, but she attempted to wind a lock of it around her finger. The gesture made her seem girlish. What are you worried about, Eira wondered. What is it you don't want to tell us?

"He asked a lot of pretty private questions, about our relationship and that kind of thing, I don't know whether I . . ."

"Just tell us what you remember, and the rest might come back to you."

"But I can't," said Cecilia Runne.

"Why not?"

"Because . . . Because I promised him I wouldn't."

"Your ex-husband is dead, likely murdered," said Silje. "Any promises you made him no longer matter, I think you understand that."

"No, God, not Hasse." Her eyes wandered, to the other side of the glass, to the phone she was anxiously fiddling with. It struck Eira just how different she had seemed last time, sitting by the bay window at home, when GG was present. How she had giggled and crossed one leg over the other, then back again, showing off like a bird during a mating ritual.

"So who did you promise?" she asked calmly. "And what is it you're not allowed to tell us?"

"It wasn't even me who did anything wrong," said Cecilia Runne.

She had called the inspector after he and Eira visited the house. *Georg*, as she insisted on calling him, had left his card.

A sense that she had more to say, there was so much stirring inside her. The grief and horror at the terrible thing that had happened. Her responsibility for their daughter, who had lost her father; the anguish over how she, as a mother, would deal with it.

"To be perfectly honest with you, I also wanted to see him again." She looked down at her hands and smiled, in a way that indicated fondness. "That's not a crime, is it? Having a little crush? Everyone needs a bit of love when things are at their worst."

The air that hit them as they came out onto the pavement was cold and raw, the wind blowing in from the Bothnian Sea.

"I need a drink," said Silje. "I'll take the bus home or check into a hotel, I don't care which."

There were construction cranes in motion around them, the afternoon traffic building, but the noise didn't seem to cut through. Cecilia Runne's voice was all that was echoing through Eira's head as they made their way to the nearest bar, the way it gained new life and energy when she finally told them what she had promised GG she would keep quiet about.

He said it would look bad, that he was in a position of power. That it would be better if we kept it to ourselves. He's not going to get into trouble now, is he? Because of this?

It was *Georg* who suggested they meet somewhere in town, at a restaurant. He had listened to her, he really had. And Cecilia had needed someone to listen, God knows that, *it was nice not to have to be the strong one for once.*

One thing had led to another. A sense of intimacy.

GG had told her that he lived alone and that he struggled to imagine himself in another long relationship, that his latest attempt had been much too complicated.

"Jesus Christ." Silje's voice broke through everything. "He slept with a witness. A relative of the victim. What the hell was he thinking?"

They continued the evening with a drink at Cecilia's place. Eira wished she could have avoided hearing the next few details. The woman didn't tell them everything, of course. She hadn't been explicit about exactly what happened when they eventually ended up in bed, but she said enough for Eira to picture it: her slim but supple body beneath his, on top.

Perhaps GG's common sense had caught up with him that night, or maybe he just wanted to leave. Either way, he had started to get dressed despite Cecilia's attempts to make him stay; he was drunk, she didn't want him to go.

It would be good if you didn't mention any of this, he had said.

A confidence, a shared secret.

Once Cecilia finally started talking, it was as though the two officers in front of her had transformed into a couple of girlfriends she could confide in. Or, thought Eira, perhaps she was hoping to get closer to him through them.

Everything had gone quiet after that night. No phone calls, no messages, no thanks for last night or I'm thinking of you or would you like to meet again?

So I did what you do, I messaged him to ask, but he didn't really give me any answers, so I wrote again, I told him how I felt, that I'd had a great time and that I understood if he needed time, that I was here for him, and, you know, I didn't want to put any pressure on him, I just wanted to be open and show him that I really do care about him, seriously . . . He hasn't said anything about me, has he?

Silje ordered two dry martinis. It wasn't something Eira usually drank, but it felt like a good fit. Strong.

They had ended up in a gloomy dive bar, a dark space where there was no need to put on any airs. Somewhere you could slump into a deep vinyl sofa, stir your drink, and prong the olive as you searched for something to say.

Tried to process what had already been said.

"And now it's in our laps," said Silje. "Should we pass this on, meaning his job might be gone when he comes back, or should we stay loyal and keep our mouths shut?"

If he comes back, thought Eira.

"It was obviously a stupid thing to do," she said. "But anyone can make a mistake."

"Not if it impacts their work," said Silje.

"We don't know that it did. Those witness statements might have been worthless, and Cecilia Runne isn't exactly . . ."

The look Silje gave Eira made her drop her attempt at a defense, if that was what it was.

"I don't know whether you know," Silje said. "But we had an affair a few years back."

"You and GG?"

"Mmm."

Her drink came to an abrupt end. There hadn't been much liquid in the glass, but the alcohol made her head spin.

"It was a pretty long time ago," Silje went on. "Lasted six months—all top secret, of course. Hotel rooms, made-up conferences, you know, the whole lot. I was the one who ended things."

There was a chalkboard listing the daily specials on the wall behind Silje. Messy handwriting. Pork noisettes. Something she couldn't quite read with potatoes.

"He started talking about getting a divorce. That was the last thing I wanted."

"But he did it anyway."

"That was later," said Silje. "It had nothing to do with me; I had no desire to change my life. I want to be in control, not deal with a load of shit that only complicates everything."

Eira thought she could see her colleague in a new light—or gloom, more accurately. She could hardly make out her expression in the dimly lit room, but she found herself thinking about what Silje had said the first time they met, that she had dreamed of becoming a geologist, working with rocks, something constant in a world that was always changing.

"You didn't have to tell me this," she said.

"Some would say it clouds my judgment."

"That's why we're not investigating his disappearance," said Eira. "We're too close, the prosecutor was clear about that."

Silje moved their empty glasses to one side and gestured to the barman to bring two more.

"I don't still have feelings for him, just so you know," she said with a smile, a laugh. "Aside from being really fucking pissed off."

Eira excused herself to go to the toilet. She didn't need it. No, she did, she needed a break, to feel cold water on her face.

How could she have missed the fact that her closest colleagues had once had an affair? That kind of thing was usually obvious, in the way people touched one another or avoided any physical contact, in the way they bickered.

She needed even more cold water, a few deep breaths, before she could bring herself to go back out. Eira ordered food, the daily special. That should mean it was quick, that she could leave soon.

"It was tricky at work, too. Keeping it from our colleagues." Silje had already finished her second drink, and was clearly drunk. "Ironic, huh? We spend all day trying to uncover the truth, and we're lying to everyone as we do it. In the end it becomes a habit. You get good at it. Our ability to lie is actually pretty impressive."

She clinked her glass against Eira's.

"Cheers to that."

Eira caught the night train back to Kramfors, the first stop on its route north through a frozen Sweden. The platform was deserted when she arrived, just after midnight. The sleeper cars and their drawn curtains began moving, picking up speed and disappearing into the distance.

She had lost count of the number of drinks she'd had, but she knew the risk of running into anyone at the station had to be small. Eira fumbled with her key card as she unlocked the door, heading straight to the toilet, where the pork noisettes she had eaten made a swift reappearance. Her new computer was ready and waiting for her on her desk, a handy laptop that would make all the difference.

She called for a taxi home to Lunde. The driver was the younger brother of an old school friend, and he turned off the meter after just five kilometers, said he lived out that way too.

"Take it easy," he told her, laughing as she stumbled out of the car.

By three o'clock, her drunkenness had started to fade, and the letters finally stopped dancing around on the screen. Eira no longer had to keep going out into the garden for fresh air.

Last year's leaves were still lying on the ground. Weeds that had shriveled, the withered stalks of flowers. She had stood out there for some time, until she managed to regain her focus and keep going. That was the best part about having the laptop. Not even the fact that she was way over the limit could stop her from working.

The night was a sanctuary; it made no demands of her. People expected her to be sleeping, which meant there was no one to watch or judge her.

The alcohol probably helped, too. The pathologist in Umeå had explained what happens to the brain when it is starved of food, trapped in a basement as Hans Runne had been. How it slowly shuts down, little by little, until you lose the ability to think. The brain needs sugar to function, but recent research had also established what many people had long suspected: that alcohol fulfilled the same function—proving all sorts of drunken geniuses right. To a certain extent, anyway.

True or not, in her fading drunkenness, Eira thought she could see things with a new clarity. They had been fumbling blindly, that was so obvious now. Jumping from one tuft of grass to another, as though they were walking down a muddy tractor track once the snow had melted. From international money laundering to more intimate, private details, this way and that, aimlessly.

All by the book, a voice in her head pointed out. They had kept their minds open, avoided becoming bogged down on anything; that was what professional police work looked like.

Had GG's leadership faltered, was that the issue? Were there things they had missed because no one had taken charge and given them clear guidelines?

She had had such faith—blind faith, perhaps—that he knew what he was doing, and felt an admiration and satisfaction almost bordering on joy whenever he thought she was doing a good job.

Eira got into the shower and let the water run from hot to cold, shivering as she came out of the bathroom. She had left the porch door open, and the frosty air was flooding in.

GG had slept with a relative of the victim, in an investigation in which no one could yet be ruled out. That realization hurt more than Eira wanted to admit.

Facts, she thought, closing the door on the darkness outside. Concrete police work. That was all they had.

She woke at five, when a message came through, surprised she had managed to drift off at all. An hour tops, in her dressing gown on the sofa.

Eira reached for her phone and saw that it was from Ricken. Typical him, so early in the morning. She closed her eyes and tried to get back to sleep. Half an hour later she gave up and read his cryptic message.

She got up to make coffee and wrote back to say that she would swing by.

Ricken never said anything important over the phone, so she knew there was no point calling him. Someone was always listening in, everything was recorded and saved and could be used against you. In the past it was always the CIA or the Soviet Union who were to blame—he claimed the latter also sailed deep into the bays and inlets of the Baltic Sea in their submarines, God knows they probably came right up the Ångerman River too, given its dizzying depths—but these days it was China and their espionage program, installed through the 5G network, and no one could convince him that the Swedish state was innocent.

The moon hung low in the sky, the early morning haze barely noticeable in the forests on the other side of the Sandö Bridge. It would be hours before the November sun rose above the horizon.

Hours of freedom, that was what Ricken called them. Despite his lifestyle, he got up at five o'clock every morning, when it was just him and the birds, the odd deer at the edge of the woods. Before everyone else woke up with their noise and their pushy ideas about how other people should live their lives.

Do your duty, get in line, report to the Employment Service, all that business. Pay into your pension pot.

Why, when life was so short, the world so unbelievably beautiful?

He was busy working on one of his junk cars when she arrived, a spotlight rigged up to help him transform the rusty, dirty white Ford with sky-blue paint.

"What did you want?" Eira asked as she got out of the car.

"I've found him."

"Found who?"

"The guy who stole Aunt Rosemarie's car."

"And you woke me at five a.m. to tell me that?"

"I didn't think about the time," said Ricken.

"What the hell, couldn't you just report it at the station? I'm working for Violent Crimes now, remember? Investigating the death up by Offer. I really don't care about a stolen car from five years ago."

Ricken smiled that smile of his that made everything cold turn warm.

"That's nice," he said. "You've got something in common with Aunt Rosemarie. She got her insurance money, and now she's worried it'll be a problem."

"So why couldn't I have another hour in bed?"

Pools of water had collected in the tire tracks on the ground, and Eira couldn't resist the urge to break the wafer-thin layer of ice beneath her shoe, to hear it crack.

"Believe me," said Ricken, putting down the spray can and taking off his mask. "You're going to want to hear this."

Eira couldn't quite follow every twist and turn, who knew who, an old buddy who had a friend who was with some girl who used to hang out with a gang up in Boteå Parish, and so on. In any case, he had found someone who knew that one Jens Boija from Undrom had dumped the Fiat in the woods four years and seven months ago.

Someone from the chain of gossip had taken the spare tire.

Eira sat down on the steps, a mug of coffee in her hands. It was freezing, but the hot coffee helped. Ricken drank his standing up, one foot on the steps, close to her.

"That means the statute of limitations hasn't passed yet," she said. The prescriptive period lasted five years for a crime like that.

"Which is why the guy was pretty stressed when I showed up at his door—that and the fact that he's built like a bit of spaghetti. I could've easily taken him down."

"If only you hadn't stopped fighting," said Eira.

"Right. I use my brain instead, my superior intellect."

"That must have scared the shit out of him."

She should be doing something useful with her time, solving the case, finding GG, but it did her good to sit on Ricken's step for a while. Joking as though it were a morning like any other. The damp but clear November air, the smell of earth and rot rising from his overgrown garden.

"I threatened him with my close contacts on the force," Ricken said with a laugh, catching a lock of her hair between his fingers.

His skin smelled like solvent and paint.

On that evening almost five years ago, after a drinking session in Kramfors, Jens Boija had fallen out with his friend. With nowhere to sleep and a need to get home, he had stolen the car. When he woke the next morning, he panicked and dumped it in the forest.

"He knows those woods pretty well, apparently. Goes out walking there all the time, poking around the abandoned houses for anything he can take. You can furnish an entire home with that stuff."

"What are you getting at?"

"If you don't mention the Fiat," said Ricken, "and there's really no point in mentioning it, because he'll never confess, he says he'll tell you the same thing he told me. But only you, no one else."

She called Silje to let her know where she was heading as she drove inland.

"They've found the car," said her colleague.

"Which car?" Eira was just about to overtake a lorry, but she held back, pulling in behind it. "GG's, you mean?"

"Covered in parking tickets. On the street, two blocks from the apartment in Härnösand."

Eira's heart began pounding at double speed.

"What does that mean?"

"That GG doesn't bother checking the signs when he parks his car," said Silje. "That he had something other than paying for parking on his mind. That they can stop looking for it on the traffic cameras in and around Härnösand."

"Shit."

Eira turned off onto a gravel track between two paddocks and pulled over. A small pack of inquisitive trotter horses came towards her.

"Have they found anything else?"

"Not as far as I know. The prosecutor is keeping me at arm's length. I'm on my way up to Saltvik, I've been granted an audience there. And you?"

"A tip from an acquaintance in Strinne, someone who might have seen something up in Offer." Eira reversed back out onto the road.

Jens Boija lived in a barn on his cousin's land, on the northern fringes of Undrom.

The first snow had fallen overnight, and the fields were frozen.

The migratory birds had left the area.

From the outside, it looked like any other aging, graying barn, a sad relic of a bygone era, but she could hear music pumping out through an open window. In the years since he stole the Fiat, Jens Boija had pulled himself together, enrolled at the community college in Hola, and transformed the barn into a fully equipped recording studio. He let her in at the gable end where he lived, a ladder leading up to a loft bedroom. Eira noticed the old drop-leaf table, the mismatched chairs, the wooden ski on the wall, the iron cauldron being used as a flowerpot.

"Did you find any of these things up by Offersjön?"

"It's not technically theft, is it?" he said, his eyes drifting over to the carved spice rack, a beautiful piece of handiwork at one point in time. "Taking stuff no one else wants, I mean, that people have dumped. It's more like recycling."

"Just tell me what you saw."

"I'm not going to get into any shit for this, am I? My cousin owns this place, and he'll flip if I cause any more trouble; he's always been good to me and I really don't want to . . ." Jens Boija shifted nervously in the cramped kitchen area marked out by a change in the level of the cast cement floor. Eira wondered if it had once been the pigsty. She could hear a heavy beat from the studio, a soft woman's voice. "And I've worked really hard on all this. Have you ever heard of the Ward brothers?"

"Uh . . . no."

"When they couldn't get a record deal in London, they built their own studio on the family farm in Wales, soundproofed it with pig feed. Oasis have recorded there, and Queen. Why shouldn't I be able to do the same thing in Undrom?"

The coffeepot began to whistle on the hob, black with soot from the open fire. It would have looked at home in one of the old charcoal burners' huts dotted throughout the forests, some preserved, many left to fall into decay; you could find the blackened wood if you kicked among the undergrowth.

"Come on," said Eira. "I don't care about your music or how you furnish your home. I'm here because Rickard Strindlund said you saw something by the abandoned house."

Jens Boija spilled the coffee as he poured it. The grounds hadn't quite had time to sink to the bottom of the pot. He was younger than her, probably closer to twenty than thirty. She wondered whether he had even had a driving license when he stole the car.

Dressed in low-slung jeans and a faded T-shirt, his hair longish.

"I can't say exactly when it was."

"Roughly, then?"

"It was September for sure, I remember feeling like summer was over—you know that sense of calm that arrives once the air gets cooler and easier to breathe? I like autumn. It wasn't cold yet, I'm pretty sure I only had a sweatshirt over my shoulders, no jacket, no rain . . ."

He looked off to one side, through the window. The flypaper hanging there was black with insects that had met their end, the spruce forest thick outside.

"I'm not one hundred percent sure it was him."

"Are you talking about Hans Runne?"

"I only saw them from behind. I was on my way to the house when I heard their voices, so I obviously didn't go in. You never know, it could be the owner or someone else with opinions. I guess it was gut instinct that made me duck behind the shed."

Eira burnt her tongue on the hot coffee. The music had stopped, or maybe she just couldn't hear it any longer.

"Them? So were there two people? Or more?"

"A man and a woman."

"Are you sure?"

"Yeah, yeah, I'm sure. I heard them talking, too."

"About what?"

"I couldn't really hear what they were saying, but I heard their voices, the melody. I'm a sound technician, I listen, it's what I do." Jens Boija had finally stopped his nervous pacing and sat down on the ladder up to the loft.

Eira tried to take in the new scene he had painted, so far removed from what she had been expecting. No ambush, no one being dragged inside, no violence.

A couple walking quietly through the woods, towards a house.

"Was their conversation calm, agitated? Was either of them being threatened? Did they know each other?"

He closed his eyes, recalled their voices.

"Calm," he said. "No arguing or anything like that. I got the sense the guy didn't want to be there. He made some irritated remark, like: 'What is this, I was expecting a manor house.' Like she'd dragged him out into the woods, you know?"

"Did they seem intimate, were they holding hands?"

"No . . . I mean, I don't know, she was holding her bag. I didn't see them kiss or anything."

"Could you describe her?"

Eira scribbled furiously. Medium height, slightly shorter than the man, hair that was neither long nor short, somewhere between light and dark.

"Mousy blond?"

"I'm not great at noticing that kind of thing. To be perfectly honest, I was more focused on him. He looked really good for his age."

Eira attempted to get more detail about the woman's clothing instead—she wasn't wearing a skirt, in any case; trousers, possibly a blazer, but he wasn't sure.

"He was humming." Jens Boija's eyes widened. "Shit, I'd forgotten that, you never think that these things might be important. Some guy, you know, humming 'House of the Rising Sun' by an abandoned house. I remember thinking, Christ, how far is he willing to go to get laid?"

Eira kept writing, the room fell silent again.

"She wasn't dressed for the woods," he said after a moment. "If the place was for sale I would've guessed she was an estate agent, also because . . ."

Jens Boija looked up at the beams, where tools from the barn's agricultural past still hung, a wagon wheel of some kind, beautiful in a rustic sort of way.

"Because . . . ?"

"The house isn't locked," he continued. "It's been like that for years. Everyone knows. You pull the door shut behind you when you leave, out of respect, to stop the snow from drifting in and the birds from building nests inside. So why else would she have the key in her hand?"

Eira remembered the handle beneath her palm, how easily the door had swung open. One of the windowpanes had rattled. That often happened with abandoned houses, someone forced the door open and the boundaries were slowly erased, people began moving freely in and out, like the squirrels whose nests they had found beneath the roof.

"I thought, shit, maybe she owns the place, and then I cleared off as soon as they went inside."

Eira called the prosecutor from the road. There were a few brief stretches where the coverage was poor and the connection dropped, but she managed to give a detailed report of everything she had found out. No one had asked her to head down to Sundsvall, but that was where she was driving. She wanted to be a part of this, not stuck at a distance, a square on a screen.

Being there might also give her the opportunity to ask questions about GG, face-to-face with people who knew something, in the corridor, by the coffee machine.

By the time she got to Sundsvall, the prosecutor had briefed Silje and a few of the others. Names that sounded familiar, bodies she had never seen before.

"Before we get carried away," said Nora Berents, "it's worth noting that the witness, this Jens Boija, isn't sure it was Hans Runne he saw."

"I think he was more confident than he let on," said Eira. She wasn't used to being the center of attention, everyone's eyes on her. "My guess is that he wanted to smooth over the fact that he didn't get in touch. He was vague about the timeframe too, but I'm pretty sure he knew."

"House of the Rising Sun," said a young civilian investigator called Josefin. "What's that?"

Sighs from the men who had been around awhile.

Eira had called Hans Runne's ex-wife from the car. "House of the Rising Sun" was one of the songs he used to play on the guitar, a typical campfire tune, once he'd had a few drinks and his dreams flared up inside him, ideas of being that kind of guy.

Someone people flocked around, who made everyone feel good.

"So we could be looking for a woman," said one of the younger investigators, Vicke was his name. "How could GG have missed that?"

He was sitting in the corner, knees spread. Eira recognized his voice, remembered him arguing strongly in favor of the criminal underworld angle. He'd been involved in the rescue of two men who were kept prisoner in a basement a year or two back, as part of an attempt to blackmail their families over missing drug money.

"An estate agent?" said someone else. "Those people just can't be bloody trusted, haven't I always said that? When we were selling my parents' place . . ."

"What about the car?" the prosecutor interjected. "How sure was he about that?"

"Dead sure," said Eira. "No doubt whatsoever on that point."

Jens Boija had seen a car by the edge of the road when he snuck away from the house, emerging from the forest to retrieve his bicycle, which he'd hidden in a ditch. A red Škoda, neither new nor old. It was parked between the trees, easily missed if you just happened to be driving by. He had glanced inside and seen a briefcase, a coat.

"It's not unusual for them to use women as a front," Vicke spoke up. "In fact, it's the best kind of bait, they get the girl to text the victim and arrange a meeting . . ."

"An amateur," said Silje.

She was leaning back in her chair, swirling a Diet Coke in one hand. She had a way of drawing out her words that made sure everyone was paying attention.

"I spent half the morning with this guy in Saltvik. He's doing time for double murder, known in both Sundsvall and Härnösand even though he wasn't based in the area, links to one of the groups operating in the east. I don't know why GG thought he would talk. In any case, he saw it as an insult to his professional pride that we'd even think he might know anything about this. His soldiers would never involve civilians without good reason, he said, or use a place where anyone could come barging in. Definitely the work of an amateur."

"What did you expect? He's going to get out of there one day."

"Oh, and he's also innocent of everything he's been charged with," Silje added. "Someone planted the weapon in his pocket and the blood on his body."

Scattered laughter around the room, quickly dying out.

"I want to know who this woman is," said the prosecutor. "Does she appear anywhere, in any of the witness statements, in the finds from the crime scene? Go back, ask again. Is there anyone else out there who hasn't made the link? A woman, dressed like an estate agent—people might have seen her and not realized. I want to find the red Škoda, too. There can't be that many of them out there."

"And GG?"

It was Silje who brought up his name at last.

The mood, which had been raised by the desire to think again, by the prospect of a possible breakthrough, quickly darkened.

"No news," said Nora Berents, getting to her feet and closing her briefcase. "I would've told you if there was."

•   •   •

Eira found Costel Ardelean in the forensic technicians' break room, where the leftovers of a princess cake suggested it was someone's birthday.

She wolfed down a piece, standing. She hadn't given lunch a single thought, and it was now afternoon.

Costel confirmed that the lock was unusable.

"From the forties, I'd guess. The door had warped to the point where the bolt no longer lined up. It probably hadn't been locked in a long, long time."

He led her through to his cramped office, cluttered with folders and books in a number of languages. Forensic science was very much an international specialty, from its emergence in China in the thirteenth century, via Germans and Italians and the Swede who discovered how to detect arsenic poisoning, to the development of DNA profiling by the British in the 1980s, a practice that had since become increasingly accurate and sophisticated.

But despite that, plenty still fell through the cracks.

The only DNA they had been able to secure from the house—aside from Hans Runne's—belonged to an unidentified individual, and came in the form of a knot of hair. That and some relatively fresh blood that turned out to be animal in nature.

A squirrel had met a violent end.

"We've been looking for signs of a struggle," he said. "For the kind of violence that leaves a trace, partly because that's when people typically leave DNA—a broken nail, a scratch, blood. And sexual intercourse, too, of course." Costel was in his forties and spoke thoughtfully, as though he were feeling his way forward. "But if they went into the house together, chatting . . ."

"Humming, even."

"Then we're not looking for signs of a crime but of normal human behavior, where the crime is a consequence of things that haven't yet happened."

Costel opened a 3D model of the abandoned house. It felt strange to see it come to life, so artificial yet true to nature. It was the kind of thing that could be achieved in an instant these days, a few photographs, a piece of software, coordinates of the findings that were then processed by the computer. Gone were the cross-strewn maps Eira remembered from her training not so long ago.

Codes and markings flashed up on the screen.

Fingerprints and other traces, dotted throughout the rooms.

"If we turn everything on its head," he continued. "If we ask: How might they have passed through the house if the intention wasn't to kill? Could we then discern the woman's movements?" His Swedish was slightly formal, with a hint of an accent; he had come to the country from Romania years ago. Eira had once heard him compare the steep hillsides of the Ådalen Valley with the area where he grew up in Transylvania. Not just in terms of the mountains and the forests, but the powerful presence of something from a bygone era—mythical and disquieting—that he was reminded of again and again, particularly at dusk.

The shimmering blue tones, fading to a minor key.

"So what do they do after the woman opens the door, once they step inside?" he thought aloud.

Eira rolled closer in her chair and peered over his shoulder. She knew how it felt to enter that kind of house, it was something she had done countless times before. A sense of reverence.

The way you lowered your voice, took in every detail.

"They look around the place," she said. "Buildings like that raise questions. They wonder about the people who used to live there, remember other houses from their childhood; the smells reawaken old memories. They might pick up anything that looks pretty or interesting, tear off a piece of wallpaper to see the layers beneath it, fantasizing about how nice it could be."

"We found only Runne's fingerprints in the basement. That led us to assume he had been carried down there, unconscious."

Eira could just picture them.

"The woman showed him around," she said. "She'd been there before, she opened the doors if they were closed."

Costel Ardelean studied her as he thought.

"The handle on the main door had been wiped clean," he said. "Ditto the basement."

"It was a warm day. Thirteen degrees in the afternoon, according to the Meteorological Institute. Sun. The witness remembered that too. She probably wasn't wearing gloves."

"A fact she only realized afterwards, once the crime had been committed." He used the cursor to move through to the bedroom. The perspective shifted and the ceiling became visible, a hole into the attic, heading through a back door into the kitchen. "They go down to the basement, perhaps he went first, and they get into an argument. But why? I suppose we've looked into the possibility that he might have been violent towards women?"

"We haven't found anything suggesting that."

Costel turned back to the pattern of findings on the screen, deselecting certain points and allowing others to form routes through the house.

"Let me know if you find anything," said Eira.

There was one free desk in the Violent Crimes Unit, tucked away in the corner against the wall, slightly worse for wear.

"Bosse's on leave," said Vicke. "He inherited a place up in Myckelgensjö and decided he wanted to try out a different kind of life. They don't even have phone coverage over there."

"Bosse Ring?" Eira had worked with him on her last investigation with Violent Crimes, and she missed the older, slightly haggard detective's quiet competence. She had found it comforting to lean back on.

"I think you're actually his cover. Everyone's convinced he'll change his mind and come crawling back, but until then the desk's yours."

Eira hadn't realized she was covering for someone, hadn't asked about the formalities. She lifted the chair down from the desk and plugged in her laptop.

The figure of a woman opening an unlocked door, did that appear anywhere in the files? In any observations that hadn't seemed relevant. She was starting to know the witness statements inside out, and only needed to see the names to hear their voices.

The ornithologist! She dug out his number. He had talked about people coming from town during berry season, but how did he know where they were from? By their shoes, in all likelihood. That was the kind of thing people in the countryside noticed. Yeah, yeah, typical townies, they thought—and *liked* thinking—*because we know better, those of us who actually belong up here. We might not earn fifty grand a month or own property worth millions of kronor, but you can be damn sure we've got enough sense to wear proper shoes—and we're not the ones who skid off the road when winter arrives out of nowhere, either.*

Eira dialed his number.

"Hullo, hullo," said Bengt Devall. "You're in luck. I was just on my way out, and the damn phone stays at home. There's enough chirping in the forest as it is."

"Last time we spoke, you mentioned something about people from town coming to the area during berry season," said Eira. "Do you remember anyone in particular?"

"Oh, there probably weren't that many."

"I'm wondering if you remember a couple, a man and a woman."

"No, I don't think so, not out this way, I'd probably remember that. Two people have a tendency to talk and talk and make a racket."

"What about anyone on their own?"

There was a moment's silence as he thought. Eira could hear classical music in the background, strings.

"The only one I remember," he eventually said, "was a young woman. But now I'm wondering if she even had a bucket."

"How young?"

"In her forties, I should think. Right by where the paths cross. I let her go first, just before the abandoned house. Strange I didn't think of it sooner. I said hello but probably only got a nod in reply, she seemed to be in a hurry. City pace. Won't see any berries charging around like that."

Eira asked another couple of questions, about her clothing, appearance. His recollections broadly confirmed what Jens Boija had said. Nice shoes, a blazer. Her hair might have been a little darker, the woman more attractive.

"Do you have your diary to hand?"

Bengt Devall put down the phone in the old-fashioned way, and she had to wait while he went off to fetch his diary. The strings had faded in the background.

Eira heard him flicking through the pages.

"Ah, yes," he said. "This must be it. Sighting of a three-toed woodpecker north of Offersjön, September thirteenth and fourteenth. A Eurasian eagle-owl too, no less."

Eira tried to keep calm, not to rush or force him. They hadn't had an exact date, just the neighbor's observations in Nyland, his phone signal disappearing two days later.

"I know this isn't easy," she said, "but could you remember which of the days it was, at roughly what time?"

"Dusk," he said, "since I was on my way home. Gets a bit hard on the eyes then. And on the fourteenth I was only out in the morning, I was invited to dinner that evening."

"So you think you saw this woman on her way from the abandoned house, at dusk, on September thirteenth?"

"I'd say so, yes."

Eira closed her eyes once she ended the call. She cursed herself for asking him the wrong way earlier.

The clues that are right there in front of us, she thought. In the things we see and don't see.

Eira quickly wrote down his statement before she forgot any of the details. She didn't hear Silje approaching, and flinched at the sound of her voice. She had something she wanted to say, but Eira got in first.

"I've got a timeframe," she said. "A sighting of the woman walking away from the abandoned house. Alone."

"Oh shit." Silje pulled a chair over. "And the description is a match?"

"Broadly speaking, though there are differences between a seventy-year-old passing a young woman in the forest and a kid in his twenties spotting a middle-aged couple."

Eira read aloud from her notes: the smart shoes, the blazer, neither fat nor excessively thin, medium height. She had already managed to google the rising and setting of the sun. Dusk lasted a long time in autumn.

"It was probably sometime around seven in the evening on September thirteenth. The sun set at 7:21."

"And his signal disappeared on the fourteenth," said Silje. "Which means she had his phone on her—assuming she took it. And then she dumped it somewhere in Härnösand, where it died the next day."

"To throw us off the track?"

"Either that or he left it in the car and she only found it the next day."

"When she got rid of it."

"But what's the motive, why did she do it?"

Silje trailed off. Her mind was likely racing too, making images emerge, a bit like doing a jigsaw—sometimes you only needed to find one piece, and other patterns suddenly came into view.

"What did you want to tell me?" asked Eira.

Silje leaned in close.

"I've got myself an inside man," she said quietly.

The prosecutor was still being strict about keeping them out of anything to do with GG's disappearance, but there were always ways.

According to Silje.

"They've spoken to his kids, his ex-wife, the girlfriend he broke up with. What a fucking hand to be dealt, having to dig into a colleague's deepest secrets—you can see why Berents wants to keep us at arm's length. This guy has been brought in from Gävle. Single, feels a bit lonely in town."

Her smile hinted at exactly how she had got him to talk. With the expectation of a glass of wine one evening, perhaps, something along those lines.

He was the one who had been tasked with the call logs.

"You have no idea how many prepaid phones GG communicates with every day. A huge mix of dates and anonymous tips; I don't know why the idiot can't manage two phones."

"He wasn't the one who ended things," Eira blurted out before she could stop herself. Perhaps she was the only one who knew. She had spoken to GG when it was still fresh. It was high summer, the tarmac soft and fragrant, and he had just gone on annual leave. She'd had things to say about the Lina case, and so they had sat down on his balcony to talk, drank red wine. "He said it was her who dumped him."

"I didn't know that. We don't really talk about our lives these days."

Eira checked a message to give herself time to think. Should she keep quiet about this, out of respect for GG, or should she be thinking like a police officer?

Acting like nothing was private, like there was no sacred trust.

"They were trying for a baby," she said. "His girlfriend broke up with him when it didn't lead anywhere. The problem was with him."

"Uff. And GG told you all this?"

"I saw him just after it happened, her things were still in the hallway."

Silje waited until a couple of their colleagues had passed and were out of earshot, then lowered her voice another notch.

"I saw his bank statements," she said. "GG went out that evening. Drank a bottle of whisky, plugged his phone in to charge, and went out."

"Where?"

"It wasn't deliberate, no one actually showed me anything, it was on the Gävle guy's screen while I was talking to him."

For some reason, Silje didn't say it out loud. Perhaps even she knew that this was a line they shouldn't cross, though Eira doubted it. She had started to realize that her colleague followed her own rules. There were no walls or fences inside her, none of the inherited hurdles Eira was constantly grappling with.

Silje grabbed a block of Post-it notes, scribbled something down, and peeled off the top sheet, sticking it in front of Eira.

Stadt in Härnösand.

"That's not possible."

"He paid a bill of eight hundred forty kronor at ten past midnight."

The letters began to flicker, black against the neon yellow paper.

"Everyone goes to Stadt," said Eira. "It's not far from the apartment. Where else is there to go so late on a weekday evening?"

"You're right," said Silje. "It doesn't necessarily mean a thing."

"Your mum is absolutely fine," said the assistant nurse who opened the door.

"I came as fast as I could."

One call from the care home and her world had been turned upside down. Eira had stayed in the fast lane the whole way back from Sundsvall, running up the stairs when she arrived with a sense of being physically torn in two.

"She's been given something for the pain, but she's really more exhausted than anything."

Eira heard the usual shouts, the sound of the TV. A woman was busy pulling the leaves off a potted plant as she hurried by.

She found Kerstin sitting up in bed, a mug of soup in her shaky good hand.

"How are you, Mum?"

"Oh, I'm fine. They've been waiting on me like a princess in here."

Her right hand was bandaged up to her elbow, and she had a large white plaster on her forehead.

"I came as soon as they called," said Eira. "I was in Sundsvall, sorry it took a while to get here."

"You didn't need to start dashing all over the place for me; I'm sure you have other things to be doing."

"Of course I was going to come."

Eira stroked her mother's hair. She didn't say a word about her reaction at being interrupted, just as things were starting to happen. She'd had to drop everything, let Silje take what she had found to the prosecutor. Ashamed that it had made her feel angry.

"You look like you've been in the wars, Mum."

"Oh no, it's not that bad." Kerstin laughed anxiously. They had found her on the floor in her room; no one knew what had happened. She had been confused, talking about how she needed to go and see to the children. They guessed she must have hit her head on the bed, hurt her hand when she broke her fall.

"Her scaphoid bone is just fractured," said the nurse, plumping up Kerstin's pillows. "Fortunately."

She left them to fetch some coffee and a bite to eat.

Eira's eyes drifted around the room, so light and bright, a life that had shrunk to eighteen square meters. But not even that could eliminate all dangers.

There was a bunch of flowers on the table, vibrant autumn colors, the kind that came from a florist, carefully arranged.

"Those are beautiful, Mum. Have you had a visitor?"

"Yes, Magnus was here."

"He wasn't, was he?"

"Oh yes, he landed his hot-air balloon outside, in the meadow. Could you pop your head out and see if he's gone yet?"

"I don't think he still has the hot-air balloon, Mum." Eira hoped her mother hadn't been rambling about him to the staff. They couldn't know that Magnus really had been a partner in a hot-air balloon firm some ten or fifteen years ago. One of his friends had the idea of arranging balloon rides over the dramatic Ångermanland landscape, but the tourists had never showed much interest and the treacherous winds had blown both the balloon and the entire project off course.

That anxiety likely still remained in Kerstin, alongside her longing.

The assistant nurse was back, with coffee and marble cake. Eira checked the card that had come with the flowers and saw an old friend's name. They could talk about her for a while, forget about Magnus and let all that disappear.

Eira lowered the head of her mother's bed.

"Do you want me to read to you? Put some music on?"

She found a CD that she knew her mother used to love, one that Eira often put on so that it wouldn't be too quiet once she left. Mozart, the music from the film about Elvira Madigan. Kerstin closed her eyes, her good hand following the romantic yet sad movements.

The room was neat and tidy, of course, the nightstand wiped down and uncluttered. Eira stacked a couple of books there, a habit she had picked up. That way anyone who came into the room would immediately know something about her mother and who she was. She had also written a long letter for the staff, a life story stretching to eighteen densely written sides of paper, covering everything from Kerstin Sjödin's childhood to who she became as an adult, what she liked to read and listen to. There were photographs, too, from when she was young. Eira had chosen the ones that were most full of life. Her greatest fear was that the staff would treat her mother as just another old woman, someone without an identity of her own. Because even if her intellectual capacity was diminished, she was still that person somewhere deep inside, behind those eyes that had become distant and inward looking.

Kerstin was dozing off.

Eira held her good hand, watched her eyelids droop and her features relax, her many different ages coexisting beneath the same skin. All the experience she had gained, the secrets that were now starting to disappear.

People lie, she thought.

She had never imagined her mother to be a liar, that just wasn't something you did. Everyone expects their parents to be true versions of themselves, until one day an unknown child turns up at a funeral or a murder investigation begins.

That was how, through her work, she had found out that Kerstin had been having an affair for years, that she had snuck out to see her lover down by the river when young Eira was asleep in bed, possibly watching a film or playing with a friend. No matter how hard she racked her memory, she couldn't find a single clear sign that it had actually happened, but still. Kerstin must have been carrying a storm of emotions inside her whenever she returned from seeing her lover.

It made Eira feel warm, realizing that her mother had experienced a bit more joy and adventure than anyone knew.

That she had pulled the wool over their eyes, at least a little.

Eira stroked her hair. The hairdresser had dyed it, and it looked good. She moved over to the armchair and opened her laptop.

She may as well stay for a while, with her mother's calm, almost silent breathing, the compact darkness outside. A jogger came in and out of view between the sparse streetlamps. She could see something bright moving on the river, a boat that hadn't yet been brought ashore for its winter rest.

Elvira Madigan was on repeat, a sad tale that ended with the deaths of the tightrope dancer and her lover. Eira had no moral objection to infidelity, people were drawn to wherever they could find love, but she couldn't get Silje and GG out of her head, the way they had kept their relationship a secret from their colleagues, police officers who were trained to sniff out that sort of thing.

Her mind turned to Stadt in Härnösand, to the Grand Hotel Lapland in Gällivare, to Mikael Ingmarsson, who traveled all over Norrland in his role as a consultant.

Nights in hotel rooms, anonymous corridors.

A woman.

Why hadn't she seen it before? The investigation had been pushed towards the organized crime angle, the mutilated fingers leading them astray, and when it transpired that the owners of the house came from Russia, that had cast a shadow over everything else.

Blocking out the light.

Eira opened her laptop and read through the interview with Mikael Ingmarsson. He had said so little that it took her no more than a minute.

I don't care whether you catch them.

I want to move on with my life, that's all I want.

She remembered the beautifully renovated kitchen, the children drifting in and out, making noise.

I'd like my wife to stay.

This is something we're processing and going through together.

Did he have any reason to lie? She remembered her doubts, that she had brought it up with Double-Antti in the car afterwards. Slightly hesitantly, so as not to question his competence, but also because she wasn't sure. Perhaps she was just trying to find cracks in the perfect family exterior because she was jealous.

Exposed beams and expanses of white, the children's voices, everything.

Happily ever after.

Eira went out onto the balcony to avoid waking her mother. The working day was over, but it wasn't yet too late.

Double-Antti didn't seem to mind being disturbed.

"Have you found something?"

"There's a chance," said Eira, "that we've received some new information that changes everything."

"I can see why you called in the middle of the match, then."

The match? What match? Ice hockey, of course; it was November, which meant the season was in full swing.

"I hope Luleå aren't playing?" she said.

"Do you seriously think I would've picked up if they were?"

Eira laughed, just to be polite.

"We have a new witness," she said. "A man who saw our victim with a woman at the crime scene. I don't know if you remember, but it's an abandoned house in the middle of the woods. There doesn't seem to have been anyone else there."

"A woman? Do you know who she is? Do you have any physical evidence?"

"Not yet."

"Anything new to link the two cases?"

"Not exactly."

Eira could almost feel her colleague's mind racing, she knew what it was like. You plowed through the investigation in your head, every scenario that had been passed over or rejected.

Barging into someone else's territory like this was a balancing act.

"I know how it is," she said. "So many details that seem irrelevant. But was there anything to suggest that Mikael Ingmarsson might have had female company at the hotel?"

"It's a big hotel," said Double-Antti. "People saw all sorts, in passing. No one actually recognized him—he doesn't stick out. Some weren't even sure they'd seen the right person."

Eira heard him talking his way past it. That there was something there. He would likely look into it once they hung up, or once the match was over.

"We asked about his private life, obviously," he continued. "But it didn't seem like the key issue, not considering the attack and everything else we knew."

"One more thing," said Eira. "Do you know whether Mikael Ingmarsson ever went to Härnösand with his work?"

"Not off the top of my head I don't. That's not something we would've asked."

"What I'm wondering is whether he stayed at Stadt in the period leading up to everything that happened—let's say in the six months before."

"I can check his bank statements in the morning, if you like."

"Thanks, that would be great." Eira moved her phone into her other hand. Her fingers were frozen stiff, her breath white in the cold air. The temperature had dropped below zero. "And I'm going to need to talk to him again," she said.

"OK . . . Are you planning to come back up here, or?"

She went inside and wrapped her mother's cashmere shawl around her shoulders. Despite the plaster and the bluish tone that had started to appear beneath her eye, Kerstin's face was peaceful.

"It would be best if we could speak to him away from home. Alone, as far from his wife and kids as possible."

The second can proves trickier. He doesn't want to think that it's because his strength is starting to desert him.

It's the kind of can that needs an opener, but of course he doesn't have one of those. Instead he does what he did with the first one: he finds a thick piece of glass from the bottom of the bottle and hammers it using his heel.

The first can contained hot dogs. He has eaten the contents and drunk the salty brine, but he can no longer remember feeling full.

The shard of glass pierces the metal, and he manages to create a hole big enough to pour the liquid into his mouth. He doesn't notice the taste, just the sense of relief.

One more day.

Then the actual contents hit his mouth, something spongey and broadly tasteless. He uses his tongue to explore the shape; it could be a button mushroom.

He restrains himself after roughly half the can. It's the second-to-last one. He has finecombed every last inch of the basement, and the three cans are all there is.

His hands have started shaking, and he is sweating despite the chill. He places the half-empty can against the opposite wall, where he won't accidentally knock it over. His hopes are pinned on the third can. He'll open it soon. Maybe he'll find that it contains something sugary. Tinned pineapple, or halved peaches in that sweet, syrupy liquid.

His body is slowly shutting down. He has been through this process with a pathologist twice before. His brain is already becoming sluggish. Darker urine is a sign of dehydration. He can't see whether it is, but he has noticed the sharper smell. And then there's the cold. The temperature in an earth cellar shifts with the seasons, and he guesses it must be somewhere between eight and ten degrees. He is no longer in charge of his will. Needs to get onto his feet. Stooping slightly when he stands, to avoid hitting his head. Raising his knees, keeping everything moving without exhausting himself.

If he ever gets out of here, he'll hand in his notice. He'll sell the apartment and buy his brother out of their grandparents' cabin, live out there with the outhouse, perfectly harmless in nature.

He sees a glimpse of their summers out there, the little rowing boat he once went out in. Everyone thought he had drowned, but he had just lost one of the oars and was drifting around in circles.

He prayed to Our Father that day, all alone out at sea.

Our Father, who art in Heaven, he thinks. He avoids mumbling to conserve his saliva. If there is a god, it's not about how loud you shout.

Forgive us our trespasses . . . No, damn it, that's not how it goes. Hallowed be Thy name . . .

He can't keep track of the words, the ones he used to know by heart when he was seven.

"I left home when I was seventeen. Hitchhiked my way south. Why on earth would I have kept any keys?"

Beneath the anger, a hint of Norrland melody was still audible in her voice. The woman, a marketing manager who now lived down south in Södertälje, was Agnes and Karl-Erik Bäcklund's daughter, the second of the siblings from Offer.

Eira had sat down with the list as soon as she finished her breakfast, with no real hope of getting anywhere.

Jens Boija could have been mistaken, and even if the woman in the woods did have a key, that didn't necessarily mean a thing. Perhaps she just wanted to make Hans Runne think the place was hers, for whatever reason.

But if . . .

The old widower in the village had managed to scribble down some of the names, taking a photograph and sending them over in the form of a small family tree. There were gaps and question marks that Eira could easily fill in with a few quick searches in databases full of names and telephone numbers, ages, civil statuses and addresses, births and deaths, but nothing about who might have a key to an abandoned house that had long since been sold.

"I haven't been there since Mum's funeral. It's not my fault if people have been snooping about in the house. I don't understand why we're even being linked to this."

Eira used the toilet, drank some water. A few members of the family had already been contacted with questions. It was understandable that they might be running out of patience.

Calling to ask people about keys was almost an affront, as though she were accusing them of stealing.

Next on her list was the only one of the children who still lived in Sollefteå. Janne Bäcklund picked up on the first ring.

Eira introduced herself as a police assistant from Kramfors. To someone from Sollefteå, that felt more acceptable than saying Violent Crimes in Sundsvall. It was in the city on the coast that decisions were made, among them to close hospitals in the region, causing the biggest political revolt in decades.

"How bloody long is it going to be before you arrest them?"

"We're doing everything we can," said Eira. Her words didn't ring true; there was always more that could be done. "I think you know my stepmother, by the way," she added. "Or did, a long time ago. She remembers you, in any case."

"Who is she?"

Eira said her name, remembered what she had been called as a girl.

There was a brief pause, followed by a loud laugh on the other end of the line.

"Marie-Louise! Of course I remember Marie-Louise—though we used to call her Marre back then. A tasty little thing, if I recall. God, yes. The women really had to watch out in those days, ha-ha."

With that, the ice was broken.

"It's different now, of course," he continued, his voice so loud that Eira had to hold the phone away from her ear. "These days, when you talk about getting someone into bed, chances are it's about trying to find them an intensive-care bed somewhere. Or a ventilator. Did you hear that they're planning to slash the number of those now, too?"

"Mmm." Eira had seen that he was standing as a candidate for the local branch of the Health Care Party. The threat of having to travel two hundred kilometers to give birth—or of giving birth in an ambulance in the middle of nowhere—had been enough to convince the residents of Sollefteå to occupy their maternity ward for years.

"And now they want to ship us off to the coast when we can't breathe—it's a bloody outrage."

"I'm sorry to bother you, but another question has come up."

"Oh?"

An underlying note of resistance.

"Is there anyone in your family," she continued, "or anyone else you can think of, who might still have a key to the old house?"

"Why don't you ask the people who bought it? That damn holding company or whatever it's called. It's a bloody outrage that they've started popping up here, lucky the old man's already dead and buried."

"We'll be doing that too, of course, we'll be asking them."

That probably wasn't true. Not because they had completely ruled them out, but because calling someone with links to international organized crime to ask about a set of keys was likely doomed to fail.

"I already told your colleague," Janne Bäcklund went on. "The arrogant one from Sundsvall. We didn't have any idea we were selling it to some shady outfit, everything seemed aboveboard. We just wanted to get rid of the place once and for all—old houses like that only end up causing trouble between siblings."

"What do you mean?" asked Eira.

His hesitation lasted no more than a second, possibly nothing but an intake of breath.

"I was in charge of registering the deeds and everything," he said. "So you can blame me for that. But I didn't keep any keys, why would I? I was just happy we'd got anything for it."

"And no keys have been stolen?" Eira pressed him. "Or left behind in the house? Lent to someone?"

It was hopeless, she knew that, chasing the key for a lock that hadn't been changed since the forties. All they had was an endless list of questions with no answers, and time was marching on. Five days since GG was right here, in her kitchen.

She could no longer feel his presence.

"Has no one told you the door was always half open?" Janne Bäcklund went on. "It happened after we sold the place, I can tell you that much. People couldn't just waltz in and out back in our day."

A message pinged. From Double-Antti, up in Norrbotten.

Janne's voice droned on in her ear.

"And if the family still owned the place, I would've gone up there to fix it—not that I want to be there, you understand, it makes me so sad to see it like that—but it's not my responsibility anymore. They should be fined for neglect. But as ever, the fat cats get away with it."

Hudiksvall, said the message. Quality Hotel.

Eira's heart began to race. She got up from the table.

"Holding companies and God knows what else, buying up properties even though they don't give a damn about the place, they're impoverishing society. If I'd known how fishy they . . ."

"Thanks, I understand," said Eira, ending the call.

She picked up Silje in Sundsvall just over an hour later.

"So, what do we know about this guy?" she asked as Eira weaved through the city traffic, back out onto the E4.

"He spent thirteen nights at Stadt in Härnösand last year, according to the investigator up there. His bank statements left no doubt. One night at a time, at irregular intervals."

"Oh shit."

Mikael Ingmarsson was now in Hudiksvall, and had agreed to speak to them. Double-Antti hadn't even needed to threaten to put the same questions to his wife. "I think he's been expecting this," he said.

Industrial and residential areas raced by, the traffic thinning out as they caught up on the latest developments. Eira's phone calls with the relatives and other fruitless attempts to find someone with keys to the house, among other things.

"Maybe she really is an estate agent," said Silje. "The holding company could've been in the process of selling."

"What, and Hans Runne was interested?"

"Didn't your witness say he'd been expecting a manor house? Who wouldn't be pissed off after reading the ad and then seeing the place in real life? Ideally situated on the High Coast, full of period features, a rare find for someone with a knack for DIY."

"It's a pretty long way from the coast."

"But you can see why someone would be disappointed."

They passed the border into Hälsingland County, a softer landscape of open fields and rolling hills, like a melody from a folk song. Eira told Silje everything she knew about Mikael Ingmarsson.

"I should've pressed him harder," she said, stepping on the accelerator slightly, though she was already pushing the speed limit. "If he's hiding something that could have stopped GG . . ."

"We don't know that."

A slow-moving German caravan was hogging the road up ahead. It was a hopeless stretch, with just two lanes and an irritating number of bends. Eira pulled towards the center line.

"Are you OK?" asked Silje.

"Fine."

"You know you're allowed to show your feelings, don't you? Even though you're a police officer?"

"I know that," said Eira, overtaking the caravan.

It was a close call, another car speeding in the opposite direction.

"It's not me asking," Silje continued. "It's HR; they're obliged to let us know that we're entitled to a chat. Some sort of crisis support. Did you get the email?"

Eira clearly wasn't on that particular mailing list, because she hadn't. The turnoff to Hudiksvall finally appeared, huge signs bringing the promise of finally getting somewhere.

"I'm working," she said. "I don't know any other way."

The grand old town hotel in Hudiksvall had, like the majority of others, been swallowed up by one of the big chains. They now all had names like Elite and First Hotel and Quality Hotel Statt.

Nineteenth-century features and high ceilings, golden banisters. Mikael Ingmarsson had left a message to say that he was running late.

They were shown into a lounge area with deep leather armchairs. Eira went on the hunt for coffee and spotted him standing by the lifts. Dressed for business in a suit and tie, a much more laced-up version of him than she had seen last time.

"Hi. Eira Sjödin, Violent Crimes Västernorrland. We spoke at your house a few weeks ago."

"I know," he said, not meeting her eye.

"We're sitting over there, waiting for you."

"Right, I was just . . ."

Mikael Ingmarsson cast one last glance at the lift, as though it might help him escape, before he started walking, incredibly slowly. Eira studied his reaction when Silje got up to greet him. The way he straightened up, pushing back his shoulders and smoothing his hair, feeling an urge to smile despite being on his guard.

He sat down in an armchair, knees wide apart.

"Is it OK if we keep this brief?" he asked, his eyes sweeping the lounge area. "I have a few meetings to go to."

"With construction contacts?" Silje flashed him her sweetest smile.

"Yes, what else?"

"I don't know," she said. "Is there anyone else you usually meet in hotels?"

Mikael Ingmarsson's face was pale. He fiddled with his heart-rate monitor, the expensive, high-tech kind that could probably also make calls and put the kids to bed.

"Can't you just ask your questions?"

"Did you meet a woman in Gällivare?" asked Eira. "Was that why you lied?"

Double questions, leading questions; this was no way to conduct an interview. Mikael Ingmarsson didn't answer either of them, but she saw him physically slump. He raised his hands to his face, shoulders shaking.

"Generally speaking," said Silje, "people's love lives are none of our business. So long as everyone is consenting and no one gets hurt, either physically or mentally, they can do whatever they like with whoever they like. But if we suspect that someone is lying in a murder inquiry, that's a different matter."

"It wasn't a murder inquiry," he stuttered, pulling on his tie to loosen it. "I thought I was going to die, but then I didn't."

"But this man did." Eira held out a photograph. "His name was Hans Runne, as you know. He was an actor, the father of a twenty-year-old daughter."

Mikael Ingmarsson looked away.

"You've never come face-to-face with death," he mumbled. "You don't know what it's like."

"We're police officers," said Silje. "Believe me, we've seen a lot."

"Of course you have."

He tugged at his watch. It could surely tell that his heart was racing, his face growing redder, his eyes glassy.

"You might have to deal with dead bodies and all sorts of horrible things every day, but you've never actually faced death. For real, I mean. No fluffy thoughts about life being finite, carpe diem and all that crap. Not sitting at someone else's deathbed, but your own. The days pass. The nights. You have no idea what's what, there's nothing but darkness. At first you think it won't be long, that someone will come along soon, but then you realize you're alone. All alone. And no one is coming to save you."

He clawed at his hand. It would leave a mark, possibly even a graze.

"They said I'd been locked up for fifteen days. They said I just kept screaming. I'd lost it, do you understand what I'm saying? Completely lost it, the whole system that keeps a person sane."

When he looked up, the gaze that met them was different. Eira found herself thinking about the treacherous ground in Malmberget, the cracks in the tarmac, the ever-present threat of the abyss.

His voice had lost its power.

"I'm sorry," he said. "I'm sorry, but after going through that I couldn't lose my family too."

•   •   •

Yes, there had been a woman.

It actually seemed to come as a relief, finally getting it off his chest. His shoulders slumped.

He had behaved like an idiot, he had been given his punishment, but he had survived.

That was how he had looked at it when he first came round and began thinking somewhat clearly.

Like a lesson.

"It was all about me—and my wife, of course. Our marriage. Who benefited from me telling the truth? What was the use in uprooting the kids, tearing their sense of security to shreds, when everything was OK again and their dad was home? They slept in my bed when I first got back from hospital, trying to protect me. Because I was no longer protecting them."

And so he had made up the story about someone attacking him from behind.

Breathed a little easier with every day that passed, slowly began to believe that his life could take it. That the sense of security was still there—something he didn't deserve.

Pathetic creature that he was, little more than an animal.

A nonperson, that was how it was. Once everything has been snatched from you.

"I'd taken my punishment. I didn't think it had anything to do with the police, I just wanted them to forget about it and stop coming back, to accept that they hadn't solved it."

He tried to be the same person as before. Doing chores around the house, playing football, tricking his children into thinking that nothing had changed. He ran mile after mile, pushing his body to the limit, popping pills to escape the nights. So that he could sleep deeply, without any dreams.

But then a new police officer showed up at his house a year later, talking about another victim. Eira saw the shame in his eyes, the way he sought out her gaze and then immediately looked down at his hands.

"I couldn't believe it when you came over and started talking about it. What could I say? That I was a fucking liar? I never for a second thought she'd do it again. To someone else. But I know that if I'd told the truth from the beginning, it wouldn't have happened. Isn't that right?"

"What's her name?" asked Silje.

He picked at a cuticle, one of his legs bouncing nervously.

"Sanna."

"Surname?"

Time ground to a halt, all sound disappeared. Eira's phone autocorrected the woman's surname to *melon* as she wrote, she had to delete it and try again, sent a message to the prosecutor.

Sanna Melin.

We need an address etc., we have to bring her in.

"And that's her real name?" asked Silje.

"Yes . . . I think so. I'm assuming it is."

Sure enough, he had met her at Stadt in Härnösand.

"It wasn't a Tinder date or anything like that. She was just sitting there, and we got talking. She seemed nice somehow, harmless. There were no strings, it was easy."

"Does she live in Härnösand?"

"Yes, but I didn't think so at the time. She had a room at the hotel. That's where we went, that first night."

He glanced from one officer to the other.

"I never normally do this kind of thing," he said. "Pick up women in bars when I'm traveling. I mean, it has happened a few times, but it's not like I planned . . ."

"We're not here to cast judgment on your sex life," said Silje.

Eira made an effort to keep quiet, took notes. What she really wanted was to slam his head into something hard.

It was all about me . . .

If Mikael Ingmarsson hadn't been so damn preoccupied with himself, if he had talked sooner, if she had seen through him right away, pressed him harder . . .

As though it changed anything, thinking that way.

"Do you have a photo?"

He didn't. A married man didn't take pictures and save them on his phone; that was the kind of thing only idiots did, that or people who wanted to be caught.

He had taken her phone number and got in touch again next time he was in Härnösand. Actually started shifting more of his overnight stays there. It wasn't something he was proud of. She became something of a fantasy to him, something forbidden that had been missing from his life.

Violent, when he felt like it.

"And what about her?" Silje asked softly. "Did she feel like it too?"

"What the hell are you suggesting? Of course she did, she was the one who took the initiative with that kind of thing—being rougher, if you like. But sometimes it was the complete opposite, tender in a way that felt a bit too intimate, if you see what I mean—given there weren't any real feelings involved. It was just sex, I never meant for it to be anything else. I was open about being married, I didn't make her any promises."

Three weeks before that fateful night in Gällivare, he met her one last time. Or that had been his intention, anyway. Something about their relationship was getting too close, he couldn't quite explain it. Just a feeling he had, that she was becoming clingy. She had started sending text messages, even when he was at home, talking about joining him on his trips.

Eira's jaw dropped.

"But the police must have gone through your phone?"

"Only my regular one, my work phone. That's the one I use. Outside of work, I mean, for personal calls too. I used my old one with her, with a prepaid SIM, but I lost it. I couldn't have shown it to them even if I wanted to."

"When did you lose it?" asked Silje.

Mikael Ingmarsson glanced from her to Eira and back again, as though the thought had only just come to him.

"I had it in Gällivare," he said.

Though he was sick of her, he hadn't been strong enough to argue when Sanna said she wanted to meet him there.

She showed up at his hotel after dinner.

"I mean, if she wanted to go up there even though I'd told her how I felt, that we had to stop, but she still . . . We had a good time together, we did. Really good, actually, even that day when I basically broke up with her. I took that as a sign she was OK with what I was saying."

"Did she book a room at the Hotel Lapland?"

"She was going to stay with me."

Eira tried to picture the woman in the lobby of the hotel, a hazy figure without a face. Had she paid for anything, would they find her bank details in the hotel's records? What evidence that she had been there could exist after so long?

Mikael Ingmarsson had told her about Malmberget. About his childhood home, which was going to be moved from the hill where he grew up. He said that he had the key and that he was planning to take one last look.

She wanted to join him, interested in his stories about the community that was on the verge of disappearing.

"I don't care about any of that, to be perfectly honest. I just wanted to see if there was anything of value left. I've always been the kind of person who looks to the future."

A flicker of a shadow passed across his face, a suspicion that things had changed. When a person was subject to a crime, even the future was affected, the belief that things would get better.

"So we went to have a look around, in the rooms where I took my first steps and that kind of thing, old pictures of relatives I'd forgotten. She started talking about how we'd live together once I was finally free." He gave a hoarse laugh. "It was completely absurd. She had this dream house back where she came from—Paradise, she called it. She talked about it like it was somewhere our kids would grow up. The whole thing was absurd—like, what was it she didn't get? I was blunt with her, told her I'd never get a divorce, that I'd never been in love with her. We were down in the basement by then. The Ping-Pong table was still there." He started shaking, as though his body had taken over as he approached the basement in his memory.

Eira fought back the natural urge to lean forward and put a hand on his anxious arm, to try to reassure him.

"God, it's really hard to talk about feelings you don't have. Like being trapped in a corner where everything you say comes out wrong, cruel somehow, even though you're not trying to be cruel. I liked her in some ways, but she was just too much. I wasn't even turned on when she tried . . ." He gestured to his crotch. "I pulled her hands off me and told her to stop, said I didn't want to do that anymore. And then I tried to lighten the mood, suggested we have a match. Back to childhood, you know? When Jan-Ove Waldner was the Mozart of table tennis and everyone wanted to go to China. I started looking for the bats in a cupboard, in the box room next door. But she was gone. I shouted for her, thought she was just messing with me."

The heavy basement door, locked. He had banged, yelled. Thought he could hear a car engine starting, saw headlights sweeping past the basement window, which was much too high for him to reach. Had he left the keys in the car? His phone? Right then, he realized everything was in the pocket of his coat, which he had taken off upstairs.

And then the hours passed. The days.

He sat quietly for quite some time, his face buried in his hands.

"Why would she do it again?"

Sanna Melin was registered at a 1960s apartment block on the outskirts of Härnösand. There was a jetty visible beyond the buildings, a playground in which the paint had worn away.

Eira had been pushing the speed limit all the way back from Hudiksvall, but the patrol car still got there long before they did, and was parked on the lawn when she and Silje arrived.

A colleague in uniform emerged from the building.

"No one home," he said, dropping his tools into the trunk of the car. They had forced entry into the apartment when Sanna Melin failed to answer. "The place is super tidy, looks like the resident has gone away—though some people actually live like that."

"OK, thanks."

Eira took the stairs to the third floor while Silje finished up with the responding officers, who had been called out elsewhere.

There was only one name on the door.

S. MELIN.

Eira pulled on a pair of shoe covers and gloves. She had lost count of the number of empty apartments she had entered lately.

There were no piles of mail on the floor this time. She checked the front door again, and saw a small plaque beside the letter box: NO JUNK MAIL, NO FREE NEWSPAPERS.

A single jacket on the coat stand. A pair of slippers pushed beneath the chest of drawers.

Tidy was an understatement.

There were no empty bottles in the kitchen, not a single glass left out on the counter. The bin was empty, the walls bare. There were no decorative touches anywhere, nothing that seemed remotely personal.

No potted plants that could wither and die.

A lack of life, so far removed from the chaos of GG's home or Hans Runne's more ordinary mess.

In the main bedroom, the bed was neatly made. There were no books on the nightstand.

The smaller of the two bedrooms seemed to be used as an office. A desktop computer, switched off. Bookshelves full of folders lining the walls. Eira took one down.

Who are you, Sanna Melin?

The folder contained business accounts. She read the company name, a car dealership. The entire shelf seemed to be dedicated to it, year after year. The next company was a copy shop. The one after that a sheet-metal workshop. Endless columns of debit and credit, Eira had never understood which was which. Balance sheets, profit-and-loss accounts.

Is this your life, Sanna?

She tried one of the drawers in the desk, but it was locked.

A sound by the front door made her jump back against the wall, keeping a line of retreat open, her senses heightened. It was sheer impulse.

Soft footsteps on the linoleum floor.

"Eira?"

"In here."

Silje appeared in the doorway.

"She has a red Škoda Fabia."

"Seriously?" The room seemed to close in around them, the shelves creeping closer. Eira took a deep breath to calm her racing heart, the adrenaline pumping through her veins. This was their link. Mikael Ingmarsson, the car by the edge of the road, Hans Runne. They were all connected.

"And we have a picture." Silje handed Eira her phone.

Eira stared down at a photograph from the passport database.

Straight longish hair, somewhere between blond and brown. Blue eyes. A slightly wide face, staring straight into the camera. Few people were at their best when they sat down in a booth to be photographed by a machine, but she seemed absent somehow.

Slightly melancholy, perhaps.

Sanna Melin looked like the kind of person you might bump into at the supermarket every week, without ever remembering you had seen them.

"Born and raised in Örnsköldsvik. Do you know her?"

Neither her face nor her name set any bells ringing in Eira.

"No, I don't think I've ever seen her before."

Silje trailed a gloved finger along one of the shelves. A hint of dust. The rows of dark folders lining the walls transformed the daylight into gray dusk.

"How long do you think she's been gone?"

"We don't know how often she cleans," said Eira. "But it can't have been long, four or five days?"

There was no need to voice her next thought. That could fit with

GG's disappearance, they were onto the sixth day now. Through the silence, she heard her colleague swallow. The distant voices of children playing in the yard. The constant hum of the pipes. The air felt stale. The windows were closed, even the narrow side window added for ventilation.

"This doesn't feel like a home," said Eira. "More like an office she could spend the night in."

"Her business is registered at her home address," said Silje, glancing down at the information on Sanna Melin that had started trickling in. "An accounting firm, started eleven years ago. They're busy digging out her annual financial reports and that kind of thing."

Eira took in the shelves and the folders without really seeing any of them, her mind still searching for someone that looked like Sanna Melin in her past, perhaps from a long time ago. She could have changed her name since she was younger. Sanna was around Magnus's age, and Örnsköldsvik was only eighty kilometers from Kramfors. They could easily have gone to the same festivals, had friends in common. Worst-case scenario, they might even have hooked up, Eira thought, panicking for a moment.

Her eyes came to rest just above one of the bookcases. The walls were papered with a beige square pattern, likely the original paper from the sixties, but she could see a white strip of wood peeping out, barely visible, almost like the top of a doorframe. That particular bookcase was also a few centimeters farther from the wall than any of the others, a fact that was barely noticeable because the folders had all been neatly lined up in a perfectly straight row, minimizing any difference.

"What's that?"

"What?"

Silje stood on her tiptoes; she was taller than Eira.

"A walk-in wardrobe? Or a guest bathroom? She probably needed the shelves more—did you know you have to keep all this crap for years, just in case the authorities come knocking?"

"There might be a door from the other side." Eira went back through to the bedroom on the other side of the wall. The door to

the walk-in wardrobe had been left open after the responding officers secured the apartment. She pushed the hangers to one side to
gauge the depth. Sanna Melin's clothes were all in muted colors, pale
pinks and icy blues. No door. And the wardrobe was too small to fill
the gap between the two rooms.

Eira returned to the office, where Silje had started moving the
folders. One of the shelves came loose when she tried to get a good
grip, and a few of them fell to the floor.

They dragged the bookcase away from the wall, revealing the
door behind.

The handle had been removed, and there was no key in the lock.
Silje pushed a knife into the gap, then peered around the room.

"The key might be in there," she said, nodding to the desk. She
tried one of the drawers. Locked. "These things are never too hard
to get into."

"Shouldn't we wait for forensics?"

They were on their way, would be there in no more than half an
hour.

"If the responding officers had seen this door, they would've
opened it," said Silje, getting to work on the top drawer. "But as it is,
we saw it. Or you did, to be specific."

"It could've been locked for years."

"If I just have to sit here, staring at the wallpaper while we wait for
forensics, I'm going to go crazy." There was something frantic about
her actions, something Eira didn't want to get in the way of.

A minute of coaxing, and the lock clicked.

"Ta-da!"

The drawer contained all the usual things: paper clips, a stapler,
Post-it notes. There was also a compartment holding a few loose
keys.

"Bingo," said Silje. She grabbed a couple that looked like they
might fit, and tried them one by one.

Eira spotted another key. Thick, heavy metal, flecked with rust.
The kind of key that might belong to a house where the locks hadn't
been changed for decades.

The third key Silje tried fit. It turned surprisingly easy, the door swinging open. Eira caught a whiff of something that didn't seem to tally with the rest of the apartment. Something she thought she had smelled before.

Musty old clothes, but also something else.

There was a heap of material of some kind. Sheets, possibly. Blankets. A rag rug? Silje bent down and carefully lifted a scrap of fabric.

A plastic bag beneath.

"What the hell is this?"

Silje took a step back. The soft daylight spilled onto the bundle inside.

Eira saw what she had seen.

A foot sticking out from beneath the black plastic, pointing straight towards her. It was wearing a sock, and she might have thought she was mistaken if it weren't for the sliver of ankle that was visible.

Eira crouched down.

It seemed unnaturally thin, gray, and dry.

"You're right," she heard her colleague's voice somewhere far away. "We should probably wait until they get here."

The walk-in wardrobe of a 1960s apartment provided the perfect conditions for the natural mummification of a body.

A dry space, free from insects.

Eira had come across something similar once before, when she entered the home of a man no one had missed until the neighbors started wondering after almost two years.

The skin was taut over the skeleton, the eye sockets gaping holes, but the person's hair was still intact. Dark, cut short.

Teeth bared in a grimace.

"How long could they have been here?"

"Impossible to say," Costel Ardelean replied once forensics had managed to get a sense of the scene. "Spontaneous mummification can be quite rapid—I've seen it on people who have only been dead a year."

"Probably not before 1964, though," one of his colleagues spoke up.

The year when the residential area was built. A golden age in which everyone would have hot running water and an indoor toilet, ideally one room per person and a ventilation system based on natural air flow running through the walls—including the walk-in wardrobes, another factor that helped promote mummification.

"But surely you'd check the wardrobes when a new tenant moved in?" Silje skimmed through the information that was still coming in. Sanna Melin had been registered at the apartment since 2005.

They carefully uncovered the body.

"A man," said Costel.

No one asked how he could tell so quickly. Whether it was the shape of his head, his eye sockets, the huge watch on his left wrist.

He was wearing a sweatshirt and jeans. His clothes were incredibly well preserved, a stark contrast to his parched skin.

He was young, thought Eira. That was a young man's style, though it didn't tell her much about the timeframe—young men had dressed that way for as long as she could remember.

"If you want my initial guess, I'd say he was dead when he was put in here." Costel pointed to the inside of the wardrobe door. There were no scratch marks, no sign of anyone having tried to get out. "And then there's the position of the body."

The dead man was slumped to one side, half leaning against the wall with his legs at a strange angle.

"I'd say he was dragged in here, or pushed—either unconscious or shortly after death—while his joints were still supple."

Eira's mind wound back to Hans Runne, the way he had curled up like a child, seeking out the corner, the last warmth of his own body. She felt a sudden darkness, a sense that this would never end.

The light bulb in the closet didn't work, and Costel's torch beam swept over the man's knees, which could have been bent when the body was pushed into the cramped space, up against the wall. Locking into position like that.

"Do you see?"

Eira tried to peer inside without getting in the way or touching anything. A spot just above the man's jeans, where his pale blue sweatshirt was dark.

"I think we have a possible cause of death."

"A stab wound?"

The torchlight disappeared as Costel got to his feet. He nodded to the photographer, who stepped forward to document everything. The position of the body, the dark spot that had spread across the floor.

The blood, which had dried a year or more ago.

A sweeping staircase led up to the restaurant at Stadt in Härnösand. There had been talk of moving it down to the ground floor, serving champagne brunch and hosting events, but the place still looked like it had in the sixties. Other than a few hotel guests eating an early dinner or enjoying a quick drink, the room was empty.

The bartender studied the photograph of Sanna Melin.

"I think I recognize her," she said, passing the image to the waitress beside her. "She's not necessarily the kind of woman you notice right away," she went on, "but if someone's been here several times you make a note of it some other way. You think, she's back again, you know?"

"Alone," said the waitress. "Isn't she usually on her own?"

"Not always, I've seen her with a few men." The bartender started unloading wineglasses from the glasswasher tray. "Sorry, but I have to."

"Don't worry." Eira had worked in a bar for a few years, and she knew how little spare time the job entailed.

"A glass of white wine, I think. No mention of the grape or anything like that, just the house white, the cheapest one."

"Who is she?" asked the other woman. "Has something happened to her?"

Eira took out the picture of Hans Runne. She had chosen one in which he looked more natural, not his passport photo. One where he looked more like she imagined him on a night out.

"You've probably already been asked whether you recognize this man."

They nodded.

"He's the one from the abandoned house, right? The actor?"

"So awful."

"And knowing that he'd been here . . . You wish you had a better idea what was going on, but it was one of those nights when the place is crazy. A Silja Line night, you know? The dining room and bar were full of tourists."

When the pandemic struck and the borders closed, the huge ferries had no longer been able to sail to Finland. One of the more creative solutions had been to start offering trips to the High Coast instead, and it had proved so popular that it had continued. For one day and night, Härnösand swelled with people out drinking and shopping, and then they were all loaded onto buses and taken to the World Heritage area.

"I saw him that night," said the waitress. "I remember because I know his daughter a bit. But it was only through the crowd, I didn't see who he was talking to or anything like that."

"Have either of you ever seen these two together?"

Hesitant headshakes.

"But on a Silja Line night," said the bartender, "they could set a wolf loose in here and we wouldn't notice."

"What's the deal with the woman?" asked the waitress. "Is she dead too?"

"No, for God's sake. Last time I saw her she was leaving with some guy, that was only a few days ago."

"Which day?" Eira grabbed her arm and immediately let go. She just wanted the woman to stop sorting the damn glasses. To concentrate.

"Hey, take it easy," said the waitress.

"Sorry," said Eira. "But it's important I know which day."

The bartender rubbed her arm where Eira had grabbed it. She left the glasses alone.

"I don't know. I wasn't working at the weekend, so it must've been towards the end of last week, I remember it was really busy."

Eira's hand was shaking as she searched for the photograph. It was one Silje had taken. They had a formal, professional headshot in the case file, of course, groomed and smartly dressed, but this one looked more like him. His thick hair slightly messy, a teasing smile on his face. He looked like he was heading somewhere, away, onwards. Silje had captured his restlessness.

"The detective? Why are you asking about him again?"

Of course. One of her colleagues involved in the search for GG must have followed up on his payment. Eira felt a brief flicker of relief, despite everything. They were taking it seriously, of course they were. A police officer couldn't just disappear in the middle of an investigation, never. There was a lot of work going on, serious police work, things that Silje hadn't managed to sniff out. Eira didn't doubt she would be told when something big happened. She could understand the prosecutor's reasoning. It was logical, by the book. She shouldn't get involved.

She touched her phone screen so that it didn't go dark.

"Could it have been this man," she asked, "who she went home with last week?"

"Hang on, I'm confused," said the bartender. "What's going on here?"

"Just try to remember what you saw that evening."

"There was a load of fuss around him, the detective," said the waitress. "But I already told the others that."

"Tell me too."

A group of drunk men had recognized GG and started causing trouble. The waitress hadn't seen everything, but the men were ac-cusing the police of protecting criminals and not doing their job. They'd had to call for the bouncer in the end.

"Do you know who they were?"

The waitress shook her head. Someone else was probably busy trying to identify and track them down now. This wasn't something Eira needed to stick her nose into.

"He wasn't exactly sober either."

"Are you talking about our colleague now?" Eira didn't want to say his name, hoped they didn't know what he was called—or that they would keep quiet if they did.

"Sorry, but he forgot the PIN for his card. Either that or he entered the wrong one. I was focused on trying to get paid, but I think he was with a woman."

"He's pretty tall, right?" The bartender spoke up again.

"Six four," said Eira.

"And he dresses really well?"

She closed her eyes for a moment. That evening, when he turned up at her house, GG was wearing muddy shoes. A graphite gray shirt.

"Yes, I guess you could say that."

"I'm not one hundred percent, but it could've been him."

"What could?"

"Who left with her."

"Left with her? What does that mean?" She had to breathe, to stay calm, even though they were dragging this out. She couldn't afford to rush their memories. They might make a mistake if she did, a terrible mistake. "I'm guessing you don't just mean they left at the same time?"

"He left *with* her," the bartender repeated. "Assuming it was him, I only saw him from behind, but I saw the woman putting a hand on his arm as they went down the stairs. I remember because I was happy she'd managed to pull. Like this."

She placed a hand on the waitress's arm to show Eira what she meant. Not gripping it, just a palm brushing a man's upper arm, an intimate gesture. A gesture that said: we're leaving here together. Perhaps it also said: I saw you were so drunk you could barely enter your PIN, but that doesn't matter, I want you anyway, *it's just us now.*

Fear made Eira's throat tighten, and she had to force out the next few words. In her mind's eye, it was no longer GG she could see, nor the bar in Stadt. It was a walk-in wardrobe, a body that had been covered in plastic and fabric until its skin and internal organs shriveled and dried.

"Thanks," she said. "You've been really helpful."

"Sorry for asking," said the bartender, "but has he done something to her?"

"What?"

"I mean, it's none of my business, but . . ."

"No," said Eira, practically snapping at the girl. "*He* hasn't done anything."

The thought didn't cross her mind until she was back out on the street, having rushed down the stairs two steps at a time. The cold air hit her face, a merciless wind blowing in from the Bothnian Sea.

Would she have been so sure if it were any other man?

Almost seven thousand people were reported missing in Sweden every year, half as a result of things like depression or dementia. Only in rare cases was there any crime involved, and the majority were found within a few days—either that or they came home, or were discovered to have left simply because they felt like it.

Those who were never found, who remained missing after several years, numbered around nine hundred.

Damir Avdic was one of them.

His body had been removed from the walk-in wardrobe overnight, and impressions and X-rays of his teeth had been taken as soon as he arrived in Umeå.

That had led to a match with a dental record in the missing persons' database.

"There's no denying we got lucky," said Nora Berents. They had gathered for a bigger meeting than usual, a striking physical presence in the room. "If this young man hadn't had issues with his wisdom teeth, it definitely wouldn't have been so quick."

It wasn't every twenty-nine-year-old that prioritized their dental health, and they didn't have access to any childhood medical records detailing all the usual obligatory visits to the dentist.

Damir Avdic hadn't arrived in Sweden until he was seventeen.

Alone, from Bosnia to a refugee center in Örnsköldsvik.

"Sanna Melin is from Ö-vik too," said Eira. "Maybe that's where they met."

Damir had been reported missing in February 2006.

"It was the principal of the community college here in Härnösand who reported it," Berents continued. "Damir was training to become an interpreter there, living in their student halls. They started worrying after he failed to turn up for over a week and wasn't in his room."

She was reading aloud from the report. Only twenty minutes had passed since they first found out his name.

"His father died in the war, when the Serbs attacked in 1992. His mother was still alive, in Sarajevo, but she'd passed away by the time of his disappearance. He has a sister—or did back then, anyway."

Someone would have to get in touch with the local police in Bosnia and Herzegovina to break the news.

What must she think after so long, Eira wondered. At what point does a person give up?

For the first time in her life, she had woken with a migraine that morning. The violent kind, with flashes of light. Taking a double dose of painkillers hadn't helped. The bright flashes were gone, but the headache was lingering like an iron grip around the base of her skull, a sensitivity to light.

"So when did they meet? How did they know each other?" The prosecutor flicked through the report. "We have the names of some of his classmates here, his teachers. They all said that Damir was popular, that he worked hard. He had a girlfriend, Hanna, another student at the school. Damir would never just leave without saying anything, et cetera. There are plenty of questions they didn't think to ask back then, of course. We'll have to talk to the school, find out whether Sanna Melin has any connection to it, whether there are any photographs of her when she was younger—how old was she when he disappeared . . . ?"

"Twenty-six."

"Talk about skeletons in the closet," said someone, unable to hold back any longer.

Only a handful of people laughed.

"You have to wonder what she's done in the years since, too."

The thought made the room fall silent for a moment.

"As yet, we don't have anything that points to more victims," said Berents. "So let's focus on the ones we know about."

"Does that include GG?" The question came from the man beside Eira, his foot bobbing up and down as though he were keeping pace with a rock track.

"Formally," said the prosecutor, "there is no suspicion of crime as far as Inspector Georgsson is concerned."

"What, so has he jetted off to the Maldives or something?"

Everyone knew they needed more than simply going down a set of stairs with someone, a suspect placing a hand on an arm, but it was the starting shot for their anxieties to explode.

"If this crazy bitch has GG locked up somewhere, then every second counts. Why are we even sitting here? Why aren't we out there looking for him?"

"And where do you suggest we look? We haven't found a single bloody trace of him since he left Stadt that evening."

The staff's statements had been backed up by the receipts from that evening. Sanna Melin had paid for a single glass of house white at around nine p.m.

She also had a room at the hotel. Checked in at seven that evening, and checked out just before ten the next morning. A room that was cleaned every day, in which new people stayed every night, sheets sent away to be washed and mixed up with hundreds of others.

"We'll search the room, of course," said Costel Ardelean, "but I'm not holding out much hope."

The check-out process was automated, meaning no one had actually seen her leave.

"Who here thinks it was a coincidence?" said someone. "That he left the bar with a serial killer."

No one raised their hand.

"I'd like to avoid that word," said Nora Berents. "Do I need to remind you that Sanna Melin is technically only suspected of one murder, that of Damir Avdic? As far as the other victims are concerned, we're looking at false imprisonment in the Ingmarsson case. And if we can tie her to Hans Runne—and I'm saying *if*—then we'll have another count of kidnapping and murder, or manslaughter, but we're not quite there yet."

She dealt out their tasks, did what was required of the leader of a preliminary investigation.

Eira cast one last glance back before she left, and saw Nora Berents slump into a chair with her head in her hands.

There was none of the usual small talk after the meeting that day.

Eira made her way over to the empty desk again. Her colleagues were delving into Damir Avdic's past, trying to track down anyone who could shed more light on the events surrounding his disappearance. Someone else was going to talk to his sister in Sarajevo. Eira planned to focus on Sanna Melin.

Who was she? And above all: *where* was she?

Eira kept her photograph open in the background as she began to look through the latest reports.

The red Škoda still hadn't been found; it wasn't parked near her apartment or anywhere else in town. The patrol cars had spent the night combing the streets, and some of her colleagues had now been tasked with trawling through footage from the roads around Härnösand over the past week, focusing on the E4, where there were far more traffic cameras.

Eira texted Jens Boija in Undrom, attaching a picture of the specific model: Does this look like the car you saw parked by the side of the road?

His reply arrived a few minutes later.

Pretty much, yeah.

They had run Melin's fingerprints against everything they had and found one match: a print from the lopsided bureau in Offer.

What had so far looked like a series of loose threads was now starting to resemble a web.

That brought with it a certain clarity and relief: we're on the right track, we've got her, it was her all along. And yet Eira's headache was worse than ever, her eyes sore from staring at the screen.

Shouldn't I have seen it sooner?

Is it my fault if it's already too late?

Other than Damir Avdic, Sanna Melin was the only person to have left any trace in her apartment. Forensics had found some blood that had seeped into the parquet floor, but it would be a few days before they knew whose it was.

Four local officers had been brought in to work overtime, knocking on doors in the area around Sanna Melin's apartment, but so far they hadn't found anyone who knew her very well. The image that was emerging was of a solitary figure. She never invited anyone over or barbecued in the yard, had neither a dog nor any children; the neighbors knew who she was and would exchange a few words when they saw her, but that was all. One man who had been living on the same floor as her for several years didn't even recognize her picture. "Oh, right, is that who lives there? I thought she must be older, maybe because I never hear a sound from her apartment."

No one had ever seen her come home with a man.

Because she always got a room at Stadt, thought Eira. They had found several bookings over the past year.

Why, when she lived in the same town?

Was it because you didn't want to take them home, so you could give the impression of being someone else, more interesting and exciting? Or was it because Damir was in your wardrobe?

Sanna Melin didn't have any immediate family. Her mother had died three years earlier, her father was unknown, and she had no siblings.

Her last period of formal employment was a decade ago, as an accountant for a company involved in the timber trade. She had started her own business upon leaving and had taken on her old employer as a customer. Outsourcing, as it was known.

Since then, she had worked from home.

Eira took out her client list and started making calls.

"I don't think we've ever actually met," said the manager of a tire-fitting firm. "It's all done online—not that I have any complaints. VAT, tax, everything's been correct and submitted on time."

"She comes over to drop off the annual report for approval," said someone else. "But that's just once a year."

"What is your impression of her?"

"Proper," he said. "There's nothing wrong with the accounts, is there?"

"No, no, it's nothing to do with that."

The man audibly exhaled, a whistle of relief. There were fifteen companies on her books, but how often did an accountant have a close relationship with their clients?

Eira turned her attention back to Sanna's family.

Her late mother, Birgitta, was one lead to follow, if nothing else—easier than trying to track down a father who wasn't even named on the birth certificate. Sanna could have aunts and cousins, other relatives she was close to.

Eira ran a search on her mother's name, bringing up her personal details. The national registration system was probably the greatest thing Swedish bureaucracy had ever achieved. The long ID numbers assigned to every citizen meant that everyone could be found, always and anywhere.

Birgitta Margareta Melin was born at Sollefteå Hospital in 1952. Sollefteå.

The fact that their suspected perpetrator had ties to the area could be a coincidence, but it could also suggest that she knew about the abandoned house. Her family might have once owned a cabin out there, had relatives to visit.

Roots were important, Eira thought as the names came up on-screen. The parents that had brought young Birgitta into the world.

Her mother, Sanna's grandmother, was Lilly Ingeborg Melin, born in Själevad in 1928.

And her grandfather.

Eira's migraine returned with full force, blurring her field of vision. She had to tilt her head to make sure she had read his name right.

Karl-Erik Bäcklund.

Born 1926, died 2011.

She leapt up, looking for someone to call over, but there was no one working on the case nearby. Her heart was racing.

Karl-Erik. Kalle, the old military man who had ruled over the house in Offer until he died, leaving it to his children, who didn't want to live there.

Eira clicked on his name, too. She wanted to see it clearly, or at least half blurred, the family photo flickering onto the screen.

There was Agnes Bäcklund, his wife. Their children, Per, Kristina, Jan, and Lars. Jan, who had once had an affair with Eira's stepmother. That didn't make them relatives, but it did wake the old feeling of being caught up in something she was powerless to influence, something that had been going on since long before she was born.

Karl-Erik Bäcklund had, between the years 1951 and 1954, been married to Lilly Bäcklund, née Melin.

The first wife, we just called her the first wife . . .

Jesus Christ, how could she have missed this? Why hadn't any of the siblings mentioned that they had a half sister? The old widower in Offer was the only one who had brought it up. What had he said? That the first wife was known as being difficult, from somewhere up Nolaskogs way.

Eira clicked through to Lilly Melin, born and registered in Själevad. That definitely counted as Nolaskogs, as the area to the north of the Skuleskogen National Park had been known for as long as anyone could remember.

Eira closed her eyes to let them rest as she took in the dizzying fact that Sanna Melin was a close relative of the previous owners of the abandoned house.

Had she inherited the key from her mother and grandmother? Did old Lilly refuse to give it back when her husband *traded her in for a better model*?

Eira opened her eyes again. It was staring her right in the face.

Lilly's date of birth, 1928, followed by a blank space.

She was still alive.

There are times when he thinks he can hear the waves outside. The soft rush of things moving inside him, the blood still pumping through his veins.

He no longer knows whether his eyes are open or closed, but he can see them. Julia, laughing and running towards him, coming out of the nursery door; she shrieks when he catches her and swings her up into the air.

He wants to carve their names into the wall so that they understand. He doesn't have the energy right now, but later.

GG shakes out the last few drops from the third can, doesn't quite know what it was. He then crawls back into his nook between the shelves, confident that he won't notice when the wave rolls in and pulls out. Death, when it comes to take back his life. He'll go to sleep then. Like a dream that simply stops: it was there, and then it wasn't.

Her fair hair above the sea of flowers in the summer meadow. A bouquet of buttercups and thistles, the girl's hand is so small when she holds it out to him. Is that for me, it's beautiful, did you pick it yourself? He can't see his son, he shouts and looks around the summerhouse, is it getting dark already, isn't it summer? For a moment he is the one hiding, but he doesn't know where. Then he spots the boy, hunched over something crawling through the grass, they're getting wings, Dad, Erik whispers, his face lighting up, look Dad, they're getting wings, and the father gets onto his knees, feels the grass and the nettles stinging his bare legs, he is wearing shorts.

And the ants lift off from the ground.

Eira set off for Nolaskogs early that morning. It wasn't like she could sleep, after all. Restlessness clawed at her.

Seven days now.

She pulled over at the truckers' café in Docksta for breakfast. The huge shadow of Skuleberget loomed in the darkness, the mountain rising sharply, the caves where robbers had once holed up. All the tourists were gone for the season. The café served both hot dogs and meatballs, but Eira could only manage a yogurt. Outside, the lorries were lined up, their drivers sleeping their regulated hours. She had always liked curling up behind the driver's seat, those few occasions she was allowed to join her father on the road. With the music on the evening radio, the headlights of approaching lorries like flying Christmas trees above the dark roads, signs warning of towns she had never visited.

The heat in the cab, his stories about the places they were passing.

The area to the north of Skuleskogen National Park differed from the more industrialized region to the south. There were factories right along the Norrland coast, of course, but the farmers there were richer, the farms themselves more impressive. She didn't know why the people living up Nolaskogs way had, at some point in time, been granted special permission by the king to trade with both the Sámi in the north and the merchants to the south, but it had given them a unique position in the country.

Sunrise was still hours away as she pulled into Själevad. One of the oldest settlements, a small church village that was now more a suburb of Örnsköldsvik than anything. Eira looked up the address of the care home where Lilly Melin lived. It was still too early, so she tipped back her seat to get a few minutes' sleep.

Dozing just beneath the surface, strange dreams that felt so real, GG following her in to talk to the old woman; Sanna Melin was there too, offering them coffee and chatting as though everything were normal.

Eira woke when her head slumped forward. The clock on the dashboard read 7:14. She had only been asleep for fifteen minutes, but her body was stiff. She checked her phone and saw that Silje had sent her a message, a moment or so earlier.

A photograph, of a young couple.

Damir Avdic laughing at the camera. It looked like summer, blue skies and water. The girl by his side was smiling softly, perhaps shyly, looking away.

Do you see who that is?

Eira enlarged the image. Sanna Melin hadn't changed much. She was younger than in her passport photo, of course, but otherwise the main difference was her hair. It was longer here, a little wilder, possibly because the wind was blowing.

She called Silje.

"Can you believe," said her colleague, "that just one year later, she'd ram a knife into his back, hitting his liver?"

"Have they finished the autopsy?"

"We've got a preliminary report."

"Who took the picture?"

"Not sure, but we got it from his sister in Sarajevo. She had it on an old backup, spent all night looking for it. They met when he lived in Örnsköldsvik, Damir was in love and his sister was angry because he didn't want to move back home—after the war, it was just the two of them left."

"So they were a couple, him and Sanna Melin?"

"Not for long," said Silje. "According to the sister, they broke up before he moved to Härnösand and started his interpreting course. That was what Damir told her, anyway. She remembered him wanting to get away from Sanna, but that it was hard."

Eira closed her eyes, tried to make sense of the timeline. Sanna had also moved to Härnösand in 2005, to a two-bed apartment. And in February 2006, Damir was reported missing.

"Did she follow him there? Is that why she moved south?"

"I'm going to meet his last girlfriend this morning," said Silje. "Damir had told her it was over with Sanna, and she believed him."

"Why wasn't there any mention of this in the files from his disappearance?"

"You know how it works—a grown man disappears, no evidence of a crime, some suggestion that he might have wanted to leave. Would you have gone round all his old girlfriends? I don't know whether the officer who dealt with the report even reacted to it, because we can't get hold of him."

"Who was it?"

"Bosse Ring."

"Shit." Eira hadn't realized that her old colleague was working in Härnösand back then, over fifteen years ago, though on the other hand she didn't know much about him at all, because he never talked about himself.

"And now he's up in his cabin in Myckelgensjö and can't be reached," Silje went on. "I've heard his stupid voice mail message ten times since yesterday, and his in-box is on auto-reply. If it was anyone else I wouldn't even consider driving to the middle of nowhere, but this is Bosse Ring, and he doesn't forget a thing—as someone once said . . ." She trailed off, growing serious. "I think it was GG. They've worked together for a long time. I wonder if he knows."

"Myckelgensjö isn't so far from here," said Eira. "Sixty, seventy kilometers, tops."

She saw someone getting off a bike by the entrance to the care home, the day staff were starting to arrive. Experience told her that the most lucid moments usually came in the morning.

Before the day came barging in, confusing everything.

"I have to go."

Lilly Melin had managed on her own for a long time, only moving into care at the age of ninety, when the home help raised the alarm about one incident too many.

"As I said on the phone, we see no reason to break our confidentiality agreement," said the manager, who had come in early to meet Eira. She was in her fifties, blond highlights in her gray hair.

"I understand," said Eira. "But the confidentiality agreement doesn't extend to her granddaughter. Sanna Melin has been arrested in absentia, on suspicion of kidnapping and murder."

"Should we tell Lilly? Her granddaughter is all she has."

"Does she ever come to visit?"

"Oh yes, every week or so. She lives quite far away, in Härnösand."

"When was she here last?"

The manager flicked through a few sheets of paper on the table in front of her.

"It's not something we keep records of, but I did ask my staff. It looks like it was a little over two weeks ago. She usually comes in on Sundays. She takes her grandmother to the church sometimes."

"The church?"

"We've got a very beautiful church here in town."

What kind of person took their grandmother to church after locking a man in an abandoned house? Was she ice cold, or was she simply looking for forgiveness?

If they didn't find Sanna Melin before Sunday, they would have to put the place under surveillance. Eira could just picture the task force, crouching behind the bare trunks in the peaceful avenue of birches.

"I've always thought she seemed like such a nice person," the manager continued. "Someone who cares about her grandmother. But my Lord, what do we really know? We appreciate the visitors who focus on their elderly relatives and don't take out their anxieties on the staff. It's more common than you might think, us having to shoulder the guilt they can't manage themselves."

"Did you notice anything unusual last time she was here?"

"I checked with the members of staff who were working, and everything seemed normal. Mind you, we don't spend our time thinking about the relatives. We're just happy when they come to visit, we take a step back."

"Is there anyone else she's close to? Family, friends?"

"Lilly's younger brother died last spring, and her friends have all passed away, too. Sanna is all she has left."

A shadow fell over the room, thoughts of the emptiness lurking in room number seven.

"Would it be possible for me to speak to Lilly Melin?"

"She hasn't been declared incapacitated, so it's up to her."

"But is it possible to get through to her?"

"Obviously I can't go into any detail about her diagnoses," said the manager, "but what I will say is that this isn't really the right place for Lilly Melin. I don't know where would be. A castle in the mountains, perhaps?" A slight smile, the first of the morning. "I can tell you what she *isn't* suffering from. Hers is no ordinary dementia, though she does seem to be in a world of her own at times."

"Stuck in the past?"

"I wouldn't say that, not unless she was a princess in a past life."

Breakfast was being served as they walked down the short corridor, cutlery clattering in the dining room, water running as someone took their morning shower.

Lilly Melin was up and dressed, sitting in a chair facing the window. Her neck was the first thing Eira noticed: a beautiful straight line, not at all crooked with age. The room was warm, but she had a shawl draped over her shoulders, her silvery hair loose. Eira caught a glimpse of the River Mo outside, treetops with dark branches, the sky slowly brightening.

"She's here now, Lilly," said the manager. "The police officer I told you about."

The old woman half turned and held out a slender hand in greeting, almost as though she expected a kiss.

"So good you could come."

"OK, I'll leave the two of you in peace," said the manager.

Eira introduced herself and sat down on a cushioned chair. The furniture looked antique without being valuable, the kind of thing amassed over a lifetime. Kitsch paintings in handsome frames on the walls: a ship on a stormy sea, a lighthouse at night, a portrait of King Oscar II.

She set down her phone on the table and told Lilly that she was recording their conversation.

"I'd like to ask you about Sanna, your granddaughter."

"Why? Has something happened to the girl?"

"I thought you might be able to tell me where she is."

"Isn't she at home?" Her confusion seemed genuine, and why shouldn't it be? "Perhaps she's gone on holiday."

"Where do you think she might have gone if she has?" asked Eira.

"No, I'm probably wrong."

"Do you remember when Sanna was last here?"

"No, no, I don't, is this really necessary?" Lilly Melin seemed nervous, though perhaps it was just the usual anxiety many elderly people felt in the face of the authorities. Eira still wasn't used to the fact that *she* now represented the authorities. The woman touched her cheek, a certain grace to her movements.

A ring on her left hand.

"Are you married, Lilly?" There was no mention of a second husband in the records, and something like that could hardly have escaped the national registration system.

"No, my dear, I'm widowed." A sad smile, a coquettish touch of her hair. "Kalle was killed in action during the war, God rest his soul."

"Is that him, is that your husband?" There were a few photographs on the chest of drawers, among them a black-and-white wedding portrait. "Do you mind if I have a look?" Eira got up and moved closer. In the corner of the image, she saw the name of a photography studio in Sollefteå. The old woman's features were repeated in the bride's face, barely over twenty, the same proud neck and wide eyes. Lilly had been blond back then, and she looked like an actress from one of Ingmar Bergman's films, at once innocent and cunning. The man was wearing a uniform on his wedding day.

"Is this your husband? Is this Karl-Erik Bäcklund?"

"Yes, that was before all the rest of it, of course. We had to go underground."

"Did you?"

"Oh yes, it was awful. I can't talk about it." A finger to her lips, a promise of silence.

"And what about this, is this your daughter, Birgitta?" Eira passed her a color photograph of a woman.

"We've no need to talk about her," said Lilly Melin. "She's never here."

Eira recognized the feeling of deliberation all too well. Should she tell the woman that her daughter had died three years ago, should she mention the cancer? There really was no reason to.

"I'm sorry to bother you, but I have to ask you about these things. I'm a police officer, you see, and I'm investigating a couple of crimes your granddaughter may have been involved in."

"I'm not stupid." Lilly pointed to her own forehead. "There's nothing wrong up here, whatever they tell you."

"Do you know where Sanna could be? Is there anywhere she goes, anyone she visits?"

"You just keep asking and asking. I'm not sure I like this."

"It's very important that we get hold of her."

Lilly Melin carelessly set the photograph down and pulled her shawl tight.

"I haven't done anything. I'm not the one barging in and stealing."

"I really just want to talk to you."

"Yes, yes, yes, that's what you always say. Just a little chat. Just a little chat." The old woman gripped the arms of her chair and got to her feet; she was clearly agitated. "As though I didn't have the right to be in my own home. Surely I'm allowed in my own house. I don't see what it has to do with the police."

"As I understand it, you live here," said Eira. "And I'm not accusing you of anything. I'm just asking for your help."

She was starting to regret turning down assistance from Örnsköldsvik, there really should be two officers present for this.

Though on the other hand, if there were any spare resources, they should be tasked with finding GG. She could handle an interview with an old woman on her own.

Or so she had thought.

"He was handsome, don't you think?" Lilly Melin shuffled over to the chest of drawers by the window on unsteady legs, picked up the wedding portrait. Her crooked fingers brushed the glass.

"It was a beautiful house," said Eira. "The one in Offer."

"Smutty, slutty strumpet, that whore fucked herself in the pussy."

It came so suddenly, so utterly out of the blue from such a frail old woman, that Eira was on the verge of laughter.

Though at the same time, perhaps it made sense.

"Are you talking about Agnes now, his second wife? Did you tell Sanna about the house in Offer? Did you tell Sanna it was yours?"

Eira studied her slender back, her veined hands gripping the old photograph.

"Damn them," she spat out. "Damn that hussy. Throwing a person out of their own home!"

Eira didn't know much about psychology, particularly not when it took this shape. She wished for a moment that Silje had come with her to Själevad, perhaps she would have been able to read the old woman's confusion the way psychologists could interpret dreams.

The wedding ring, the story about the war—did Lilly really believe the things she was saying, or were they deliberate lies? A way to maintain her pride?

The first wife.

A marriage that lasted only a few years, perhaps she had been mentally ill even then. Or perhaps she simply loved too much, refused to let go of her vision of love as eternal?

If she had kept the key . . .

Gone back to the glade in the forest, a woman who had been cast aside, possibly kicked out, *inclined to feeblemindedness.* Eira could just picture her stepping into a house she still considered hers, finding another woman in her kitchen, her bed, with the man she believed she was married to.

Had they called the police, driven her away? In those days, that might have meant the psychiatric hospital, one of the terrifying places like Gådeå, Sidsjön, or Beckomberga.

She would be able to find out, but was it relevant?

Eira got to her feet.

"I came to talk to you about Sanna," she said to the back of the woman's head. "We need to find her. It's urgent."

Lilly Melin didn't turn around. Her eyes left the wedding portrait and drifted out of the window, but Eira was convinced she had heard what she said.

"I think you know more than you're letting on, Lilly."

"Yes, yes, yes, you just talk and talk."

Eira repeated that she was a police officer, that Lilly had a duty to tell her what she knew. That wasn't entirely true, of course—no one was required to testify against their closest relatives, there were clauses that protected people from that kind of thing.

"Did you tell your granddaughter she would inherit the house? Did you keep the key all these years? Where is she, Lilly? Where is Sanna hiding?"

The old woman clamped her hands to her ears. Eira felt like shaking her, waking her up, forcing out whatever she knew, and she gripped her thin wrist. That feeling would stay with her: how much resistance it put up, despite being so slim.

"What's going on in here?"

The manager was standing in the doorway.

She woke with the feeling that she was in the wrong place. The sofa she was lying on was old and lumpy, the scent of age and dust ingrained in the material. Eira sat up. Afternoon sun, slanting in through a window. The net curtains painted handwoven patterns of light onto her body. She could hear a radio somewhere, the weather forecast. An area of low pressure moving in from the northwest, bringing snow to central Norrland.

She remembered.

The sixty kilometers to Myckelgensjö. Her hands had started shaking as she drove, away from the care home where she had come so close, so worryingly close. She had sat in the car afterwards, listening to the recording. Could you hear it? The way she had shouted in the old woman's ear, wanted to grab her, shake her. Snap out of it, for God's sake, you're just pretending. You know, and I know that you know.

When she reached the small community, she'd had to pull over and ask for directions. The address was nothing but a mailbox, and didn't come up on the satnav.

"Isn't he the one who moved into the Gransveds' old place? The Stockholmer?" said one of the men outside the shop. "Right at the old petrol station, then left by the big yellow house with the sign for sourdough bread."

"They're Dutch, the people who've moved in there," another man spoke up. "But you can still get an ordinary loaf from the shop."

"Keep going straight ahead 'til you get to the crossing, then past the old chapel. You'll see it up ahead."

"Yeah, their girl passed away last spring, we've been waiting for it to be put up for sale."

Eira had spotted her colleague in the distance as she approached, perched at the top of a ladder. He seemed to be nailing a plank of wood over a hole in the side of the building. The black woodpecker had been at it, Bosse Ring explained once he climbed down.

"Are they so desperate for me to come back that they sent out a patrol?" he asked.

"GG is missing," said Eira.

And then her legs gave way beneath her.

It only lasted a moment, that weakness, barely even the blink of an eye. She had got back onto her feet and followed him inside. Told him everything there was to say about GG. Bosse Ring had listened, asked a few questions, narrowed down the timeframe, but he hadn't revealed what he thought might have happened. Perhaps he was in shock, Eira couldn't tell. She had summarized everything they knew in an incoherent torrent of words, cases crossing over, Sanna Melin and who she was, how they had gone on a wild-goose chase. And then she had closed her eyes, just for a moment or two.

That was two hours ago.

Bosse Ring was now busy frying diced sausage, onion, and po-tato, wearing some sort of Hard Rock T-shirt.

An old clock on the wall, ticking loudly. The sun quickly disap-peared. It was almost three in the afternoon.

"I only meant to get a few minutes' rest," she said.

"A tired cop can do more harm than good," he said. "Not to men-tion what it does to you as a person."

"But I set an alarm."

"I switched it off," said Bosse Ring.

Eira tried to check her messages, but it was true: there really was no coverage in Myckelgensjö.

Bosse set out some plates, put the pan on the table.

"I should go," she said. "I haven't even called in my report from the care home. I came straight here."

"You said it didn't lead anywhere."

"Still . . ."

"You can't solve this on your own."

"I'm not on my own," Eira mumbled, her mouth full. The hash tasted incredible, like butter and salt and childhood. "And now that we know who she is, someone will find her—on a traffic camera, through her bank card, or if she has a new phone . . ."

"That's not what I'm talking about," said Bosse Ring.

Eira got up to fill a glass of water from the tap. There was some-thing fatherly about the way he was looking at her that she couldn't quite get used to. The kitchen was original, eighteenth century or so, a wood-fired oven with a brick hood, thick floorboards.

"Help yourself from the bucket instead," he said. "It's from the well, tastes better."

His hands were flecked with paint, and he looked thinner than she remembered. Had grown a longish beard.

"What are you doing up here?" she asked.

"I inherited a house. Had to do something with it."

"I always had you down as a city person." Eira remembered them searching the woods together, her colleague lagging behind as she ran through areas without any trails.

"I grew up in Stockholm, Södermalm," he said. "Mum ran away there when she was seventeen, never wanted any of this. No roots going back here, either. She came to the country as a child, as an evacuee from Finland, and ended up staying. Managed to fall and break her arm in May 1945, and they only sent the healthy kids back after the war. She never belonged anywhere."

"And you?"

Bosse pushed the frying pan towards her.

"Have some more."

"I'm OK, thanks. It was good, but . . ."

"Coffee?" He didn't wait for her to respond, might not even have been asking. He simply filled the coffeepot and set it down on the wood-burning stove, which was already hot. His brief burst of openness was over.

Eira slumped back on the daybed. They needed to discuss what she had come here for, she had almost forgotten.

"Damir Avdic," she said. "Do you remember when he disappeared?"

"He lived at the community college," said Bosse. "I think it was his tutor who reported him missing."

"People always say you remember everything."

"We didn't find anything of note in his room. Neat and tidy, as I recall. Worried friends, but nothing concrete. I didn't see any reason to suspect a crime."

"Nothing that made you hesitate?"

He thought for a while.

"I don't think so. Possibly also because he was who he was."

"Bosnian?"

"I thought maybe he'd just gone home, or to a third country. That maybe he was a fighter, that he'd given false information; I probably wasn't really thinking at all. It was a rough period, there'd been a double murder of an old couple, that's what everyone was focused on. You know how many refugees go missing every year, either leaving the country or just living in the shadows?"

"But Damir had papers, he wasn't at risk of deportation. He'd become a Swedish citizen. He was in education, spoke fluent Swedish; he'd chosen to stay."

"You're right." The pot started whistling. Bosse took it off the heat, let it stand for a while to allow the grounds to sink. "I followed my gut, and that was wrong. Looking back now, I should've given it another go."

"Do you remember anyone mentioning Sanna Melin?"

"Not by name," he said. "But I think one of his college friends said that Damir had been having trouble with a girl, someone who wouldn't leave him alone. That he was in love with the new girlfriend, but it was tricky. Hurting someone's feelings. He couldn't quite manage it."

"There was nothing about any of that in the report."

"Because it sounded like your typical relationship problems, the kind of thing all young people go through," said Bosse Ring, filling two cups. "I'm sure I would've reacted differently if it was a girl who'd gone missing, who was having trouble with her ex. I made a huge mistake."

Eira closed the file of notes, there was nothing else to say. The coffee was almost too hot, but she gulped it down.

"Is there anywhere I can get a phone signal nearby?"

"And you don't want to climb up on the roof?"

"Rather not."

"Then we'll have to go down to the crossroads, it usually works there."

Bosse Ring pulled on a jacket. He was already wearing his shoes, and he didn't bother locking the door behind them. Instead he made his way over to Eira's car, which was parked at an angle on the grass.

"You're coming, are you?" said Eira. "I thought you liked the freedom of being disconnected, of not having people call you constantly."

He had said something along those lines, that it had only taken a month or two before he no longer missed any of it.

Before he started listening to the birds and that kind of thing instead. The poem of the day on the radio. The wind's never-ending battle against the treetops.

Thinking about getting a cat, and so on.

He got into the passenger seat, called out as they approached the right spot. There were already two people there, phones raised in the air. Their screens glowed in the dusk.

"It's one way of seeing other people," said Bosse Ring.

A moment later, Eira's phone began serenading her with missed calls. Silje had left several messages.

Where the hell are you?

They've found her car.

Check your emails.

She had sent the footage from the speed camera. Eira linked her phone to her computer, a larger image.

The camera had caught the Škoda on the E4, making its way up onto the High Coast Bridge. Six days earlier, at ten thirty in the morning. Sanna Melin was going way over the speed limit, at 130 kilometers per hour. It was an open-and-shut case of speeding, the kind that would see her lose her license.

There was a glimpse of the driver. Eira zoomed in.

A heart doesn't just stop, not like that. It keeps on beating.

The image quality was poor, but for the traffic police it was probably good enough. They simply needed to know whether it was the owner of the car who was driving or not. You couldn't convict someone of speeding with only the car as proof.

Sanna Melin was suspected of many crimes, but speeding was not one of them. It wasn't her behind the wheel.

Eira stared at the image as she felt herself sinking. Plummeting into the darkness inside herself, into a place where there was no sound and no world around her.

His sharp jaw and familiar features, his graying hair. His mouth was open, caught midconversation. His eyes were focused up ahead, the same gaze that made Eira feel at once strong and small, towards the bridge, the north. Where were they going?

She hadn't heard Bosse Ring get back into the car, and jumped when she noticed him beside her.

"Look," she said, turning the screen towards him.

"Christ," he muttered, followed by a string of expletives, so loud that the other people turned to look. "Where are they?"

"Heading north on the E4," said Eira. "Over the High Coast Bridge."

"And then?"

"Nothing."

"Petrol stations?"

"They haven't had time to check the footage from every one in Norrland, but there's nothing on her card after this, she hasn't filled up the tank."

"And when was this?" The question was as much to himself as to Eira; the answer was right there in front of them.

That morning, some thirty or so minutes after Sanna Melin checked out of Stadt.

The day after the last known sighting of GG, when he followed her down the stairs in the hotel.

Or was it the other way around, was she following him?

Eira's mind was racing, thoughts barreling around without any guidance or purpose. Had they gone back to her room? She didn't want to think about it. Where were they going? Had he tricked Sanna Melin, or had she tricked him?

Was he a complete idiot?

Eira couldn't manage anything other than sending a text message to Silje, explaining why she had been out of reach. Nothing important to report, speak later.

She fumbled for some sort of coherent thought. What could she do? Set off along the E4, looking for them on every turnoff in Norrland? How long would that take? Half of Sweden stretched out to the north of the High Coast Bridge, an area the size of France or Italy, countless small roads without a single traffic camera on them. And forest, never-ending forest.

What she should do was write up her report from the care home. It just seemed so pointless.

Bosse Ring had got out of the car again and was pacing back and forth with his phone like a divining rod, raised to the wilderness surrounding them. A mast in the distance somewhere, a weak signal. Until recently there had been a fixed telephone line to Myckelgensjö, for a hundred years or so, but Telia had ripped it out.

Eira put in one earbud. Dutifulness, her grandfather would have called it, the virtue of keeping one's promises. Listening to the conversation and the long silences, writing down a confused old woman's statement. She managed to get lost in it for a short while. Back to Offer, to the early 1950s.

If Lilly Melin had been mentally ill, that could explain the divorce. It took a little more than an absence of love back then. A cousin's aunt had been granted a quick divorce on grounds of infidelity, and Eira's mother had spoken about it with dismay. Not over the infidelity, but over the fact that it was left to the courts to decide whether a person was free or not.

There was a soft thud on the recording when Lilly Melin put the photograph of her daughter to one side. What had happened to her in all this, three-year-old Birgitta?

Eira called Janne Bäcklund in Sollefteå.

"Why didn't you mention that you have a sister?"

"I have two," he said.

"Three."

He didn't speak for a few seconds.

"OK, OK," he said. "I see what you're getting at. But I've never met her. Not as far as I know, anyway—we could've bumped into each other on the street. When I was a kid I didn't even know Dad had another child."

"How did you find out?"

"An argument at home. Mum was ranting and raving, Dad had been seeing the girl in secret. She wanted to know whether he still had anything to do with her mother, accusing him of all sorts of things a young boy doesn't want to hear, telling him to take care of his real family first. What does this have to do with anything?"

Bosse Ring was back in the passenger seat. Eira saved her document. She had managed to get most of it down, hadn't left it floating in the ether like GG.

"There's always a logic," he said.

"What do you mean?"

"We like to think that a madman's world is irrational, but even a madman wants to create order." He pinched a wad of tobacco between his fingers. "It wasn't fate that chose these crime scenes; this woman didn't just go trudging about in the woods at random."

"I know," said Eira. As though she hadn't already thought of that, during every waking moment—sleeping, too; wandering through those damned houses at night, constantly thinking about places GG could have chosen to go to. "The house in Offer belonged to her relatives, and in Malmberget it was Mikael Ingmarsson's childhood home. As far as I know they've already searched everywhere GG has ever cared about—the island in the archipelago where he went as a child, his ex-wife's parents' summerhouse . . ."

"And hotels are hardly relevant anymore," Bosse continued. "She probably knows we're onto her, otherwise she wouldn't have left her apartment."

"So what are you getting at?"

"Lilly Melin had a brother."

"I know, they said so at the home, but he died last spring."

Bosse pushed the tobacco beneath his lip, wiped his fingers on his trouser leg.

"I called the Tax Authority, checked with the National Land Survey, that sort of thing. His estate hasn't been fully settled yet. The old bloke was registered at a rented flat in Örnsköldsvik, so that's gone back to the owners, but the cabin he owned hasn't been sold. It's listed in the inventory."

"Where is it?" asked Eira, starting the engine.

"By a lake north of Gålberget, near the Västerbotten county line."

One of the neighbors leapt out of the way as she swerved across the road.

"Aren't you meant to be on leave?" she asked.

It wasn't far as the crow flies, but on the narrow country roads snaking between lakes and hills, it took them over an hour.

The lake wasn't named on the map, a forest tarn with dark waters. A few squares marked the cabins set back among the trees.

"Did you call the prosecutor?" Eira asked as soon as she knew which way to drive.

"I know Berents. She does everything by the book," said Bosse Ring. "I'm not technically on duty, which means that in practice you're on your own. Do you really think she'd let us go in? Unarmed? You are unarmed, aren't you?"

Her gun was back at the station in Kramfors, locked in a cabinet.

"I don't give a damn if they fire me," he said. "Just tell them I forced you. No one's closer than us."

They pulled over on a forest track. According to the Land Survey records, the cabin was some five hundred meters up ahead.

"Should we keep driving?"

"Better to walk."

Eira left her car blocking the road, an obstacle in case anyone tried to escape. Making any sort of intervention was out of the question, they were agreed on that. They would simply approach the cabin and check, from a distance, whether there was anything to see.

"That way, if it turns out to be a dead end, we haven't wasted resources for hours," said Bosse.

They set off along the track, each carrying a torch. Below them, the cabins sat in a sparse row, embedded in the forest around them. Eira had been to cabins like this in the past, often by small fishing lakes. Simple, single-story wooden buildings from a time when people were encouraged to get out into nature and lead healthy, outdoor lives. She remembered visiting a cousin up by Saltsjön every summer, lighting candles and fires around the lake to celebrate the end of the season before they closed up for the winter.

There was nothing to suggest that anyone was still out here now, in November. The boats were all lined up beneath tarpaulins, the cabins dark in their winter slumber. On the other side of the lake, a tawny owl hooted.

They left the trail and slowly made their way towards the cabin, hidden from view behind the spruce trees. Bosse Ring checked the terrain against the map; it was the fifth cabin. He had the ability to move without making a sound, light footsteps. The owl flapped from treetop to treetop, but otherwise the forest around them was still, not a single breath of air. Even the trees seemed to have stopped their usual whispering.

Eira switched off her torch, needed to give her eyes time to get used to the darkness. The moon hadn't yet risen.

"Can you see anything?" He crouched down beside her in the moss.

Eira pointed. A faint hint of light on the far side of the last cabin. Maybe it was the moon on its way up, maybe it was all in her mind.

"Let's go around," Bosse Ring whispered.

They moved on all fours, slowly feeling their way forward. Twigs broke, Eira's hand sank into an anthill. She felt the needles sting her palms, the sleepy, slow ants on her skin. She paused to shake them off.

Bosse Ring was ahead of her, and he made the sign. She could only just make out his hand. There, forwards, then off to the right. Eira crawled up alongside him, and now she could see it too: the narrow chink of light spilling from one of the windows, possibly around the edge of a blind. It painted a bright path through the garden, where there was a small scrap of lawn. An outhouse at the treeline. Eira heard her colleague take a deep breath, felt a hand on her arm, and then she saw what he saw.

The car.

She couldn't make out the color, only the dull sheen of the metal. Bosse Ring slowly backed up among the trees at their most dense and gestured for her to send a message.

He wasn't on duty, but he had taken charge—and with every right: he had thirty years' more experience than her, and Eira was grateful for that. Keeping her phone hidden among the ferns to minimize the risk of anyone spotting its glow from the cabin, she wrote a brief update for Nora Berents and Silje. There was some coverage, and the message sent.

They waited. Still no movement by the cabin.

Eira could feel the chill through her clothes, and she shuffled to one side and found a rock to sit on instead of the damp moss. There was a touch of frost in the air, and she folded her arms, pushed her hands deep into her armpits—the warmest part of the body, other than between the legs. She guessed the temperature must be somewhere around zero, but it would quickly drop.

A responding unit had just left Örnsköldsvik. That meant over an hour, at least an hour and a half.

Bosse Ring groaned and dragged himself up, moved a few meters back. Eira heard the sound of a zip, a stream of urine. The smell mixed with the earth and the moss, the decay.

He crouched down behind her.

"You think he's in there?"

How could she answer that? He probably wasn't even expecting an answer. Just needed to get it out.

"There's no basement," Eira whispered back.

"How can you tell?"

"Trust me."

The cabins were for ordinary workers, that was the point. Often self-built, according to standard plans, which meant no expensive groundwork; they had only ever been meant for summer use. They were typically constructed on forest slopes like this, joists resting on the granite bedrock.

No excavations, no basements.

Eira was shivering.

"Unless there's an earth cellar."

"Let's go in," he hissed.

"Unarmed?"

The moon had risen above the forest on the other side of the lake.

"You do what you think best," he said. "I don't have the right to give you orders."

Before Eira had time to think or make any decisions, Bosse Ring was on the move, branches breaking underfoot. She heard him reach the track. Firmer ground.

Now in full view, he approached the cabin. The reflection of the moon painted a silvery trail across the lake, its glow spilling in between the trees where she was standing.

The light went out in the window.

Eira couldn't stand still any longer. She aimed for the outhouse, moving in a quick yet silent arc to avoid being seen. She paused beside the narrow wooden building, the stench of the toilet pail seeping out to where she was standing. Bosse Ring had almost reached the porch, a dark figure in the shadows cast by the moonlight. He seemed to hesitate, or possibly steel himself.

Then he stepped up onto the porch and vanished from sight.

The car was only a few meters away. Colors became warped in the moonlight, but she could see the emblem glittering. A Škoda.

Eira crouched down behind it.

Bosse's knock echoed through the forest, carrying across the lake. The light came on outside.

A door opened.

She heard her colleague's voice. He was lost, he said, wanted to know how far it was to the next village. A torrent of words about nightfall taking him by surprise while he was out on the lake, his phone battery running out; he'd been wandering around for hours now.

Could he borrow her phone?

Eira held her breath, listened for the reply. She couldn't make out any words, but the voice was bright and soft.

Then the door closed. She should be able to hear her colleague's footsteps on the porch now.

Something stirred in the brushwood, a bird flapped up into the air.

Twenty seconds. Thirty.

He must have gone in.

Another light came on inside, flooding out through several windows. Eira tried briefly to catch sight of them inside, to make out their movements and work out exactly where they were. Then she started running. Across the lawn, towards the gable end of the building. Pressed up against the wall, she made her way over to one of the illuminated windows, pausing right beside it. She could hear his faint voice inside. It sounded conversational, no hint of agitation, no arguing.

Right then, there was a louder sound, a bang of some kind. Someone cried out, the voice shrill. It was the woman. Another thud. A few quick steps and Eira was on the porch. She crossed it in two strides and tore open the door just as Bosse Ring pulled the woman to the floor.

He twisted her arm behind her back, pressed his knee to her spine. Her legs kicked and she cried out. No words, just noise.

"Where is he?" Bosse Ring barked.

"Let go of me, you bastard!"

"You know who I'm talking about. Georg Georgsson, a detective with Sundsvall Police. He was last seen driving your car, which is now parked outside, so tell me where the hell he is."

Eira could hear the anger in his voice. He raised his free hand, fist clenched.

"Stop!" she shouted.

He froze. Bosse Ring turned to face her, and she saw something wild in his eyes; he hadn't heard her come in.

"Police," said Eira, taking out her ID and angling it so that the woman could see. Her colleague was still pinning her down, and she placed a hand on his arm, tried to hold his eye. Calm down. Don't do it. For God's sake, Bosse.

"Sanna Melin," she said. "I'm arresting you on suspicion of murder and kidnapping." There were other crimes too, but none of them came to mind.

"Get him off me," the woman whimpered.

Bosse Ring had regained control of himself. He lifted his knee from her spine, but maintained his grip on the arm behind her back, let her up. The suspect didn't put up any resistance, just slumped onto one of the wooden chairs like a rag doll.

"Thank you," she whispered, massaging her arm. Her hair hung forward over her face. She looked so harmless, like any other woman.

They weren't supposed to interview someone suspected of such a serious crime. Instead they were meant to inform her of her right to a lawyer. If she confessed to anything, they had to interrupt her and prevent her from saying any more until the lawyer arrived.

"Answer the question," Eira said slowly.

"What question?"

She was still gripping her ID tight. The rage she had seen in Bosse Ring was also simmering inside her.

"You heard. Georg Georgsson. Where is he?"

Sanna Melin's face was pale and oddly blank, her gaze steady.

"I don't know who you're talking about."

It took almost an hour for the first car to arrive. They had to keep watch over the suspect, which meant they couldn't leave the room, but they did open a window to get some fresh air, quickly closing it again to avoid getting too cold. At just over thirty square meters, the cabin was claustrophobic. A dining table and chairs, a sofa and TV, bookshelves full of cheap American thrillers.

Searching the place took almost no time at all.

"Don't let her fool you," Bosse Ring had whispered as they stood in the doorway, keeping an eye on Sanna Melin. "She's stronger than she looks."

"What happened before I came in?" asked Eira.

"She turned her back to me. Going to get her phone, she said, so I could call someone. But there was something about the way she moved. My mind went to the knife drawer."

They had feigned friendliness, offering her both tea and a glass of water. She took the water.

"Thanks very much, but would you mind letting me go now?"

"As soon as you tell us where he is," Bosse Ring lied.

"I don't know anyone by that name."

In the end they saw torchlights dancing down the forest track, their colleagues running towards them. Eira's car was still blocking the road, and they had been forced to abandon theirs and approach on foot.

While one of them ran back with Eira's keys, the other officer handcuffed Sanna Melin. The patrol car soon came bouncing over to the cabin.

Eira stepped outside to call the prosecutor. Forensics were on their way, an air ambulance on standby in Umeå.

By the time she got back, Sanna Melin was in the back of the patrol car. The light inside illuminated her blank face, completely void of all emotion.

"We need to borrow some spotlights to search the area," said Eira.

"Do you think there's anyone else here?"

"We don't know."

Bosse Ring plugged in the lights as the sound of the car's tires on the uneven ground faded into the night. They worked methodically along the edge of the property. No sign of an earth cellar. No other hidden spaces. The outhouse was empty.

"Maybe there's a boathouse?" said Eira.

They made their way down to the lake. A well-trodden path, frozen reeds on the shore. There were a couple of small, upturned boats. Eira looked out over the thin new ice, the forest tarn. They could be frighteningly deep, like pits into times long past. Farther along the shore, she spotted something and turned the light towards it. A jetty, pulled onto dry land.

"Community," she said. "There's usually a sense of belonging in a place like this—people help one another, share all sorts of things. They might have a common storage space somewhere."

Bosse Ring opened the map again, Land Survey entries that led them to the names of the owners. There was slightly more reception down on the shore, but it took them another few minutes to find the owners' contact details.

There was no answer from the first, so Eira moved on to looking up the details of the next property. She heard her colleague asking whether there were any earth cellars in the area, noted the shift in his voice.

Bosse Ring switched his phone to loudspeaker, a man on the other end.

Yes, there was an old earth cellar. It had belonged to the property that stood there before the cabins, though he doubted anyone actually used it—people had fridges nowadays.

"Where?"

Behind the third cabin. To the rear. Maybe thirty meters into the forest, just before the rocky area on the hill.

Eira ran towards the cabin and made her way around the back, slowing down to count her steps. She shone the torch all around. Twenty steps, thirty. She heard Bosse Ring fussing over something, and then the forest lit up, the bright glare of the spotlight. The cable didn't quite stretch far enough.

There was the rocky spot. And just in front of it, a slight rise, barely noticeable. It could easily be mistaken for a natural feature of the landscape, but it was made of brick, the roof covered in grass and fallen leaves. At the front, an old wooden door. A large iron nail, slightly bent, was jamming the lock. Eira gave the door a shove with her shoulder, knocking the nail out. They didn't speak, but Bosse was right behind her. The hinges creaked and groaned.

Something dark brushed past Eira's cheek, and she cried out, bumping into her colleague.

"Fucking bats," Bosse Ring muttered.

The scent of earth. Something dull and old. He angled the light inside. A few lopsided shelves. Cans, empty bottles. But otherwise, the cellar was empty.

"Damn it."

Eira dropped to her knees.

"I really thought . . ."

Her voice gave way. There was nothing else to say.

"This is madness," said Bosse Ring. "What the hell are we playing at? GG can be an idiot sometimes, but not this bad."

Eira wiped something from her eye, whatever it was.

"She could've been armed," she said. "Threatened him. We've got no fucking idea what happened."

"Did you see a weapon?"

"She could've dumped it somewhere."

The door was wide open when they got back to cabin number five. Eira found another heater, and they sat down in the warming room to wait for the forensic technicians. They had already contaminated the space, so there wasn't much hope of finding anything there. It was the car that really mattered, the red Škoda brooding between the trees.

Sanna Melin should be in custody now, at least if they had taken her to Örnsköldsvik rather than driving straight to Sundsvall. Maybe they had. Either way, it would probably be morning by the time her lawyer showed up and they could really start interrogating her.

An endless night.

"Thanks," said Eira, taking the cup of tea Bosse held out to her. She was chilled to the bone, hadn't noticed until now. "Thanks for coming with me."

"Do you think this bread counts as evidence?"

Bosse Ring buttered a few slices and sat down at the other end of the daybed. Eira's mind whirred in the silence: was there anything they could have done differently, anything they had missed? She replayed the evening's events over and over again in her head.

"Did you know I was a boxer at one point in time?" he said. "At the Linnea Club in Södermalm. More or less legendary."

"Yes," said Eira. Everyone knew. His crooked nose betrayed him.

"I'm going to tell the truth about what happened. That I lied my way in and then wrestled her to the ground, that I came close to hitting her. It could easily have ended badly. Don't even think about lying for me."

"OK," she said.

"That would really mess up the case."

"I said OK."

"OK."

He ate his two slices of bread, both thick with butter. Eira took off her shoes and raised her feet to the radiator. Something rustled in the forest outside. A fox, possibly the owl again, nocturnal hunters. The silence took over once more.

"I don't have any issue spending time on my own," he continued. "I've been living like this since things went to pot the first time, just never had the energy to try again, you know? I don't spend a lot of time with friends, don't have a gang of guys to drink and curse life's unfairness with." He gazed out of the window. In the glare of the light bulb, all she could see was a reflection of the room, themselves. "I guess work was my gang, GG was my guy."

Eira wanted to say something, but she also felt reluctant. The moment passed. Bosse Ring got up and moved into the small kitchen nook. She heard him rummaging through the cupboards.

"I'll be damned, Lilly's brother died and left his schnapps." He pulled the cork from the bottle and sniffed the contents, read the handwritten label. "St.-John's-wort. Not bad stuff."

"I've heard that was used to treat depression in the past," said Eira.

"Do we agree that you're driving?"

The room at the station in Kramfors had never been so infuriatingly quiet. Time had never felt so slow but pressing.

"I'm innocent."

Eira read the few short lines again and again, as though something might miraculously jump out at her from the brief, strictly legal text.

An interrogation room in Sundsvall, late the night before. Sanna Melin had been read her rights, as required ahead of the initial interview. She had been informed of her right to a lawyer and of the charges that had been filed against her, a long list comprising murder, kidnapping, false imprisonment, another murder—or, in the alternative, manslaughter. And then a few more points, which seemed to grab Eira's gaze like flies to flypaper:

The kidnapping or, in the alternative, false imprisonment of Georg Georgsson.

The degree of suspicion was lowest there. "Reasonable grounds to suspect," was the term, rather than reasonable grounds to believe, as in the other two cases. When it came to GG, they had next to nothing. Vague witness statements, an image from a traffic camera.

Eight days of silence.

Seeing it in writing did something to Eira. Perhaps that was why she kept reading it again and again. She needed to achieve distance, to find enough professional objectivity to carry her through, but all she had was anger and a degree of fear that frightened her. Fear was something she had never quite learned to deal with, or maybe she had, a long time ago: learned that the only thing that helped was to act, to get to grips with things. She wasn't afraid of the dark, for example—she had been born in darkness, taken her first steps in darkness. It was the fear itself that was the real threat, of losing control and becoming weak.

As though everything would fall apart if that happened.

She wished that Bosse Ring had come back to Kramfors with her, that he had broken his leave of absence rather than insisting on being dropped off in Örnsköldsvik in the middle of the night, so he could be on the first bus back to Myckelgensjö.

"Is there anything you would like to say, with regards to the charges?"

The last question in the transcript, once the suspect knew what she was accused of.

"I'm innocent," Sanna Melin repeated.

That was her response to every point.

Innocent.

Over in Sundsvall, the interview with Sanna Melin had resumed an hour or so earlier, in the presence of a lawyer this time.

Eira grabbed a cup of coffee that tasted like crap. There was nothing wrong with the coffee; it was her. She hated that she was stuck in Kramfors, on the fringes of everything.

When reception called to let her know she had a visitor, Eira gathered up the photographs of women around age forty. She tracked down August on the way, so there would be two of them present.

The witness, Jens Boija, had been shown into an interview room. He was sitting down, nervously picking at the edge of the table with his nail.

"Why did I have to come all the way down here? Couldn't you just show me the pictures on FaceTime? I don't know what era you people live in; shouldn't the police be a bit more tech savvy?"

Eira considered giving him a lecture on legal certainty, but decided against it.

"We'd like you to take a look at these images," she said, setting them down in front of him. "Do you recognize anyone here?"

"What if I point out the wrong person?" he asked, flicking back and forth through them. "What happens then? I don't want to ruin someone's life."

"Have another look," said August.

In the end, he settled on two photographs. One was an unknown woman, the other Sanna Melin, in profile. Her blank expression was broadly the same as in her old passport.

"It was her," said Jens Boija.

"What was?"

"Who I saw in the woods with the guy who died."

"Are you sure?" Eira asked, keeping her voice neutral. "You said you only saw her from a distance."

"Yeah, can I go now?"

"Yes, you only saw her from a distance or yes, it's her?"

"It's her."

Eira asked August to escort Boija down to reception while she went straight back to her office to let the prosecutor know that their witness had picked out Sanna Melin.

That meant another witness statement for the lead interviewer to use against her, to bring the case home.

They also had her fingerprints from the abandoned house, and the ornithologist was on his way to the station, due to arrive in thirty minutes or so. The net was closing in. They had managed to place Sanna Melin at the scene of the crime, that was the key thing. What was it GG had said?

Just show me someone who has actually been in Boteå Parish.

We're doing that now, she thought. We're doing it too late.

What else did they have?

Eira found herself thinking about the witness statement she had never managed to find, from the woman who had been with Hans Runne in Stadt.

Why hadn't she taken that any further?

Because she hadn't found a single mention of any such statement, no tip that had been called in. It was something she thought GG had mentioned during a fragmented telephone conversation. She had thought maybe she was simply mistaken, though she could now recall the conversation in detail, could remember exactly where she had been standing in the corridor.

It wasn't him she had doubted, it was herself.

Always herself.

"I'm glad you called," said Silje when she eventually picked up. "You don't know how we can bring back torture as an interrogation method, do you?"

"Is she still innocent?"

"She admits to being in the house with Hans Runne, but claims she has no idea what happened once she left. He wanted to stay, she says. Amazing that the lock on the basement door could have jammed, but it is an old house."

"Her fingerprints were only on the bureau," said Eira, feeling her confidence start to wane. "The witnesses only saw her outside."

The ornithologist had now been to the station and had picked out Sanna Melin as the woman he bumped into in the forest.

"She's smart," said Silje. "She makes only the slightest adjustments to the story whenever she needs to."

"And Damir?"

"An argument. He attacked her, and the knife slipped. Her lawyer might be able to talk it down to manslaughter and preventing the lawful burial of a body." Silje hadn't been in the room herself, but she had been allowed to listen in on the interview. "She says she left Mikael Ingmarsson because he was being an idiot. How could she have known that the door locked behind her?"

"And GG?"

A brief pause as her colleague took a deep breath. Eira knew she didn't have good news. If she did, she would have mentioned it right away.

"She's never met him," said Silje. "Can't understand how he ended up in her car. Are the police really allowed to borrow people's cars like that? Her lawyer will probably question whether it's really him in the picture. You sure you don't have any idea about the whole torture thing?"

The chair took Eira's weight as she slumped down onto it, but she felt herself continue to sink. They still hadn't found Sanna Melin's mobile phone, and she didn't have a contract registered in her name. Nor had they found GG's fingerprints anywhere—not in the cabin, not in the Škoda. It had been cleaned, wiped down.

Silje's voice was distant, in a reality that was rapidly losing all definition.

"What did you want, by the way?" she asked.

"What?"

"You called me. Seven times, it looks like, while I was in various meetings."

"I think they might have met before," said Eira.

She told her colleague about the mysterious witness, the woman who supposedly met Hans Runne at Stadt. Eira had gone over and over it as she tried to call, becoming increasingly convinced that she had heard GG right.

"But the strange thing is that there's no mention of this woman anywhere. I can't find any telephone tips, no other witnesses mentioning her."

"So what are you thinking?"

"That she might have got in touch herself," said Eira. "Gone straight to GG. That she'd seen him somewhere, knew who he was."

"To challenge him?" said Silje.

"Or give her version of events. Sanna Melin has been to Stadt plenty of times, the staff know her there. She must have realized that someone might have seen her with Runne. Maybe she gave GG a false statement, something that convinced him she wasn't connected. She could have given him a completely different name."

"GG still should have made a record of it."

"But what if he didn't?"

"So he goes out to Stadt that evening." Silje was thinking aloud. "He's already been drinking whisky, we know that, and she's there. She recognizes him. Does that turn her on, the fact he's a cop? And then GG recognizes her, they start talking."

"He seemed confused somehow, that evening," said Eira. "I couldn't really understand why he'd come to my place. He seemed low, almost like he was depressed."

"A woman's embrace?"

She didn't speak. Silje's words were left hanging in the air. A feeling she'd had, but never wanted to admit.

Was that why he had come over?

Eira cleared her throat.

"If this is right," she said, "then they might be able to find her number among all the calls from prepaid SIMs on his phone. That day, or the day before."

She gave her colleague the date. The tightness in her throat was still lingering.

"I'll look into it," said Silje, ending the call.

Tracing a prepaid SIM wasn't easy, but was not impossible. If they managed to narrow down the provider they should be able to follow the signal, which would tell them where Sanna Melin had been.

It could tell them about routes, directions.

Eira's eyes were drawn to the map on the wall, to the huge expanse of land to the north of the High Coast Bridge.

They had checked every single speed camera in the region by now, as well as every petrol station with CCTV all the way up to the border with Finland. Several of them no longer took cash payments. GG hadn't used his card anywhere, and nor had the suspect; it was a mystery where the fresh bread in the cabin had come from.

Her grandmother, thought Eira, immediately sending an email to one of the officers working on that kind of thing. Have we checked Lilly Melin's bank accounts?

She spent a long time standing in front of the map.

Norrland and its endless forests, its countless small roads. The air in the room felt suffocating.

What could make a police officer break the speed limit, she wondered, if the person he was looking for was in the car with him? And why would he then slow down?

A woman's embrace.

She drove past Lunde and continued towards the High Coast Bridge. Its sky-high pillars reached for the stars like the gates to a temple, dotted with glittering lights. Down below her, the river disappeared, opening out into the sea.

When she reached the other side, she turned off and pulled over.

The traffic flowed on to the north. The emptiness took over. Pine forests and brackish water, the High Coast, a never-ending darkness in which they couldn't make out a single trace.

The wind tugged at her hair as she got out of the car.

A woman's embrace.

We're all idiots, thought Eira. In certain situations, we are.

Why would GG have suspected anything? The prospect of a female perpetrator hadn't even crossed their minds at the time. If Sanna Melin was just a woman he met in a bar and vaguely recognized, possibly only enough for his gaze to pick her out.

And her?

If Eira's hunch was correct and they had previously met, then Sanna Melin knew exactly who came into Stadt that evening, already pretty drunk. She had contacted him once before.

The branches whipped against one another in the breeze. The cold air followed her as she got back into the car. Eira dug out the interview with Mikael Ingmarsson, what was it he said?

She seemed nice somehow, harmless.

There were no strings, it was easy.

Did you want it easy, GG?

Eira could understand that. She really could. Wasn't easy precisely what she had been looking for lately, one source of love that placed no demands on her and another that was more an old memory than anything, barely existing in the present?

She forced herself to imagine how his night might have gone.

A shabby, faded hotel room with wall-to-wall carpets and synthetic sheets, that was how she pictured it.

At once sweaty and cold, void of all emotion.

That kind of night, and then the following morning.

Where had he wanted to go then?

Clearly not to work, nor to his neglected apartment in Sundsvall. GG hadn't even gone back to the police apartment a few blocks away to pick up his phone.

It was a spur-of-the-moment decision, she thought.

Seize the day, run off with me. Away from here, let's forget reality, just you and me, we can go out to . . . where?

Into the forest, up into the mountains, to an art gallery in Umeå, out to sea?

Eira struggled to imagine an accountant in that kind of situation, but the line of thought itself felt realistic.

Particularly the scenario involving the sea.

She put the car into gear and pulled back out onto the E4.

Eira herself had no real connection to the sea. To her, it existed only as something nearby, a faint saltiness that made its way upriver, but GG had talked about the archipelago that day on his balcony. She thought she could remember a hint of longing, a melancholy over something he had lost, his childhood, summer holidays, whatever it was.

The exit for Nordingrå was the first to appear. Deep lakes and steep hillsides, houses that had been shut up for winter.

Signs illuminated in the headlights of her car.

She couldn't just drive around looking for him, that was impossible. The High Coast stretched out for over eighty kilometers as the crow flies, full of the elevations that gave it its name, inlets and fishing villages and rocky beaches. She considered calling one of her colleagues, but quickly realized that she wasn't the first to think along these lines. What were they going to do, comb the entire region with sniffer dogs?

Eira drove slowly on as the hills grew higher around her. She passed the house where Magnus's last girlfriend lived. The lights were on. The woman ran a small art gallery out of her barn, but it was shuttered up right now. Eira wondered whether she wrote to him. She hoped so, that he had someone else who cared about him, who loved him. She briefly considered pulling over and knocking. Maybe the woman would be able to manage what Eira had been unable to: convincing Magnus to change his statement and take back his confession, to try to regain his freedom.

There was a sign pointing to Barsta, one of the fishing villages popular with tourists, and to Högbonden Lighthouse, on a small island off the coast.

An image of the lighthouse came to her, perched high on the rocks above a violent sea. Eira was sure she had never been there, she had never visited a single lighthouse in her life. It wasn't that kind of memory, either; not something she had experienced herself. It was something she had seen, and recently. A painting, probably on the wall in her mother's care home. The corridor and dining room were full of local images.

She slammed on the brakes.

The pastel tones on the walls were similar, but they weren't in her mother's home. They were in Lilly Melin's room. The paintings in beautiful frames. A king, a lighthouse, a ship on a stormy sea.

Eira could see headlights approaching from behind, so she pulled onto the verge and searched for a picture of Högbonden Lighthouse. There, that was exactly what it had looked like.

A white lighthouse on top of a cliff, surrounded by water.

Wasn't that how most lighthouses looked?

Eira dug out the phone number for the care home in Själevad and asked to speak to the manager, who wasn't on duty.

"Whether Lilly has ever mentioned a lighthouse?" The nurse who picked up the phone seemed confused by Eira's question.

"Or anywhere else on the coast," Eira pressed her. "I noticed the paintings on her walls, and I know that people often keep hold of the things that mean most to them when they move."

"I think I need to check with my boss whether . . ."

"I can always call the prosecutor and try to get a written order, but I'm sure you've read the papers. You know what this is about, and you probably also realize that we don't have any time to lose."

It was out there now. A HIGH-PROFILE DETECTIVE, that was how they described him, with links to the murder investigation. MISSING.

"I think you can see the difference between any information about Lilly's medical condition," Eira continued, speaking slowly though she felt like screaming, "and the question of whether a lighthouse has ever been important to her."

"But I don't know if she's ever mentioned it," the girl replied. She sounded young. "Do you want me to go and ask her?"

Eira's conversation with the old woman was still fresh in her mind, and she knew that question could lead anywhere.

"Or should I ask my colleagues, maybe they . . ."

The road had narrowed, snaking onwards. A lake glittered and was gone. She was driving slightly too fast.

"There might be something written down," she said. Right then, it came to her: "A life story?" The dense pages in which she had tried to summarize her mother's life. Everything she had been, her childhood and youth, what kind of music she liked; a desperate attempt to make the staff see her as the person she once was.

"Didn't Lilly's relatives write anything like that when she moved in?"

"I'm sorry, but I haven't had time to read it yet," said the nurse. "We're supposed to, but there's been a lot of turnover here, and I'm pretty new."

"Could you have a look now?"

"OK, give me a minute."

It wasn't a minute, it was an eternity, and Eira had time to reach the fishing village, slow down, and start looking for the road down to the harbor.

The nurse sounded short of breath when she came back.

"I found the folder in her room. It was *her* who wrote it."

"Lilly?"

"No, the woman they think did all that stuff. Sanna, her granddaughter."

"That makes it evidence in a murder investigation," said Eira. "And we can seize it in the same way we would during a raid."

"Uff."

The nurse didn't ask any more questions, perhaps her curiosity was too great. As the car rolled slowly past mostly dark houses, down towards the fishing huts in Barsta, Eira asked her to skim through the text and read aloud if she found anything relevant.

"Högbonden!" she heard the girl shout down the line. "That's a lighthouse, isn't it? Yeah, it is, it says so right here!"

A lone caravan was parked in the small campsite, the restaurant boarded up for the winter. Eira wound down the side window and breathed in the sharp scent of seaweed and salty air. She knew the island was out there in the darkness somewhere, but she couldn't see it. Accompanied by the sound of waves rolling in to shore, she heard Lilly Melin's story.

In 1945, the summer after the end of the war, she found work in the kitchen at Högbonden Lighthouse. Lilly was seventeen at the time. The island could be quite lively back then. There were a lot of staff, and it was hard work. Lilly's duties included cleaning and washing up, but she also did simple tasks in the kitchen, like peeling potatoes.

Guests came to stay in the lighthouse keeper's house from time to time. Once, a military ship docked and the soldiers wanted to be fed, even though their arrival was unexpected. Lilly was asked to help serve them, and that was how she met the man who would go on to become her husband.

The language sounded like an old school essay, old-fashioned yet childish somehow. Perhaps Sanna Melin had fallen into her grandmother's tone of voice, replicating the way she had been told the story as a girl.

"Do you want me to go on?"

"Go on."

Lilly stayed at Högbonden until 1951, when she got married. She took me and my mother there several times, to show us the lighthouse and tell us about that time in her life. Lilly said that she felt free there. She liked being by the sea, but she also enjoyed the sense of community. She has often said that those were the happiest years of her youth.

The lighthouse had been automated for more than half a century, which meant that the island was now uninhabited. The boat that usually took the tourists and bird-watchers out there was moored at the very end of the jetty. It ran only one trip a day during the winter season, but Eira found the captain's phone number on a handwritten sign.

She called Silje, too, but went straight through to voice mail.

"I'm in Barsta," she shouted over the wind and the waves, the creaking of the jetty and the moorings. "Her grandmother used to take her to Högbonden Lighthouse. I'm going to check it out."

Not long later, she heard a quad bike approaching.

The captain, whose body was hidden beneath layers of fleece and waterproof fabric, shook his head when she showed him the photographs.

"I would've remembered them, what with so few people going out there in November."

"Is there anyone else who runs people out to the island?"

"Not regularly, there isn't."

Eira didn't ask how much a special trip would cost, and nor did he bring it up. He just ducked down into the cabin and tossed a lifejacket to her, then started to unmoor the boat.

"How long does it take?"

"No more than ten minutes."

Given how close the island was to the shore, she hadn't been prepared for the violence of the sea. The way the waves would toss the boat around like a toy. The powerful nausea.

"It's better if you stand up," the captain shouted. "But hold on!"

Eira had been planning to call Silje again—someone should check the boat register to see whether Sanna Melin owned a boat they had missed—but it was pointless with the waves raging around her. She gripped the doorframe to the cabin. It would just have to wait until they reached the island, assuming they weren't thrown into the rocks first. She studied the captain. He seemed perfectly calm.

"It's a bit choppy," he shouted over to her. "But it almost always is."

The lanterns on the jetty came into view, the cliffs rising sharply out of the water and blocking the moon high above them. He moored the boat, which was rocking back and forth, rattling ropes and chains.

"Do you want me to wait here?"

"How far is it?" Eira could see the start of a path that snaked off up the hill and then disappeared. The island was densely wooded.

"You'd probably be better off asking how high it is."

"I'd appreciate it if you came with me."

Högbonden was the second-highest lighthouse in the country, he told her as they began climbing the steps that appeared at intervals along the path. And it was on the other side of the island, of course. That was the whole point of a lighthouse: that it shone out onto the open sea.

Guiding the lost into harbor.

The captain had brought a powerful lamp with him, and they were both wearing headlamps. Eira started running, but soon had to slow down. She was in good shape, but the path was just too steep and too long. Eventually she saw the beam of light sweeping across the water on the other side of the island. The sea looked even wilder over there, lashing at the rocks.

One last set of stairs up the rockface. There was a rope pulley system that had been used to carry building materials and food to the lighthouse during its hundred-year history, the captain shouted behind her. In its heyday at the start of the last century, over twenty people lived on the island, but that eventually shrunk to a lone light-house keeper during the last manned years.

The lighthouse keeper's residence now functioned as a youth hostel during the summer months, but otherwise all overnight stays on the island were forbidden.

The wind was blowing from the east, bringing with it the raw chill of the sea.

The lighthouse keeper's residence rose up above them, the light-house itself perched at the very edge of the cliff. The house was bigger than she had expected, with two stories and a basement. There was a freestanding cabin, too. A row of outhouses.

Eira tried the main door. Locked, of course. A set of stairs led down to the basement door. She pounded on it and strained to listen, but couldn't hear anything other than the roaring waves.

"If I owned a place like this," she told the captain, "I'd make sure there was a spare key somewhere. It would be a real pain to come all the way out here and realize you'd left it back on the mainland."

"Do you want me to give them a call?"

"Have you got their number?"

He knew the people who ran the youth hostel, of course. Stupid that she hadn't thought of it sooner. He took shelter from the wind to make the call while Eira did a loop of the house. On the sea side, there were a number of large windows in the basement, which looked like it had been refurbished as a dining hall. She inspected the cabin, also locked, and walked along the row of outhouses, checking the coverage on her phone. No problems there. She sent a message to Silje about the boat, about her being out on the island now.

Back in the yard, she found the captain with the keys in his hand.

They tried the basement door first. The room smelled fresh. There were showers and a laundry room, no locked cupboards, easy access to water and windows; escaping wouldn't have been a problem. Getting off the island would have been trickier, she thought, particularly if you'd left your phone in Härnösand. Easy to get lost in the forest—she had sensed a number of ravines on the way up.

Eira made her way up to the ground floor. Large rooms full of bunkbeds, windows out onto the water, a shared kitchen. Out of sheer habit, she checked the fridge. It was switched off, nothing but a few ketchup bottles and tins inside.

The cabin was also empty. It seemed to serve as a restaurant during the summer months, with huge refrigerators and a dishwasher. The outhouses had been fitted with modern toilets, and she took the opportunity to use one of them.

Over by the cliff, the lighthouse loomed in the darkness. A solid

door with two locks, none of the keys fit. She made her way around
the edge, pressed up against the wall. Stood on tiptoe to peer in
through the lowest windows. The emergency lighting was on inside.

Nothing.

She felt dizzy as she approached the edge.

Eira wanted to believe that she was wrong, that GG hadn't decided to take a trip out to sea, to an island where the rocks dropped
away so suddenly. Anywhere but here.

A simple push.

How high was it? She had seen that detail somewhere, seventy
meters above sea level.

Her mind began to drift to places she didn't want it to drift: realizing that they would have to bring dogs out to the island, launch a
search party. Tomorrow, once the sun came up. But that was almost
twelve hours away, a long November night.

She thought about getting back into the boat, setting off across
the hostile sea.

"What do you reckon?" the captain asked behind her. "There anyone out here?"

Eira couldn't remember his name, the wind was probably blowing
too hard when he introduced himself. Her mind had been elsewhere.
On the dizzying feeling of being onto something, on the right track.

"Are there any other buildings?" she asked.

"Not that I know of. If it was light you could've searched the
caves, but I'm not going down there now."

"There are caves?"

"Yeah, but you'll need a professional with you." He had been enthusiastic at first, at the prospect of being able to help her by doing
what he did best: taking her across the sea, setting out in an emergency. But Eira could see that he had reached his limit.

"You head back," she said. "I'll stay here overnight."

"That's not technically allowed," he said.

"I'm a police officer, we can usually manage to get permission.
We're going to need to launch a search party in the morning, so I
may as well be here."

That wasn't the whole truth. Eira didn't want to get back into his boat, not while the sea was so dark and hostile. But it was more than that: a sense that she couldn't leave the island. A numbing resistance.

"I'll pass on your details," she said. "So you should expect a call. We're going to need your services again in the morning."

"You're not scared of the dark, then?"

"I'm not scared of the dark," said Eira.

She watched as his torchlight bobbed down the hillside. A flash between the trees, and then it was gone.

The rumbling of the waves, a lone seabird's cry.

Left alone, her professional facade came crashing down. The sheer force of it pushed back everything else. Eira dropped to the ground, both hands clawing the gravel.

She had held it back so effectively, hiding it so well from herself, explaining away everything she knew she shouldn't feel. He was her boss, of course she wanted him to notice her; she admired him. Those were emotions that were closely related to love. The way she sometimes found herself watching his hands, still slightly tanned after the summer, a thick ring on his right little finger. Touching something, a phone, a pen, anything. The warmth she had to drag herself away from.

If he was out here somewhere, then at least he wasn't alone.

If they found his body once dawn broke and the beaches came into view, the sheer drops and the jagged rocks, then at least she was here.

It took Eira a while to realize she was shivering.

She got to her feet and headed back into the old lighthouse keeper's residence, turned up the radiator in one of the bedrooms. She found a half bottle of cordial in one of the kitchen cupboards and mixed herself a glass, grabbed a packet of digestive biscuits. Sugar, a quick burst of energy.

She wrote an email to the prosecutor suggesting a dog patrol on the island the next morning, as well as a number of questions to ask Sanna Melin.

She read through the latest updates from the preliminary investigation. They had released Damir Avdic's body, and his sister wanted to fly him back to Sarajevo so that she could lay him to rest beside their parents. The autopsy had confirmed that he died from a single knife wound to the back. The assailant was right-handed, slightly shorter than him, which fit Sanna Melin's description.

Someone had also locked horns with the bank and managed to get hold of Lilly Melin's statements. There were a number of transactions that the ninety-three-year-old simply couldn't have made herself, like a payment at a petrol station in the vicinity of Örnsköldsvik just over a week ago, another at a supermarket.

One of the dates caught Eira's eye. That terrifying, all-important date.

Two hundred and twenty kronor on alcohol at Systembolaget.

The same morning Sanna Melin checked out of Stadt, she had used her grandmother's bank card at the Systembolaget in Härnösand. Two hundred and twenty kronor, that sounded like two bottles of wine—or one, if she had expensive taste. And shortly afterwards, another payment at a supermarket.

Then she got into the car, thought Eira, and GG stepped on the gas.

Eira switched her phone to low-power mode so that it would last through the night. She realized that she needed to do the same, so she opened one of the tins she had found—meat soup—and heated it in the microwave.

The sounds of the sea made their way in. Eira couldn't allow herself to start thinking about the cliffs outside. The drop. The waves crashing in against the rocks.

The seabirds' cries whenever they found something.

Instead she tried to picture the island in the late 1940s, back when it was home to over twenty people. She had seen traces of old tiled stoves in some of the rooms, a modern electric cooker that had replaced the old wood burner. Lilly Melin had worked in the kitchen, just a young girl. Life must have been so hard back then, yet she had experienced such freedom. Perhaps that was simply hindsight talking, a vision of a bright youth that she painted much later, once she knew how her life had turned out and wanted to believe she was made for something else.

Eira thought about the love affair that had begun here on the island, the handsome man in uniform. Perhaps Lilly had found herself pregnant, and he had stepped up to his responsibilities—for a few years at least. Eira tried to imagine the seventeen-year-old girl sweeping around in her apron, standing right there as she did the dishes by hand, peeling potatoes. Hauling water, but from where? Did they have running water then, or did they have to carry it up the hill? Baskets of food, the rope pulley, how economical they must have had to be in such a barren, isolated place. They could hardly have had a refrigerator at the time, not until the fifties, when Electrolux made its grand entrance into every Swedish home—Eira had seen the ads featuring plucky housewives in snug dresses in the magazines her grandmother had saved, one of the many things she had saved. What had they done before then?

She hadn't seen any sign of a cold store in the basement. Eira pulled her down jacket back on, did another loop of the building. No stone cellar, no food store.

The treetops shook and bowed in the wind. An island, cut off from the mainland by an unpredictable sea. They must have stored their food somewhere.

Eira could feel the presence of the cliffs close by. The path leading away from the yard wasn't entirely dark, a little raking light from the lighthouse followed her as she walked.

She let the beam of her torch sweep from side to side. Saw roots creeping over the trail. After thirty meters—she was counting her steps—she turned and chose another direction, behind the cabin. She tried to picture seventeen-year-old Lilly, to imagine her running her errands. Meat and potatoes and sweet, low-alcohol beer. Not too far, particularly not on this terrain, no further than was necessary. When she caught sight of the rope pulley on the hillside, she turned and went slightly deeper among the trees, where the bare rock broke through the ground. Perhaps there had once been a trail here, snaking between the rocks.

For a moment she thought she could see it, but then it was gone, and she clambered over the trunk of a tree that had fallen years ago.

If she hadn't stumbled, she might never have noticed it. A slight
hump, that was all, but the stones below it seemed a little too even,
man-made. Eira shuffled down, and her torchlight hit an iron door.
She kicked it, a muted sound.

Down by her feet, something caught the light. A wine bottle. She
nudged it with her toe. The label was still intact.

Chateau something.

It couldn't have been there long.

Eira grabbed a stone and began hammering the padlock. She
cried out as she hit it, but the damned thing wouldn't break. She dug
out her Swiss army knife instead, her fingers freezing again, stupid
fiddly fucking thing. Finally, the tiny screwdriver. She pushed it into
the keyhole, turned and prized and shouted, overpowering both the
wind and the waves.

It clicked. Eira tore off the padlock, pulling the door with all
her might. The smell that hit her wasn't cold earth, it was the same
stench of life and death she had encountered before.

The torch was shaking in her hand. She saw a few cans on the
floor. His shoes, his trouser leg, his body curled up on the shelf
above the bare earth floor.

"GG?" she whispered.

No movement, no answer.

There was his hand, so awfully cold. She dropped to her knees
and fumbled for his wrist, searching for a pulse. Her other hand
managed to find his throat.

Tell me you're alive, you damn idiot.

She felt something weak beneath her fingertips. Was it a figment
of her imagination, her own blood pumping through her veins? She
pressed her lips to the skin on his neck, the thinnest point, held her
breath and felt it again, as soft as a raindrop.

A pulse.

Her phone wouldn't work inside, and she had to leave him, first
draping her coat over his body. I'm coming back, GG, I'll be back
soon, I'm not going to leave you.

Outside, a call to the emergency operator, 112, air ambulance

to Högbonden Lighthouse, then the prosecutor, who picked up—
thankfully.

Once Eira had said everything she needed to say, she ran back to
the lighthouse keeper's residence and grabbed an armful of blankets,
filled a few bottles with water. She returned to the earth cellar and
wrapped him up. Wet his lips, warmed him using her own body.

Whispered until she was hoarse, telling him he had better not
fucking die on her.

She didn't hear the helicopter circling overhead, but she later found
out that it had taken some time to land.

The darkness and the wind, the lighthouse guiding them to safety.

The climb up the hillside.

It was only when their searchlights broke into the earth cellar that
she realized help had arrived. Hands gripping her arm, leading her
out. Blinding lights and voices. She watched from a distance as they
struggled to get the stretcher inside, tanks of oxygen, and everything
else.

The helicopter lifted into the air, its lights mixing with the stars.

The sky had cleared.

DECEMBER

There had been snow on the ground for the past few days, the first time that winter. A white landscape, a pure blanket over everything that had happened.

Powder swirled around the tires as Eira drove south to Sundsvall.

Other than a brief glimpse through a hospital door, she hadn't seen him since that night on the island.

A life-threatening condition, those were the words she had read.

Dehydration. It had been two days before GG woke up and the doctors were able to say anything with certainty. Eira had spent those days cleaning the house, scouring away all thoughts of everything she could have done to find him sooner.

He had been hooked up to a drip when she got to the hospital, surrounded by his nearest and dearest, sleeping or busy with the doctor.

"Sit here with us, I'll go down to the café and get us something," his ex-wife had said, but Eira told her she would come back. The next time she tried, his two grown children had thanked her in a way she couldn't quite handle. Telling them "I was just doing my job" sounded fake and wrong, as though their father's life was just part of her job description.

Eira knew she had done more than that when she warmed him with her lips and her breath, whispering things she had never told anyone.

She had turned down all interviews since the press found out about what happened. Not once had she ever felt any urge to be in the spotlight.

In the end, she had blamed her mental health—though she called it exhaustion—and was signed off sick for two weeks. She had gone on long runs with Rabble, who was starting to get fat from his lazy life at Allan's place; she had picked up her mother for dinners at home and at the whisky distillery. Kerstin had got tipsy during the latter, started talking about a boy she had a crush on. "I can't see him anywhere, has he gone?"

"I'm sure he'll be back," Eira had told her. It was an attempt to avoid souring the mood, but it was also true. Anything could come back to someone who was lost in time, youth and love and the dead, who had never ceased to exist.

"Magnus is coming, isn't he? Is he late again?"

No, Mum, Eira could have replied. He hasn't even requested day release. He's hiding in his cell in Umeå with the ancient Greeks. I don't think he dares look you in the face, because everything will come crashing down.

She had spent most of her time alone at home, with the recordings from the interviews as company. The wildly different statements were like a dance in which the two had been in the same room, at the same time, but never quite met, only ever brushing up against each other.

Eira had never heard GG mumble before. Searching for the right words, his voice so weak those first few days.

GG: *She came over to me in the bar at Stadt. I thought I recognized her, but I couldn't remember where I'd seen her before. I guess I'd already had quite a bit to drink by that point.*
NO: *We found an empty bottle of whisky in the apartment. Among other things.*
GG: *I drank some of it the night before.*
(Pause)
Guess I (coughs) needed to get away from myself.

Eira didn't recognize the initials NO, the voice unfamiliar to her. The interviewer had been brought in from Stockholm, from the national unit. The squeaky-clean type, who had probably never made a single mistake in their life—or certainly made it sound that way.

GG: *I don't know what made me leave with her. I hadn't been doing too well beforehand. She looked nice, but I can hardly remember what we talked about. It was more what she saw—in me, I mean. That feeling, you know?*

NO: *I can't say I do.*

GG: *The sense of fitting, somehow. It's hard to explain. Like she could give me something I needed, like she saw something in me. I bought her a drink. There might've been something else there too, something wild. That's what I thought, anyway. The look of a woman who has decided she wants you. When she's made up her mind to take whatever she wants.*

NO: *Did that scare you?*

GG: *Well, yes. But not just that.*

(Pause)

And then I wake up. I think it's night, but I don't check the time. I'm in a hotel room, and I feel awful. My head's aching and . . . You know what it's like, when you wake up with someone you don't . . . And you're not entirely sure whether you . . . or at least not what it was like.

NO: *No, I don't.*

GG: *Right, no. Of course.*

NO: *So what can you tell me about it?*

(Pause)

GG: *You don't want to be that person who sneaks off at dawn without even leaving your number.*

NO: *But Sanna Melin already had your phone number. She contacted you. You'd already met.*

GG: *That didn't cross my mind at the time, in that context.*

In that context.

Eira pictured the scene again. GG waking up beneath a tangle of sheets, the anxiety of not knowing what they had done. Who she was. The urge to leave as quickly as he could and the knowledge that he would feel even worse if he did.

And then, when the woman woke up and smiled at him.

"Thanks for last night."

"Sorry for asking, but I don't really remember much of yesterday evening . . ."

"Don't worry," she had said, laughing and giving him a quick caress. "It was nice. To be perfectly honest, I think you were a bit drunk."

The relief, making him stay awhile longer. A sense of forgiveness.

NO: *You interviewed her about Hans Runne. Didn't that make you hesitate, when you realized she was a witness?*
GG: *A witness who hadn't seen anything. No, I can't say it did.*
(Pause)
It's not something I'm proud of.
NO: *OK. Moving on to what happened next. You said that you decided to stay with the suspect.*
GG: *She wasn't a suspect at the time.*
NO: *It would be best if you took me through it.*

They had sex that morning. GG thought he owed her that, for some reason, though his feelings of guilt didn't ease afterwards. Around nine, when he told her he had to leave, she saw straight through him.

"But you said you had the day off."

"Did I?"

"I asked if you were going to arrest me, as a joke, and that's what you told me."

GG had squirmed, telling her that a police officer was never really off duty, that his phone was back in the apartment, that he really needed to check in.

"You can't let your work own you," she said. "Not on your day off."

The woman, whose name he still couldn't quite remember, definitely had a point there. Or at least that was how he felt in the moment. Why not cut loose for the day, enjoy life a little?

Once he had taken a shower, he felt ready.

There was a sense of rebelliousness to the whole thing. Lust and something reckless. The fact that she didn't have anything more important to do than be with him, that her entire focus seemed to be on him.

Her kisses softer than downy feathers.

"If you peel away everything other people want you to be, who are you? What do you dream of, Georg?"

Ordinarily he struggled with that kind of nonsense, finding oneself and all that. But he had started talking about the sea.

About the longing he felt for the open horizon. Being able to gaze off into the distance without focusing on anything.

"I know a place," she had said.

Sanna Melin's version wasn't a million miles away from his, yet it was undeniably a different story. The same bar and the same hotel room, but they had recognized each other the minute their eyes met.

She admitted that only once GG came round and NO confronted her with his account.

SM: *I'm sorry I didn't say anything earlier, but I didn't want him to get into trouble. With him being a high-ranking detective and everything, I knew there could be issues with a relationship like this.*
NO: *And what kind of relationship is that?*
SM: *It's much too early to say.*

According to her, it was Georg who insisted. She pronounced his name with a hard G, revealing that she had seen it written down before ever meeting him in person. Read his name in the paper and then reached out.

NO: *Why did you get in touch with Inspector Georgsson?*
SM: *I wanted to tell him the truth. I didn't end up saying much that*

first time, and I apologize for that. I find it difficult to trust people I
don't know sometimes. We needed more time.

They had a wonderful night together—and she wasn't just talking
about the act itself, but a deeper understanding. The pain of then
having to go their separate ways, the longing for more time together.
A place where nothing could bother them.

She knew of a small boat they could borrow. An old friend of her
grandmother's had a fishing hut in Barsta. He was one of the last
fishermen there, now that Stockholmers had started buying up the
little red huts along the harbor.

As Sanna Melin described it, they had a lovely day. She showed
him the places that had meant so much to her family, the rugged
nature of the island, the lighthouse. They took a picnic with them,
wine. It was cold, but they kept each other warm.

And then GG had gone off to do his business. When he didn't
come back, she had looked everywhere for him. She thought he
might have gone back down to the boat. And no, she didn't check
the earth cellar. Why would he go there to relieve himself?

According to GG, it was windy as hell, the temperature close to zero.
He had realized what an idiotic idea it was almost as soon as they got
into the boat, but found himself drawn to the barren, brutal nature
of the place. He didn't want to back out before they had climbed to
the highest point of the island.

When they got to the lighthouse, the doors were locked. They
had sheltered from the wind for a while, shared one of the bottles
of wine without a single thought as to who would be driving later.
He stood on the rocks and looked out at the horizon. Then he
thought they should start heading back, before it got dark. Sanna
suggested going into the old lighthouse keeper's residence instead,
lighting a fire and making love. She knew where the spare key was
hidden.

In the earth cellar.

NO: *And you weren't suspicious?*

(Pause)

GG: *The thought did cross my mind as I stepped inside. The minute I felt the chill and smelled the earthy air. But not before then. Do you think I would've been so stupid as to go with her if I was? It seemed absurd.*

And then the door swung shut.

Eira turned off onto Esplanaden. She had to drive up and down the broad avenue before she managed to find a parking space.

There was no such thing as a single truth, always several versions of a sequence of events. She believed GG, of course, but she also knew that that made her a worse police officer. What was most likely and who was most credible were for the courts to decide.

"I'm so glad you could come."

He was still weak, she saw that the minute he opened the door. Gripping the doorframe as she stepped inside, quickly slumping down into an armchair. It had been turned towards the TV, which he immediately switched off. Someone had tidied his apartment, and it smelled clean and fresh. Eira suddenly became aware that she had come empty-handed. There were a couple of magnificent bouquets in vases, she should have brought something too, but the very thought of buying flowers for GG was embarrassing. It was too intimate, too emotional. And it might make him feel like an invalid, which she doubted he wanted. She had considered bringing a bottle of whisky, but decided it probably wasn't the right moment.

"It feels like such a trivial thing to say," he said, "but thanks for everything."

"How are you feeling?"

"Good."

"Should I make some coffee or something?"

"Only if you want some."

It didn't feel right to be rummaging around in his kitchen. Eira also couldn't shake the suspicion that GG had heard what she said out on the island. He had been unconscious, there was no doubt about that, but it could still have seeped in somehow, like a dream, a memory he couldn't quite trust to be true. A small part of her hoped it had.

"The evidence is strong as far as Damir Avdic is concerned," Eira said once the coffee was brewing and she was back in the living room, "but it's trickier with Hans Runne. No one saw her lock him in the basement, and we don't have any physical evidence."

"She'll get a few years, at the very least."

"And as for you . . ."

"I only have myself to blame," said GG.

"You know how often victims feel that way."

GG groaned as he shifted in his chair. Someone had cut his hair, and he was well dressed, clean shaven. She remembered his rough stubble against her cheek.

"I let her trick me," he said. "They should give me the boot. I mean, what did that callout cost, all that work . . ."

"I've listened to the interviews," Eira said without looking at him, there was something shameful about hearing him beat himself up. "I'm not sure Sanna Melin consciously tricked anyone. It seems like she thought it was about love every time."

"Believe me, it wasn't."

He sought her eye.

"I think the coffee is ready," said Eira.

She filled two cups and managed to avoid touching his hand as she passed one to him, took a seat on the edge of the sofa. Over the past few weeks, alone, she hadn't been able to hold back her feelings. They had cleared and become purer since that night on the island; what she had felt was about so much more than a fear of losing him, it was much bigger.

"I thought I deserved to die," said GG.

"You didn't."

"But I still reached for the last can," he said, finally smiling. "Tinned mushrooms. Do you think I could get those banned?"

Eira laughed, and for a few seconds she actually dared to hold his gaze. There was so much she had been planning to say.

"Oh, right, I've just remembered why I asked you to come," said GG, straining to stretch out one leg at a time. "Well, other than wanting to thank you, obviously. You'll have to forgive me, but I'm still exhausted."

"Don't worry."

"Did you hear about a fatal stabbing in Täby, just north of Stockholm? It was a few weeks ago now."

It did ring a bell. Something she had heard about on the news, perhaps. No, she had changed the channel, her mother was at home at the time.

GG wasn't on duty, and there were rumors that he was going to resign, so why did he want to talk to her about this?

Eira put down her cup. The coffee made her feel queasy.

"What's going on?"

"Stockholm police got in touch about a DNA match. Costel was here this morning. They were asking about a woman they've definitively placed at the crime scene, there were traces of her all over the house."

"Sanna Melin?"

Eira felt the floor sway. There couldn't be more victims, surely this had to be over now? But then she saw the look on GG's face.

Searching and doubtful, the detective in him was back.

"Another old friend," he said. "Lina Stavred."

A wave of nausea rose up inside her.

"You're joking."

"That's probably what they thought too," said GG. "Given that she was officially declared dead twenty years ago."

"Is she a suspect?" Eira managed to stutter.

"Of course."

There was nothing to say. Images of Lina flickered by in her mind: the school portrait of the pretty young girl who vanished one July day in 1997; standing in the ruins of the old sawmill in Lockne, an iron bar in one hand. Magnus, who had come so close to death that evening.

Other than those two, Eira was the only person who knew what really happened back then. Her brother had confessed to the crime, and she had let him do it. It was his choice. Magnus had threatened to confess to killing Lina too, if Eira told anyone. He might have faced a life sentence then.

The lie had been niggling away at Eira ever since, but it was always her brother who was on her mind. She hadn't for a single second imagined that Lina might do it again.

"Do you remember what I told you that day?" she asked quietly, her words sluggish and dangerous. "About Lina Stavred possibly still being alive?"

They had been sitting right here, in GG's apartment, out on the balcony. It was summer.

"And I told you the case was closed," he said. "Which it was."

"What did you tell Costel this morning?"

"That I'm on sick leave, but that I'll take a closer look at the old preliminary investigations as soon as I'm back."

"So you are coming back?"

"I did briefly think about moving out to a cabin by the coast—Dad left it in his will—but my brother can sell it. I think I've had enough of the sea."

Eira just wanted to swing by the station while she was in Sundsvall, to return the laptop she had been given. She had actually started to feel like it would do her good to take a step back from everything for a while.

To make the most of the break, as her doctor had suggested.

There was nothing left for her to do, nothing she still needed to understand. Some things simply couldn't be explained. The preliminary investigation was closed and Sanna Melin would be charged, likely in the morning. She was currently in custody in Härnösand. There were some weaknesses in the evidence, but they had enough to keep her locked up for a very long time. A brief psychological exam had revealed that the woman suffered from a personality disorder, but a more thorough assessment would provide clearer results.

"She couldn't bear for anyone to leave her," Silje had said when she called to update Eira, something she did from time to time. "She stabbed Damir in the back. What does that tell you?"

"That he was about to leave?"

"And Mikael Ingmarsson told us he'd already ended things with her. We're not sure about Hans Runne, but he hadn't told anyone about their relationship and he was annoyed that the house was a wreck, so maybe he told her the truth that day."

"Did she think she would be able to hang on to them if she locked them up?"

"Or that no one else could have them, in any case."

Psychological guesswork wasn't Eira's thing, but Silje had mentioned something else that she couldn't stop thinking about. It wasn't directly linked to the case, but still.

"It struck me how invisible Sanna Melin's mother was in all this, as though she never existed or wasn't allowed to exist," Silje had said after Eira recapped everything she knew but hadn't yet had time to write down. "There's a name for what happens when the new woman drives the man's previous kids out of the nest and he lets it happen. Wicked stepmother syndrome, like Cinderella. No one wants to believe it's as common as it is."

Eira was on her way to the bathroom, and she was in a hurry, when she bumped into Nora Berents.

"Eira, hi, great to see you. I thought you were on sick leave. How are things?"

"Good," said Eira, trying to make it seem like her stomach wasn't churning. She felt an immediate pang of guilt for being on sick leave when she clearly wasn't ill, when she was running around the station. She managed to smile. "I just came in to drop this off."

"Why?"

Eira told the prosecutor that she would be off work for a while if the doctor got her way. That she had only really been brought in to work on Hans Runne's case, and that even if that had now turned into her filling a temporary vacancy, it was probably time for her to return to Kramfors.

"That's not what I heard," said Nora Berents, lowering her voice. "I just received an inquiry about you and your work. It seems the person you've been covering for has resigned."

"Has he?"

"I've been flat out, so I haven't had time to reply yet, but obviously I'll be recommending you for the post. Without you . . ."

"Sorry," said Eira, gesturing to the bathroom. "I have to . . ."

She only just managed to lock the door behind her before she slumped down over the toilet seat and vomited. Coffee and mineral water, a Snickers she had found in the car. That was all she had eaten since she left home. It wasn't nearly enough. Her stomach cramped. She was going to have to learn to eat better and more often, that was the only way—or so she had heard. A carrot in her bag, a pack of crackers.

She splashed her face with cold water and then sat down on the toilet lid for a moment once the worst of the nausea had passed.

The regularity of her period hadn't exactly been top of her mind lately, otherwise she would have reacted sooner. She just didn't understand how it could have happened. Had she missed a pill, or had it somehow managed to latch on anyway? These things happened.

When the two lines appeared on the test, she hadn't been able to stop laughing. If August had a wife in Stockholm and a baby in Ådalen, how was his free-loving life going to work out?

The whole thing was too big, she just didn't have the energy to process it.

But then the realization had hit her with full force.

Ricken.

How many days had it been? She obviously hadn't made a note of the dates, Eira didn't keep track of her private life like that, but if she went by the preliminary investigation she could narrow down those two evenings. With August: she had been to Umeå, visited the pathologist there, seen her brother in prison. That was why she had felt lonelier than usual. And then there was the evening when GG came to see her, she remembered feeling an urge to get away from both him and herself, grabbing the bag containing Ricken's aunt's schoolwork and driving over to Strinne.

Not many days between them at all. Very few, in fact.

Eira held her wrists beneath the cold tap, the way she used to whenever she drank too much as a teenager. Maybe it would help with this kind of nausea, too.

Nora Berents was still waiting in the corridor when she came out. She finished a call and said a few more words about the job.

As though it were that easy.

"I'll have to think about it," said Eira.

ACKNOWLEDGMENTS

A heartfelt thank-you to everyone in Ådalen for answering my strange questions, giving me a ride when I didn't have the energy to ride my bike, sharing tales and stories and checking local details for me: Ulla-Karin Hällström Sahlén and Jan Sahlén, Mats De Vahl, Tony Naima, Fredrik Högberg, and many others. I would also like to send a posthumous thanks to the poet Birger Norman for piquing my curiosity and creating such a sense of place, and to his children, Bosse and Kerstin, for allowing me to use his words.

A huge thanks to Veronica Andersson with the Violent Crimes Unit in Sundsvall and to other police officers in the region. To Per Bucht, my cousin and former detective; Johanna Loisel at the National Board of Forensic Medicine in Umeå; and to Peter Rönnerfalk for his medical expertise. Thanks to Hans Granqvist, Mario Velasquez Castro, and Fredrik Palmqvist for the excursions through forests, mines, and running tracks.

Any mistakes or excesses are entirely my own.

My warmest thanks also go out to everyone who stood by my side during the writing process, making it so much less lonely: Göran Parkrud, for the difficult questions and long chats; Liza Marklund, Gith Haring, Anna Zettersten, Boel Forssell, Kicki Linna, and Malin Crépin for reading and for casting your eagle eyes on my characters and manuscript. I'd never be able to do it without you.

To my publisher, Kristoffer Lind, Kasja Willén, and everyone else at Lind & Co—it's always such a joy to work with you. To Astri von Arbin Ahlander, Kaisa Palo, and the rest of the gang at Ahlander Agency. I'm so glad to have you representing my books.

And to Astrid, Amelie, and Matilde, most important of all. Thank you for every single minute you're around me, your love and support, and for being the wonderful people you are.

ABOUT THE AUTHOR

TOVE ALSTERDAL is the author of five critically acclaimed stand-alone novels. Her American debut, *We Know You Remember*, won the award for Best Swedish Crime Novel of the Year as well as the Glass Key Award for Best Nordic Crime Novel.